THE MURDER COLUMN

Brian Cooper

CHIVERS
THORNDIKE

This large print book is published by BBC Audiobooks Ltd, Bath, England and by Thorndike Press, Waterville, Maine, USA.

Published in 2003 in the U.K. by arrangement with Constable & Robinson Ltd.

Published in 2003 in the U.S. by arrangement with Constable & Robinson Ltd.

U.K. Hardcover ISBN 0–7540–7312–2   (Chivers Large Print)
U.K. Softcover ISBN 0–7540–7313–0   (Camden Large Print)
U.S. Softcover ISBN 0–7862–5668–0   (General Series)

The text of this Large Print edition is unabridged.
Other aspects of the book may vary from the original edition.

Set in 16 pt. New Times Roman.

Printed in Great Britain on acid-free paper.

British Library Cataloguing in Publication Data available

Library of Congress Cataloging-in-Publication Data

Cooper, Brian, 1919–
      The murder column / Brian Cooper.
         p.   cm.
      ISBN 0–7862–5668–0 (lg. print : sc : alk. paper)
      1. Lubbock, John (Fictitious character)—Fiction. 2. Tench, Mike
   (Fictitious character)—Fiction. 3. Police—England—Norfolk—
   Fiction. 4. Norfolk (England)—Fiction. 5. Large type books.
      I. Title.
   PR6053.O546M87 2003
   823'.914—dc21   2003053313

Author's Note

According to an ancient rhyme, apart from 'London, York and Coventree', there are 'Seven Burnhams by the Sea'.

To those who live and work within their bounds, I must apologize for having added an eighth. Burnham Northgate does not, of course, exist. Like the people who wander in and out of these pages, it is merely a creation of the author's somewhat eccentric mind.

Acknowledgement

I would like to express my thanks to the Society of Authors, acting on behalf of the Bernard Shaw Estate, for permission to quote the passage from the Preface to *Three Plays for Puritans* on p. 325.

To
Bert and Olga and Alan and Hilary,
my friends and willing helpers in Norfolk

CONTENTS

My wife is dead and here she lies,
Nobody laughs and nobody cries;
Where she is gone to, or how she fares,
Nobody knows and nobody cares.
Epitaph on a memorial in Kingsbridge Church

PROLOGUE

THE STORM

The storm is up, and all is on the hazard.
William Shakespeare: *Julius Caesar*

The storm, some said it was the worst in a generation, broke over the Burnhams early on a summer Sunday in 1952.

The day before had been hot, and the night that followed was close and breathless. From midnight onwards thunder could be heard away to the south, perhaps over Norwich, and sheet lightning lit up the distant sky. Then at exactly half-past two a savage clap of thunder seemed to split the sky apart over Burnham Northgate, a vivid fork of lightning illumined the church and the gravestones around it, stopping the clock, and rain began to fall as if a dam had been breached on some celestial lake.

At Burnham Overy Staithe, as the lightning flashes continued with little intermission, the creek seemed to bubble and seethe behind the heavy grey curtain of tumbling rain, and the yachts, sails furled, yawed and strained at their moorings, intent, so it seemed, on escape to the open sea. In a field near Burnham Deepdale a heifer was struck and killed; at

1

Burnham Thorpe an ancient oak tree was riven down the middle by a bolt; in Burnham Market the roads flanking the Green were, for a time, awash; and in Burnham Norton a cottage lost a chimney which fell through the roof, showering slates and debris on a bed which sleepers had vacated in terror only minutes before.

The storm continued to rage for another two hours before it left Norfolk and moved out to sea. The rain ceased abruptly, and with the dawn beginning to show over Wells, the Burnhams were left with saturated fields and still-dripping gutters, and memories of a night that many would recall to the end of their lives.

But those who lived in Burnham Northgate would remember that night for another and even more terrible reason. To those who knew their bibles, and there were many in the village, it came to be known as the Night of Retribution, the night when the wrath of the Lord descended; and they quoted the lines from the twentieth chapter of the third book of Moses which is called Leviticus: 'And the man that committeth adultery with another man's wife, even he that committeth adultery with his neighbour's wife, the adulterer and the adulteress shall surely be put to death.'

The great day of God's wrath had come, so they said, and He had struck down the sinners.

I

THE TOMBSTONE

Take me upon your back and you'll know what
I weigh.
English proverb

1

At half-past six that morning, ex-Detective Chief Inspector John Spencer Lubbock pushed open the churchyard gate at Burnham Northgate and, placing the metal tip of his cherrywood stick precisely between the puddles left by the storm, set out up the path that led to the church.

Not that St Andrew's was, to him, of any special interest. He was merely intent on taking a short cut through the scatter of gravestones to Northgate village, where he hoped to purchase a Sunday paper.

A sturdy, white-haired figure in corduroy trousers and thick-soled boots, he strode ahead up the path at a steady pace till his eyes fell on something that was, to him, of considerable interest.

He paused and looked again, just to make sure that what he thought he'd seen wasn't some preposterous mirage: a trick of sunlight on the grass. And it might well have been, for what he saw was hardly the kind of thing one expected to see on a sunny Sunday morning in a staid Norfolk churchyard.

Two pairs of naked legs, one a woman's, one a man's. The woman's legs spread wide, the man's close together, posed as if he lay face down on the woman, caught in some sacrilegious act of copulation.

Whose legs they were he couldn't possibly see, for their owners were hidden, pinned to the ground by a heavy, blackened gravestone that had fallen on top of them.

2.

Mike Tench was dreaming.

He was being kissed by Dorothy Lamour and stroked in all his most erogenous zones by Hedy Lamarr when, somewhere in the distance, a bell began to ring.

Brr-brr.

Brr-brr.

He groaned, rolled over in bed and groped for the bedside phone.

A familiar voice grated in his ear. 'Would that perhaps be Detective Chief Inspector Tench?'

Tench glanced at the clock and swore beneath his breath. 'D'you know the bloody time?'

'Yes,' said Lubbock. 'It's seven twenty-eight and a half.'

'And it's Sunday morning.'

'I know that, laddie. I've just come from a churchyard.'

'Confessing your sins?'

'No. Simply taking a morning stroll.'

'And you've rung me up at this ungodly hour just to tell me?'

'Not exactly,' said Lubbock.

Tench gave another groan. 'Don't tell me you've stumbled across another body.'

'Not this time, laddie, no. This time it's two.'

'Two?'

'That's what I said.'

'I don't believe it,' said Tench.

'Then you'd best come and take a look for yourself.'

'Where are you?'

'Burnham Northgate.'

'What the hell are you doing there? It's a dozen miles from Cley'

'Just enjoying a little holiday, I needed a change of scene.'

'And you take a morning stroll and discover two bodies? Incredible,' said Tench.

'Nonetheless, it's true.'

'Then inform the local plod, and let me go back to sleep.'

'I've done that already. Three-quarters of an hour ago, as a matter of fact. Now it's your turn, laddie. You need to get down here, and sharp. These two didn't just lie down and die. They've been murdered. So you'll need to get the whole team down at the double, before the locals do any more tramping around.'

Tench groaned a third time. 'Stay there,' he said, 'and don't move an inch. I'll be down in an hour.'

3.

It took him longer than that to reach the Burnhams from Norwich. A couple of elm trees, felled by the storm, had blocked the road north of Fakenham and he had to turn back and make a detour through Walsingham. But just before nine o'clock he was standing with Lubbock in the churchyard at Northgate, inside an area sealed off by canvas windbreaks and guarded by the local constable.

His old Chief was sombre. 'Messy business,' he said.

'I can see that,' Tench said sourly. 'Looks as though a herd of elephants has been charging around.'

'Unavoidable, laddie. We had to raise the headstone and topple it backwards. They were pinned underneath it. Took the local chap, Barnes, and five of the strongest lads in the village to lift the damned thing, and they only managed it at the third attempt. By that time, of course, the damage was done.'

'It's not damage. It's destruction. If the scene-of-crime boys are hoping to find any clues, they'll have a hell of a job.'

'True enough,' said Lubbock, 'but we had to raise the stone. That was the first priority. At that time there was nothing at all to suggest foul play. All we could see were two pairs of legs, and we simply assumed that last night's storm had blown the stone down and trapped them in the act. It wasn't till I lifted the man's head by his hair and we saw what was left of their faces that we realized we were dealing with more than an accident. At that point I cleared everyone away, told Barnes to stand guard and went off to phone you.'

Tench squatted down and gingerly raised the man's head.

'He was lying on top of her,' said Lubbock. 'and the stone must have hit him on the back of the head. There's no way it could have mashed up their faces like that. There's hardly anything left. You'll have a job to identify them, even using dental records. And there's no blood around. Whoever did this, he didn't kill them here in the churchyard. He brought the bodies here, laid them out in some grisly act of fornication and pushed the headstone down on top of them. If you look at the base of the stone, you'll see that on this side the ground's been cut out. Made it easier to topple.'

Tench peered down and nodded. Then he straightened up. 'This chap Barnes,' he said, 'how well does he know the village?'

'Pretty well, I should think. He's been here three years and there isn't a lot of it to know: just the church, the church hall, the rectory and a handful of cottages. According to what he says, he covers four of the Burnhams— Deepdale, Norton, Overy, Overy Staithe and here. Burnham Thorpe and Burnham Market

9

are Jack Vernon's province.'

Barnes was a young man, fresh-faced and eager. Tench called him in. 'Constable,' he said, 'I suppose you've no idea who these two people are.'

Barnes shook his head. 'None at all, sir, no.'

'No one's been reported missing?'

'Not so far, sir, but it's a bit early yet.'

'Check round the cottages. See if there's anyone who didn't come home last night. Report back to us here.'

'Right, sir.'

'And don't waste any time. We need some facts, and fast.'

They watched him stride away down the slope to the churchyard gate. Lubbock stared at the grave. 'I've a feeling you're not going to get them,' he said. 'Unless I'm reading all the signs wrong, you're in for a long haul. Whoever killed these two was determined to keep their identities a secret, and he did a thorough job. Even their mothers wouldn't be able to put a name to them now. And remember what I told you at the time of those murders at Red Lodge Wood. They may not be locals. They could well be a couple of the travelling dead, ferried in by car from Bedford or Stepney or God knows where, and left here in Norfolk. This county's an ideal dumping ground for bodies.'

Tench gave a shrug. 'Well, let's hope they're not. And let's cling to the chance that Ledward can come up with one or two clues.'

'You'll be lucky,' said Lubbock. 'You know what Reg is like. And it's Sunday morning. He won't be in the mood to do anyone any favours.'

'He'd better be,' Tench said grimly. 'If he isn't, he'll get the sharp edge of my tongue. I've had just about enough of Dr Reginald Ledward.'

4.

His frustration was understandable.

Dr Reginald Blake Ledward, the long-serving Home Office pathologist for Norfolk, had, even in Lubbock's time, earned himself something of a reputation in the county. A taciturn man with a voice that crackled like dried-up parchment, his method of working appeared to many to be excessively cautious. He refused to be rushed and was reluctant to commit himself to any conclusion until he felt certain that what he said was irrefutable. He was also possessed of a caustic tongue that reserved itself for the odd sardonic comment and, being a notoriously bad sleeper, was never at his most approachable till mid-afternoon; added to which he regarded his Sundays as sacrosanct, and was always likely to be at his most churlish when called out to view a body early on the Sabbath.

That morning proved to be no exception. As

11

he trudged up the slope and deposited his bag outside the windbreak, it was clear that he wasn't in the best of tempers.

'Well, well,' he said, 'if it isn't Detective Chief Inspector Tench! Tell me, Chief Inspector, is it perhaps a perverse sense of humour that directs you to summon me with such regularity at this ungodly hour of a Sunday morning?'

Tench was tight-lipped. 'No, sir,' he said.

'Then all I can assume is that our local murderers have equipped themselves with a clutch of faultless alarm clocks and set them to sound off at midnight on Saturdays. Or am I mistaken?'

'Unfortunately, Doctor, murderers don't consult with either you or me before they commit a crime. If they did, we wouldn't need to call you out at all.'

'That would be bliss indeed.' Ledward turned the words sour. 'So, Chief Inspector, what visual delight have you uncovered today to soothe my jaded eyes? Is the body male or female?'

'Both, sir.'

'Both?'

'Two bodies, sir, not one.'

'Are you telling me that on this glorious midsummer Sunday morning you've deliberately contrived to double my workload?'

'I apologize for that, sir. The killer failed unaccountably to warn me in advance.'

'But I suppose, as usual, you'll be demanding the impossible.'

'Time of death, sir,' Tench said curtly. 'As near as you can get.'

*   *   *

It was another half-hour before Ledward repacked his bag.

'Well?' said Tench.

'As far as I can tell without a closer examination, they died between nine and twelve hours ago.'

'Both of them?'

'Yes. As near as makes no difference.'

Tench glanced at his watch. 'Between eleven o'clock last night and two o'clock this morning?'

'Counting on your fingers, are you, Chief Inspector, or questioning my grasp of simple mathematics?'

Tench ignored the question. 'Can't you narrow the time down?'

'I may be able to, once I get them on the slab. Till then, quite impossible.'

'Then can you tell me this? In your opinion, Doctor, have the bodies been moved?'

'You know me better than that, Chief Inspector. Mere opinions are for others. Before answering that question, I need to check the bodies for hypostasis.'

'And I need to know. Surely you can at least

hazard a guess.'

'Off the record?'

'Of course.'

'Then . . . possibly.'

'Can't you do better than that?'

Ledward raised his eyebrows. 'You want me to say "probably"? All right then, probably But don't quote me on that.'

'And what would you say was the cause of death?'

'All I can do at this stage is to state the obvious. There are massive lacerations to the skull, inflicted with force by some very hard implement.'

'Such as what, Doctor? A hammer?'

'No, there are no marks to indicate the head of a hammer.'

'What then?'

'Your guess, Chief Inspector, is likely to be just as accurate as mine. You'll have to wait for forensic evidence.'

He pulled out a note pad, checked on the time, scribbled a few figures, tore the sheet off the pad and handed it to Tench. 'Death was certified,' he said, 'at eleven twenty-six. Get them down to my lab as soon as you can, but don't expect any results before midday tomorrow . . . At the earliest,' he added.

He picked up his bag. 'Well, a good Sabbath day to you, Chief Inspector. See that you spend it in profitable pursuits. You could perhaps make it a day of atonement. That would be most appropriate.'

He gave a brief nod and made off down the slope.

Tench watched him through the gate. 'And the same to you, Dr Ledward,' he said, 'in spades.'

5.

The feud between Constable Will Barnes at Burnham Northgate and Constable Jack Vernon at Burnham Market had been simmering ever since Barnes had arrived on the scene three years before. Vernon wasn't his type of copper. A dour, melancholic, monosyllabic man who'd held fort in Burnham Market for twenty-five years, he'd come to regard the town as strictly his own province, and resented any encroachment on his authority. Now nearing the age of retirement, he tended to regard his confidential files on the few more dissipated residents of the town as the Vernon Archives, accessible to no one else but himself.

This, as Barnes very soon discovered, had made co-operation between them difficult to achieve, and so when, an hour later, he reported back to say that no one in Burnham Northgate was missing, he was more than a little irritated to hear from Chief Inspector Tench that Constable Vernon had already been instructed to make house-to-house inquiries in Burnham Market.

By that time the aspect of the churchyard had changed. Screens had already been erected round the grave, Sergeant Lester and his scene-of-crime squad were busily at work subjecting the ground to detailed inspection, photographers were taking shots of the bodies, and the whole area had been taped off apart from one short path that led to the church door.

'You'd better check the rest of your villages,' Tench told him. He turned to a heavily built man at his side. 'Mac,' he said, 'take Constable Barnes wherever he has to go. This,' he said to Barnes, 'is Detective Sergeant McKenzie. He'll give you what help he can. And you'd better check Burnham Thorpe as well. Vernon's got enough on at Burnham Market. Even with the extra couple of men I've sent down there, he'll have a long job. If I'm not here when you get back, make your report to Detective Inspector Gregg.'

Will Barnes needed no further urging. To turn up the missing couple, especially if they lived somewhere on Vernon's patch, would be a feather in his cap and at the same time put one over on Vernon.

'Right, sir,' he said. 'If you're ready, Sarge, let's go.'

*　　　*　　　*

16

The trouble, as he discovered, was that no one at all appeared to be missing. He and McKenzie knocked on every door in Burnhams Deepdale, Overy, Overy Staithe and Norton, and repeated the process down at Burnham Thorpe. In each they drew a blank, and the only consolation that awaited him when eventually he reported to DI Gregg, was the news that Vernon's search had proved equally unproductive. Whoever the two victims happened to be, no one, it appeared, in any of the Burnhams was anxious to claim them.

A fact which Tench, later that day, imparted with some misgiving to Detective Chief Superintendent Hastings in Norwich.

6.

The Chief Super frowned.

'So, Mike?' he said.

'It looks as if they may be "travelling dead", sir: bodies brought in by car and dumped here in Norfolk.'

Hastings nodded slowly. 'Well, it's always a possibility now that petrol's no longer rationed, but I wouldn't be too ready to jump to that conclusion. They could be from somewhere relatively close. You've put out a call?'

'Yes, sir. We've contacted all the stations in the county. If anyone's reported missing, we should know right away.'

17

'Then pending the autopsies and any clues that Sergeant Lester finds on the ground, we'll just have to wait.'

'I don't think Lester's likely to find very much. The whole area was roughed up by six of the heaviest men in the village.'

'Then we'll have to be patient. It's early days yet. Someone's bound to report them as missing, and you've one suspect at least to question right away. You know the old saying: "Whoever finds the body . . ."'

Tench shook his head. 'Not in this case, sir,' he said.

The Chief Super raised his eyebrows. 'No? Why not?'

'Believe me, sir, you don't want to know.'

Hastings leaned back. He peered at Tench keenly. 'You're not going to tell me . . .'

'I'm afraid so, sir, yes.'

'Not John Lubbock . . . again.'

'It's incredible, sir, isn't it?'

'Out at Burnham Northgate? What the devil was he doing there?'

'On holiday, so he says.'

'He never goes on holiday.'

'Well, it seems it's part holiday and part business venture. He's staying at the windmill at Burnham Overy'

'Hasn't he had his fill of windmills?' Hastings said testily. 'He's restored Kettle Hill and lets out the cottage to visitors in the summer. What more does he want?'

'The one at Burnham Overy's been taking in visitors for a quarter of a century. Apparently he's been hoping to pick up a few tips.'

'And turns up two bodies? At half-past six on a Sunday morning? The man's unbelievable. What the hell was he doing in a churchyard at half-past six? And don't tell me he was going to early morning service. He's never admitted to a sin in his life.'

'Taking a morning stroll to buy a Sunday paper.'

Hastings snorted. 'And that's another thing. He's never strolled in his life. All he does is stump around on that cherrywood stick. Doesn't he ever sleep?'

'Not for long after daybreak. He never has.'

'And I suppose he's already given you some sage advice.'

'Not yet, sir, but he will.'

'Good God! The man's already been retired five years. And he trained you, didn't he? Why can't he trust you to deal with a case on your own?'

'I don't think it's that, sir.'

'No? Then what is it? Apart from continually tripping over bodies, why does he keep popping up whenever there's a murder?'

'It's just that he's been dealing with murder all his life. It's grown to be a habit. He can't let it go. He needs to be involved.'

'It's none of his business, Mike. Isn't it

19

about time you told him so?'

'Perhaps it is, sir, yes.'

'But you never will, will you?'

Tench seemed to hesitate. 'No,' he said at last. 'I don't think I could. He's irritating, yes, arrogant at times, but I owe him a great deal. He's always treated me as more of a son than a subordinate . . .'

'The son he never had.'

'Yes, maybe so, but he's an uncanny gift for tracking down killers. You've said so yourself.'

'It isn't by any means a flawless gift. He'll fly off at a tangent chasing wild geese.'

'Yes, I realize that, sir, only too well, but there's another thing too. He knows more about Norfolk than I'll ever know.'

'So you'll bite that tongue of yours and let him ramble on.'

'He taught me to listen. "When you're dealing with a murder," he always said, "listen and learn," and that's what I do. I listen when he talks, and sometimes I learn.'

'Well, remember what I've told you before. Don't play the submissive son. This is your case, not his.'

Tench gave a faint smile. 'I don't think there's very much danger of that, sir. My father's a canon. He's rambled on for years, and made me what I am: a dyed-in-the-wool agnostic.'

Hastings' eyes twinkled. 'Keep me informed,' he said.

7.

Whether Lubbock was in fact chasing wild geese was a matter for conjecture, but he seemed to spend the rest of that day with a purpose in mind. Returning to his billet in the windmill at Burnham Overy, armed with a morning paper, he treated himself to a larger breakfast than he normally enjoyed in his cottage at Cley. He then retired to his room, methodically filled his pipe and, ignoring the columns of the *Sunday Times*, prudently ordered two days in advance, he picked up his stick, wound himself behind the wheel of his ageing Morgan and drove back to Northgate.

Leaving his car by the church, he ducked under the tapes which read 'Police. Do Not Cross' and plodded through the still-wet grass to the further, vacant side of the graveyard, where he spent the next hour moving from stone to stone and subjecting the inscriptions to close examination. Every now and then he reached into an inside pocket of his jacket, pulled out a notebook and pencil and, hooking the stick across his arm, jotted down a name and, after it, a date.

He worked systematically, crossing the graveyard from side to side. Then, leaning on his stick, surveying the ground, and seeming sure at last that he'd examined every stone, he stumped back to the car, executed a less than

21

perfect three-point turn and drove back to the coastal road. Once there, he swung right and followed it through Wells, Stiffkey and Blakeney till he came to Cley Mill, where he turned right again and, a couple of minutes later, braked to a halt in front of his cottage below Cley church.

For the next half-hour he remained in the parlour, slumped in his armchair, puffing at his pipe, turning the pages of a couple of pamphlets he'd retrieved from a bookshelf, and making more notes; after which he took the road through Holt to Norwich, treated himself to poached egg and haddock at his sister Meg's Riverside Restaurant and then made for the offices of the *Eastern Daily Press.*

Pushing open a rear door, he made his way up to the reporters' room where the staff were busy on Monday's edition. There he sought out Dave Ransome, the crime correspondent, and passed the next couple of hours sifting through the dusty files of the *EDP.*

By the time he reached the windmill at Burnham Overy it was half-past six, but he hummed a little tune as he parked his car. Ex-Detective Chief Inspector John Spencer Lubbock was, so it seemed, more than a little pleased with the results of his day.

II

THE PATHLESS PINES

There is a pleasure in the pathless woods,
There is a rapture on the lonely shore . . .
Lord Byron: *Childe Harold*

1.

It was at half-past ten the following morning that Detective Sergeant Bill McKenzie, pursuing a report from the Duty Sergeant at Wells-next-the-Sea, pushed open the door of the Queens Hotel at Holkham and, somewhat sourly, thumped the bell on the bar.

Turning fifty, broad of beam, overweight and long inured to the tragic absurdities of death, McKenzie's attitude to life was persistently cynical. Thirty years of investigating violent criminals had taught him to be wary, not to say pessimistic, and he'd long ago concluded that to hope for the best was to court disaster. He therefore made a point of expecting the worst, and consoled himself with the thought that, once off duty, he could make for a pub and relax with a pint of good Norfolk ale.

Not that he was inclined to waste any time licking his lips once a brimming tankard had been placed in front of him. Patience had never been a virtue that he'd taken much trouble to cultivate, and it was typical of him that, presented with a pint, it took him no more than a couple of gulps to empty the glass. It irked him to see the level of the beer remain static, and what irked him still more and strained the seams of his temper was the need to spend time in a pub when duty precluded

25

the consumption of alcohol in any shape or form.

He was consequently not in the best of tempers that midsummer morning when, despatched in haste to Holkham's Queens Hotel, he found himself facing a multitude of bottles and no landlord in sight.

He thumped the bell with some impatience.

No one appeared.

He thumped it a second time and waited.

Still no one. Not a sound.

He brought his fist down hard on the bell half a dozen times.

Still no response.

Steam began to issue in wisps from McKenzie's ears. He was just about to pick up the bell and ram it down with force on the face of the bar, when a pudding-faced youth in a much-soiled apron materialized through a door at the back.

'We ent open,' he said.

'Where's the landlord?' McKenzie wasn't in any mood to fraternize with minions.

'Ent here,' said the youth.

'Where is he then?'

'Clacton.'

'What's he doing in Clacton?'

'Holiday. Allus goes there.'

'Then who the hell's in charge?'

The youth scratched his head. Flakes of dandruff descended. 'Reckon it be Jake.'

'Then fetch him,' McKenzie said.

'He's out back. Beer's just arrived.'

'I don't give a damn if the Archangel Gabriel's turned up in a Spitfire.' McKenzie flashed his card. 'Detective Sergeant McKenzie,' he said curtly. 'Norwich CID. Now fetch him. If he isn't here inside the next couple of minutes, you'll be spending tonight in a cell for obstruction.'

He took the watch from his wrist and laid it on the bar. 'Two minutes,' he said. 'And not a second more.'

*   *   *

If the pudding-faced youth was sparing of words, Jake, a diminutive man with a stoop, proved to be barely more than monosyllabic.

McKenzie eyed him with some dissatisfaction. 'You Jake?' he said.

'Aye.'

'You in charge here?'

'Fer now.'

'You reported an abandoned car.'

The man nodded.

'Where is it?'

'Outside.'

McKenzie refrained from the obvious, scathing comment. It cost him an effort. 'Show me,' he said.

The car was a new open-topped Ford Consul convertible. White and gleaming in the sun, it was parked some fifty yards from the

27

pub up the side road that led to the gates of Holkham Hall.

McKenzie slid into the driving seat and opened the glove compartment. There was nothing inside. He felt in the side pockets. Nothing there either. He couldn't see any keys, and the boot was firmly locked. He looked up at the man. 'You've no idea who owns it?'

'Nah.' Jake grimaced and tossed his head.

'How long's it been here?'

'Sin Sat'dy night.'

'Was there anyone drinking in the pub who might have owned it?'

A shrug. 'Coulda bin.'

'Who?'

Jake threw out his hands. 'Pub were full. Sat'dy, weren' it.'

'You mean you've no idea?'

'Aye. That'd be right.'

McKenzie made a note of the registration number. There was only one way to deal with the Jakes of this world. 'Phone?' he demanded.

A jerk of the thumb. 'Inside.'

'Lead me to it,' McKenzie said.

2.

Whenever there was an incident room to be organized, the task always fell to Detective Constable Desmond Lock; and since the only building in the whole of Burnham Northgate to boast a large enough room was the Northgate church hall, and since the Rector had felt a strong moral obligation to provide what assistance he could to the police, it was Lock who was in charge there to answer McKenzie's call.

'Incident room,' he said.

'This is Mac, Des. I'm in Holkham. You remember that report from Wells about an abandoned car? I want a check on the owner. It's a Ford Consul convertible, CL9547. Be a good lad and ring me back, will you? The Queens Hotel.'

He told Lock the phone number, replaced the receiver, lit a cigarette, and spent the next five minutes in thirsty frustration staring at a large framed poster depicting a tankard of foaming Norfolk ale. When at last the phone rang, his throat felt as dry as a chunk of the Sahara.

'Mac?'

'Speaking.'

'It's registered to Two Furlong Autos, Mill Road in Wells. They're a car-hire firm. Looks like you could be chasing someone on holiday.'

'Well, whoever he is, he must be staying somewhere. Thanks, Des.'

'Best of luck.'

He put the phone down and considered ringing up Two Furlong Autos; but since sounds from the bar indicated that opening time was more or less imminent, he decided

29

that discretion was the better part of valour, and, kick-starting his motorbike, roared off towards Wells.

*   *   *

The twin facts, first, that he used a kick-starter, and second, that he roared away from the Queens Hotel, were sufficient in themselves to mark out McKenzie as something of a non-conformist.

Those officers in Norfolk fortunate enough to be issued with motorbikes were normally allotted a Velocette 'Noddy': silvergrey, powered by a near-silent 149cc engine, started by a pull-handle, and with a maximum speed of fifty miles an hour. But if he'd ever been offered one, McKenzie would have viewed it with utter disdain. Its limited power would have left him as deeply depressed as if he'd been condemned, a confirmed city dweller, to live out the rest of his life in Burnham Northgate.

His own pride and joy was a machine of a very different colour and calibre: an ageing 490cc Norton, which he swore had once won a TT race in the Isle of Man. Painted bright red, incredibly noisy and spitting clouds of acrid blue smoke, it could still be coaxed to reach a sweet sixty on a straight stretch of road; and though Gregg had once described it as a death-trap on wheels, and Tench had more than once compared it to Lubbock's burnt-out old briar, it was, to him, a jewel to be treasured.

But not to Joe Scanlon.

The part-owner and joint chief executive of Two Furlong Autos, he was adding up three long columns of figures when his frail concentration was shattered abruptly by an ear-splitting racket that sounded to him like a battery of machine-guns loosing off a prolonged burst of fire. So, when McKenzie flung open the door, strode towards him and laid two gauntleted hands on his desk, Mr Scanlon was in no frame of mind to offer him a welcoming smile and a handshake.

He looked up and scowled. 'Don't you ever knock?' he said.

McKenzie had been asked that very same question hundreds of times before. He preferred to ignore it. 'Police,' he said, showing his card for the third time that morning. 'You hired out a Ford Consul convertible, registration number CL 9547.'

Scanlon studied the card. When he spoke, he still scowled. 'So what?' he said.

'Did you or didn't you?'

'Might have done. Why?'

'Is that a yes or a no?'

Scanlon gave a shrug. 'All right. Yes, I did. Not a crime, is it?'

'Who did you hire it to?'

'Young fellow, thirtyish. Why? What's the

31

trouble?'

'Don't you know his name?'

Scanlon sighed. He pulled open a drawer, took out a ledger and turned the pages. 'Gave his name as Bolton, Edward Bolton. Hired it last Saturday. Wanted it for a week. Paid on the nail.'

'Address?' McKenzie said.

'Creek Cottage, Common Lane, Brancaster Staithe.'

'Much obliged.' The sergeant turned on his heel and began to walk out.

'Hey. Hang on.' Scanlon raised a hand. 'What's he done? Crashed it?'

'No, the car's safe enough.'

'Then why all the questions?'

'It's Mr Bolton,' McKenzie said. 'He seems to have vanished. But don't worry, we'll be in touch.'

3.

At much the same time as McKenzie was fretfully eyeing the poster that advertised tankards of Norfolk ale, Detective Constable Robert Ellison was ringing the bell of a brick-and-flint cottage four miles to the east in the village of Stiffkey.

Bob Ellison's approach to such a situation bore little resemblance to the sergeant's brusquely impatient method. In his early twenties, fresh-faced, intelligent and

32

something of a scholar, he preferred to adopt a more courteous procedure. When the door was opened and he found himself facing a well-dressed young woman of obvious refinement, he politely inquired if she was, by any chance, Miss Erica Westaway.

'That's right,' she said. 'Are you from the police?'

Ellison produced his card. 'DC Ellison, ma'am,' he said. 'You reported your sister missing?'

She nodded and stepped to one side. 'You'd better come in . . . Would you like a coffee? I was just going to make one.'

He gave her a winning smile. 'Thank you, ma'am,' he said. 'That would be most acceptable.'

*   *   *

It was only ten minutes later, sipping a cup of well-sugared coffee in Miss Westaway's comfortably furnished parlour, that he felt it was time to resume his inquiries. 'Your sister, ma'am,' he said.

'Tamara.'

Ellison made a note. 'Tamara Westaway.'

'No, not Westaway' She corrected him. 'She was married last year. Her name's Tamara Scott.'

He made an amendment. 'Then she doesn't live here?'

'No,' she said. 'Binham. In Priory Court. She was just staying here.'

'And she's been missing since Saturday?'

'Yes. Saturday evening. She left here about seven. Said she was going to catch the bus into Wells. I haven't seen her since.'

'But you expected her back?'

'On Saturday evening? Yes, I thought she'd be back, but I wasn't surprised when she didn't turn up. It was only when she didn't come back again last night . . .'

'You thought something might be wrong?'

She was suddenly troubled. 'I don't want to think so, but it's strange that she hasn't given me a ring.'

Ellison watched her carefully. 'You said you weren't surprised when she didn't come back on Saturday. Why was that?'

She took a deep breath. 'Perhaps I'd better tell you about Tammy,' she said. 'We're sisters, yes, but we're very different. I'm mother's daughter. She's more like my father. I was always the quiet one. She was the wild spirit. She was younger than me by a couple of years, but she'd had half a dozen boyfriends before I'd even ventured to snatch a kiss in the dark . . . Well, to cut the tale short, she got herself into trouble early last year with an older man from Binham. He did the right thing, I suppose, and they were married, but then she had a miscarriage and that was that. It didn't work out . . . Anyway, she turned up here last

Friday saying that she'd left him and she wasn't going back.'

'So you offered to take her in.'

She nodded again. 'She's my sister. I had to. She'd nowhere else to go.'

Ellison glanced down at his notebook. 'And she went out on Saturday to catch a bus to Wells . . .'

'That was what she said. She couldn't settle. She was restless. She needed, she said, to find a bit of life.'

'And what would she mean by that?'

'In Tammy's case, probably finding a pub, and after that a man.'

Ellison nodded. 'And you think she may have found one and stayed out all night.'

'It wouldn't have been the first time, not by a long chalk. But I thought she'd have phoned me sometime yesterday, just to let me know. Set my mind at rest.'

'And you're worried.'

'Apprehensive. That's a better word. I know Tammy. She's never been a very good judge of men.' She paused for a moment. 'You don't think I'm panicking without good reason?'

Ellison shook his head. 'No,' he said, 'I don't. You were right to report it. In a case like this it's always best to err on the side of safety.' He closed his notebook and dropped it in his pocket. 'But don't worry too much. She's probably safe and well. We'll set some inquiries moving, and let you know just as

35

soon as we find her . . . If she does turn up, you'll give us a ring, won't you?'

'Of course.' She gave a faint smile. 'And pray God you're right. There are times when Tammy's so . . . irresponsible.'

'Aren't we all, ma'am?' Ellison said.

4.

Creek Cottage at Brancaster Staithe was yet another brick-and-flint structure with a steep pantiled roof, a couple of dormer windows and a bed-and-breakfast sign. McKenzie surveyed it sourly and pounded on the door. As he fully expected, it evoked no response.

He raised his fist again and delivered a series of hammer blows that raised a flock of seabirds from Brancaster Marsh, and was just about to repeat the process when a small sash window in one of the dormers was thrown up with a rumble and, looking up, he saw, projected from it, a dark, tousled head, an even darker beard and a chest of matted hair.

Before he had time to speak, he was assailed by a voice like a bass bombardon. 'What the hell's all the bloody racket down there?' it roared.

'Police,' McKenzie said. 'Are you Edward Bolton?'

'No, I ent,' the voice roared, 'so bugger off sharp an' let a bloke sleep.' The window slammed shut.

Detective Sergeant William McKenzie was not the type of man to be trifled with by a surly-sounding oaf from those parts of Norfolk that he chose to call 'The Sticks', and the owner of the voice, on his way back to bed, was roused from semi-stupor by a noise like a rock being thrown at the door.

The window was savagely thrown up again. 'Bugger off,' he shouted.

McKenzie flashed his card for the fourth time that morning. 'Get down here now,' he said, 'and open this door, or you'll be under arrest. You've got thirty seconds.' He started counting. 'One . . . two . . . three . . .'

*　　　　*　　　　*

He'd reached twenty-eight when the door was flung open, and a barrel-chested man clad only in trousers stood blocking the entrance. 'You ent comin' in,' he said.

McKenzie looked him up and down. 'Name?' he said curtly.

'None o' your know.'

'Name?'

'Jelf,' the man said sullenly. 'Charlie Jelf. What's yours?'

'Detective Sergeant McKenzie, Norwich CID. Where's Edward Bolton?

'Who?'

'Edward Bolton. Lives here, doesn't he?'

'Lodges, that's all.'

37

'Then where is he?'

'God knows.'

'I think,' McKenzie said, 'you'd better let me in.'

'Then reckon ye'd best be thinkin' agen. I'm off back ter bed.'

The sergeant breathed deeply. 'Mr Jelf,' he said, 'if you don't move aside and let me come in, I'll have no alternative except to arrest you and take you back to Norwich.'

'Fer what?' Jelf was menacing.

'Murder,' McKenzie told him. 'We suspect that someone may have had it in for Mr Bolton, and as things stand you're the most likely suspect.'

The man's jaw dropped. 'Ye must be bloody well shanny. I ent never done no murder.'

'Then stand aside and prove it to me,' McKenzie said.

*   *   *

It was another half-hour before he left Creek Cottage, ten minutes of which was spent prising the facts out of Charlie Jelf and a further twenty in subjecting Bolton's room to a pinpoint search, which in the end had yielded a sizeable wad of significant information.

Mr Bolton, it seemed, had turned up at the cottage the previous Saturday round about midday in a taxi from Norwich. Telling the driver to wait, he'd inspected the room,

38

booked it for a week and paid the rent in advance. The taxi, which had borne the name of Excelsior Cars, had then driven off towards Wells, and Mr Bolton had returned an hour and a half later in possession of a new Ford Consul convertible. He'd spent the afternoon in his room, then left about six o'clock telling Jelf not to worry if he wasn't back that evening. And that was the last that Charlie Jelf had seen of him.

'And you weren't bothered when he didn't turn up last night either?'

'What were there ter bother about?' Jelf was still grudgingly reluctant to help. 'Rent were paid, weren' it? Wouldn' have mattered if he'd stayed out all week. Ent none o' my job what he does with his time.'

That was the point when McKenzie demanded to see Bolton's room. There he found a suitcase, and in one of the back flaps a number of documents that he studied with interest.

Edward Bolton was, like himself, a sergeant, but not in the police. He was a soldier from a Royal Army Service Corps unit stationed in Munchen-Gladbach, West Germany.

He was also on fourteen days' embarkation leave.

5.

It was at three thirty-five that same afternoon that Mr Alexander Rouse squeezed himself and his fiancée, Miss Penelope Layton, into a phone box at Holkham and asked to be connected to the police station at Wells.

*   *   *

Not far from the Queens Hotel, and competing with it for custom, stood the old Victoria facing the coastal road, and from there a tree-lined drive ran down to Holkham Gap, where a twisting path through the thick belt of pine trees planted by Thomas Coke a century and a half before gave access to the broad stretch of sand flanking Holkham Bay.

As he later confessed, not without some embarrassment, to Detective Inspector Gregg, he and Miss Layton had parked their Morris Minor at the edge of the Gap, walked down the path and stretched themselves out on the golden sand. After the storm of the night before, the day was warm and still, and Miss Layton was a girl of irresistible charms. That being so, one thing, as he said, had led to another, and seeking seclusion they'd found it at last deep among the pines. They must, at one point, have dropped off to sleep, and it was nearly an hour later when, picking their way back between the trees to the path, they'd stumbled across what remained of the carnage.

'It was sickening,' he said. 'There was so much blood that Penny turned white as a sheet. I thought she was going to faint. She was shaking from head to foot. I had to help her all the way back to the car.'

*   *   *

Gregg, standing among the pines, could well believe what he'd said.

There were items of blood-soaked clothing thrown about haphazardly: what had once been a white shirt, a pair of trousers, shoes, socks and underclothes; a silk blouse and skirt, nylon stockings, a suspender belt: all scattered across the pine needles, as if they'd been ripped off in some kind of frenzy and tossed aside with no respect for the wearers.

At one point between the boles of two of the pines, the needles themselves were dark-stained with blood and heavily scuffed as if someone had writhed and twisted on the ground.

And, peering more closely, Gregg saw what he thought were fragments of flesh and bone.

Ten minutes later he was ringing Mike Tench from the phone box at Holkham.

6.

That was how it began: the affair at Burnham Northgate.

Two naked bodies grotesquely laid out in the graveyard adjoining a Norfolk village church and, four miles to the east, a clutch of bloodstained clothes discovered deep among the pine woods that fringed a sweep of shimmering golden sand.

To Detective Chief Inspector Michael Bruce Tench they presented what seemed, at least for a time, an intractable problem, and one which developed its own peculiar blend of mysteries.

A double murder. Yes, that was plain enough to see. But who was it who'd savagely struck down the victims and then left them trapped beneath an old weathered gravestone in a parody of passion?

And not only that. Why had he done it?

When, in the months that followed, he looked back on the way that events had unfolded, Mike Tench never called it The Northgate Affair. To him it was always The Rionero Case.

And that, in itself, was something of a mystery.

III

PATIENCE

Patience is a flower that grows not in
everyone's garden.
English proverb

1.

When, at the end of the war, Mike Tench had been cast adrift from the army, he'd been faced with a decision. Should he go back to Cambridge and complete the degree course broken in half so rudely by his call-up, or should he elect to train for a different kind of life?

The two years he'd spent at Cambridge reading history until the war and the army had wrenched him away, had left him with a fierce, pervasive love for the town. It was there that he'd begun to grow from a boy into a man. It held memories that would stay with him for the rest of his life: boating on a summer afternoon up to Grantchester; wrestling with pointless examination papers as the flashes of war lit the Dunkirk beaches; nights spent talking with friends as the shadows lengthened and night closed down on the age-weathered stones; and sunlit days on the Backs, watching the clouds as they drifted across the pinnacles of King's . . . And other reminders, too: the wistaria hanging in purple cascades from old college walls; the silence of ancient courts deep in the snow; and the sound that still for him held everything of Cambridge: the bells ringing out from innumerable towers on a Sunday morning . . .

But what Cambridge had started, the war and the army, between them, had finished. The boy was now a man, and the man had very different ambitions from the boy; and that was why, after much troubled thought, he'd chosen in the end not to go back, but to join the police and train for the CID.

Drafted first to Fakenham and then, as detective sergeant, to work under Lubbock's guidance in Norwich, he'd suffered a great deal, but learnt even more. That was when Bill McKenzie, his fellow sergeant, already middle-aged and completely unambitious, had offered him a few words of timely advice. 'You want to get on?' he'd said. 'You want to make inspector sooner or later? Well, you could just be lucky. You're with the right man. Watch him and learn. Don't assume that he's past it because his hair's white. The Chief's more than simply a competent copper. He's a legend here in Norwich. Follow him around. Keep your eyes and ears open. He may seem to you to be painfully slow. You'll find yourself saying he's just wasting time. Well, think it but don't say it. He'll drop on you like a ton of bricks if you step out of line. So be careful, watch your step. Learn to duck and weave, and never forget that his conviction record's the best in Norfolk.'

He'd taken Mac's advice, and he'd learnt. He'd learnt the hard way; not without the bricks; but he'd kept his head down, taught himself to read the signs: the frown, then the glare and the tightening of the lines around Lubbock's lips that always warned of the scathing comment to come. There'd been months of frustration: months when he'd seemed to act as nothing but a teaboy, laying on pots of strong Darjeeling tea to quench the old boy's seemingly insatiable thirst. It had been a disconcerting apprenticeship, full of uncertainties, riddled with doubts, but he'd slowly come to realize that Lubbock's methods of training were, like the man himself, unique. He'd been content to let his young assistant trail after him, learning by example to weigh all the evidence, not to move too fast, to think before he jumped to any conclusions. He hadn't spared him the frequent explosions of wrath; had cut the ground from his feet on more than one occasion; but, once he'd felt it was time to let him off the leash, he hadn't been reluctant to trust him with the chance.

If his training had been harsh, it had nonetheless been effective, and Tench had, in course of time, come to see the old man in a different light. He'd marked him down at first as an irascible old devil, difficult to work with, devious in his crab-like approach to a problem, yet intolerant of any step that diverged from his tried and tested procedures; but, almost imperceptibly, he'd come to appreciate that, behind the short temper and apparent illogicality, there was a thoroughness that laid bare the bones of a case, like a surgeon's knife probing the source of an infection. He got the results, and results, as Tench knew, were what counted in the end.

More than that, the old boy had mellowed. Or perhaps that wasn't the whole of the truth. Perhaps Tench himself, as his confidence increased, had found him easier to work with. What he'd first condemned as faults, he'd come to see later as nothing but foibles; and whereas, in the early days, he'd always watched him with suspicion, that suspicion had gradually melted away, to be replaced by a kind of amused affection.

Since Lubbock's retirement, the bond between them had strengthened. He'd spent more than one evening in the cottage at Cley, drinking the coffee that Lubbock kept stowed away against such a visit, tapping into his inexhaustible fund of local knowledge, seeking answers to his own unfamiliar problems, and listening to his old Chief, through clouds of pungent pipe-smoke, rambling on about his wonderful windmills.

He owed him more than a little, and though—a DCl himself now for more than two years—there were times when he resented his continued interference, he knew very well, as he'd confessed to the Chief Super, that he'd never be able to bring himself to warn the old boy off.

Old loyalties died hard, old affections

persisted and, as Tench secretly admitted to himself, there always lurked somewhere that weary appreciation that Lubbock's fund of knowledge about his own county was an asset far too valuable to be thrust aside out of sheer exasperation.

So, yes, he'd bite his tongue and let his old Chief ramble on. It was better that way.

2.

And he was ready to admit another thing, too: that wherever he was and whatever he did in the years to come, Lubbock would, in a sense, always be with him. Even when his old Chief was laid to rest beneath his own gravestone, as sometime had to happen, he'd still hear the gruff voice striving to reach him through clouds of tobacco smoke, repeating its principles of crime investigation: 'Listen and learn . . . Let the case simmer. It'll come to the boil in its own good time' . . . and the most frequently repeated of all his dicta, 'Patience, laddie, patience! That's what you need in a case of murder, and it isn't a flower that grows in everyone's garden. Plant it firmly in yours. Tend it with care.'

The old boy had a fondness for horticultural metaphors, and there was one in particular that he, Mike Tench, would never forget. He'd heard it first of all in the cottage at Cley, and again and again in the years that ensued.

Solving a murder, Lubbock insisted, was much like the business of cultivating roses. You needed to prune the evidence you'd gathered, discarding most of it as quite immaterial; you scratched yourself from time to time following clues that led absolutely nowhere; and then one day, after weeks or perhaps even months of waiting, the case would open out like a beautiful flower.

That, of course, was why patience was needed, but, of all his old Chief's virtues, it still remained the one he'd found hardest to cultivate. The lack of it had brought strictures down on his head, not once, but many times, yet always in the same rigid pattern of words: 'Don't rush things, laddie. Most murders solve themselves if you give them the time. Hold your horses. Watch and wait.'

There'd been more than one occasion in the past two years when his patience had been tested almost to the limit—when clues had run dry and cases had seemed insoluble, when paths that he'd been following had led to brick walls, and when normal procedures had failed to produce the results he'd expected.

The Medford case had been a classic example. It should have been easy to establish her identity—the young woman found dead on the sands at Blacknock—and yet time had dragged on, and four full days after the body had been discovered he still hadn't been able to say for certain exactly who she was.

That was why, standing with Lubbock in the graveyard at Burnham Northgate, he'd had the unwelcome feeling that events were about to repeat themselves. Looking down at the two naked bodies, their faces battered into pulp, he'd prepared himself to face another Medford, and Lubbock's words had confirmed his own fears. There might very well be a long haul ahead.

That had been Sunday morning, but on Tuesday afternoon, when he swept up his files, made his way down the corridor and knocked on Hastings' door, he did so with a mixture of relief and satisfaction. Up to that point, at least, there'd been little need for patience. Although the main questions—who killed them and why—still demanded resolution, he knew who the victims were, and that was the first and very necessary step to tracing their killer.

As Lubbock might have said, the case was beginning to simmer—and, seemingly, on time.

3.

'So they weren't Lubbock's "travelling dead",' Hastings said.

'Well, they travelled, sir, it's true, but not very far. Only from Holkham. Roughly four miles.'

'And you've identified both of them?'

'I think so, sir, yes. The evidence we have is pretty compelling. When we get the dental records, it should be confirmed, but I don't think there's any doubt about who they were. The woman's husband and her sister identified the bloodstained clothes that were found at Holkham, and her blood group was AB. That's comparatively rare. It only affects some four per cent of the population. And the man had a scar on the thigh, an old war wound, apart from other distinguishing body marks. He was a serving soldier. They were listed in his pay book.'

The Chief Super frowned. 'He wasn't a deserter?'

'No, sir. Sergeant Edward Bolton, stationed in West Germany with BAOR. He was on a fortnight's embarkation leave, prior to posting to the Suez Canal Zone. He'd already spent five days in Norwich, staying with his brother, and had just booked into a bed-and-breakfast at Brancaster Staithe. Not a good choice as it happened. The place was run by a Mrs Ada Jelf, but she walked out on her husband the following day, and according to McKenzie, Jelf's the sort of chap who wouldn't know how to fry an egg. So if Bolton had lived he wouldn't have got any breakfast.'

'And the woman?'

'Mrs Tamara Scott. Lived with her husband at Priory Court, Binham, but, like Mrs Jelf, she'd just done a spot of walking out, too.

Gone to stay with her sister over at Stiffkey Went out on Saturday evening to find some night life in Wells, and never came back.'

'So what d'you think happened?'

'Well, we don't know for sure, sir, but it looks very much as though somewhere en route she met up with Bolton. He'd hired a car from a firm in Wells, and we found it abandoned by the Queens Hotel at Holkham. We don't know for certain whether or not they were drinking there, but at some time they must have wandered down to the pine woods at the Gap, and that was where they were murdered. The question is, were they followed? And if they were, who followed them and why?'

'Robbery?'

'No, sir, we've ruled that out. Among the things we found at Holkham were Bolton's wallet and Mrs Scott's handbag. Thirty pounds in the wallet and seven in the handbag. As far as we can tell, nothing had been taken.'

'Then what about the woman's husband? Sounds to me that he's the most likely suspect.'

'Gregg's bringing him in, sir. At the moment we're trying to trace back their movements. It looks very much as if Bolton met up with her somewhere in Wells, and then drove her to Holkham. We've no evidence that they knew one another before they met, so it was probably just a random meeting in a pub.'

'Is it possible it could have been a random

killing?'

'Let's hope not,' said Tench, 'but that's what I'm afraid of. Random killers are always difficult to track down. If it was, we've got a violent maniac on the loose. According to Ledward, the attack was frenzied. Both of them were struck some twenty or thirty times.'

'What with? Was he able to say?'

'Some heavy implement.'

'A hammer?'

'No, sir. He ruled that out. Could have been an iron bar, but we just don't know.'

'Any sexual interference?'

'No, none at all, but they'd both been drinking and there was evidence of recent sexual intercourse. Semen from Bolton was found in the woman. It's pretty clear that's the reason they went down to the woods. They were looking for a place where they wouldn't be disturbed.'

The Chief Super nodded. 'But they were, and savagely. Have we any clues at all that could lead us to the killer?'

'At the moment, sir, few, and they aren't very likely to be of much use till we get to lay hands on a viable suspect. Ledward says he was right-handed, but so are most people. He did find hairs adhering to Bolton's fingers, and passed them to the lab. We're hoping that Merrick may be able to tell us something when he's put them under the microscope. And the scene-of-crime squad turned up one thing at least that might provide a clue. There's a patch of the churchyard that's been recently seeded. The ground's soft there and almost bare. They found a footprint, ribbed, possibly made by a wellington boot. They took a cast of it, but of course there's no guarantee that it was left by the killer.'

Hastings frowned. 'There's one thing, Mike,' he said, 'that puzzles me about this case, and perhaps it's something that you should start puzzling over, too. A man beats the living daylight out of two lovers in the woods at Holkham, but he doesn't leave the bodies there. He drives them four miles to Burnham Northgate, carries them into the churchyard, lays them out as if they're still making love, and pushes a gravestone down on top of them. But why?'

Tench gave a shrug. 'At the moment, sir, I haven't the slightest idea.'

'But he must have had some reason. Maybe it's worth a few serious thoughts. If only we knew why, it might give us a lead.'

'It might, sir, yes, but he's the only one who can tell us just why he did it. We have to find him first.'

There was a pause. Hastings looked at his DCI. 'Think about it, Mike,' he said. 'This man must have had some compelling reason for acting as he did. After all, he was taking an unnecessary risk. The whole procedure must have taken some time. He could easily have been seen.'

'It was after midnight, sir. The church stands on its own, and there's a band of trees between the graveyard and the village . . .'

'Even so,' said Hastings, 'what he did seems irrational.'

'Well, he must have been irrational, mustn't he, sir,' said Tench, 'to beat two innocent people to death. So the sooner we find him, the better.'

'It could be the husband.'

'It could, sir, yes, but somehow I've a sneaking feeling it isn't.'

'What makes you say that?'

'Too simple, sir,' said Tench. 'Maybe I'm a pessimist, but I get the impression that this isn't something we're going to wrap up in a matter of days.'

The Chief Super looked down his nose. 'Then it's up to me to play the optimist, isn't it, Mike? Just keep me up to date. And remember, if you need any help, I'm available night and day. I'm not like Reg Ledward. My phone bell ringing at three in the morning isn't likely to bring bricks raining down on your head. Let's get this sorted out just as soon as we can. We don't want the Chief Constable calling in the Met, and if it drags on, he will.'

'And that'll be the worst of all possible worlds.'

'Chaos,' Hastings said, 'and chaos we can't

afford. So let's look on the bright side. It won't come to that.'

4.

It was unlike Mike Tench to be pessimistic. Cautious, yes; but expecting the worst was something more akin to McKenzie's line of thought, and as he made his way back along the corridor to his office, he asked himself why, when the case was already beginning to simmer, he'd resigned himself to a long investigation.

The only reason he could find was that what he'd seen on Sunday morning in Burnham Northgate churchyard had been so bizarre— the two dead bodies so gruesomely juxtaposed, the gravestone deliberately toppled to trap them—that it had invested the whole business with an improbability that seemed to defy any logical solution. And the logical solution was, of course, that Robert Stratton Scott, devastated by the fact of his wife's desertion, had followed her and killed both her and her lover.

No, he just couldn't convince himself that, in a case such as this, the first and most obvious solution that came to mind would prove to be the right one. That would be far too simple, too swift an answer to what appeared to be a demented piece of grotesquerie.

He just couldn't believe that a few straightforward questions posed to this man, the first apparent suspect, would reveal the whole truth behind what he felt was a complicated case.

But that remained to be seen.

*   *   *

Gregg was waiting in his office.

'Where is he?' said Tench.

'Down in the interview room, sir. Rayner's with him.'

'Any trouble?'

Gregg shrugged. 'Protested a bit. Didn't see why he should have to come all the way to Norwich. To put it mildly, he's not in the best of tempers.'

'Too bad.' Tench was blandly unsympathetic. 'How long's he been waiting?'

'A good ten minutes.'

The DCI pulled out a chair and sat down. 'Another five,' he said, 'won't hurt him. Then we'll go down and see what he has to say for himself.'

*   *   *

Scott had plenty to say and was determined to say it. A small, but stocky and powerful man, he seemed unimpressed by the two six-foot detectives facing him across the table. 'Why

58

am I here?' he said. 'Am I under arrest, and if so, what for?'

Tench opened a file. 'You are Robert Stratton Scott?'

'You know damned well that I'm Robert Stratton Scott. What the hell am I here for?'

'You live at 7 Priory Court in the village of Binham?'

'You know that as well, so give me an answer.'

'There's no question of you being under arrest, Mr Scott. You're free to leave whenever you wish to do so . . .'

Scott pushed back his chair. 'Good. Then I'm off. I've a business to run.'

'. . . but it would be most unwise for you to take that course.'

'Would it indeed? Why?'

'I don't think you appreciate the position you're in.'

'Don't I? Then perhaps you'll explain it to me. Otherwise I'm on my way back to Binham.'

'We're investigating a case of murder, Mr Scott.'

'I'm well aware of that.'

'The murder of your wife.'

'That's nothing to do with me.'

'Then you'll have no objection to answering a few questions.'

Scott drew a deep breath. 'And just how long's that going to take?'

'That depends on you. Not very long if you're prepared to co-operate.'

'I don't see why I should, but go ahead, ask. What is it you want to know?'

'You run an antiques shop in Binham?'

'Yes, and I've had to close it. I'm losing money.'

'How long were you married to your wife, Mr Scott?'

'We were married in March last year.'

'Not very long, then.'

'More than long enough.'

'It wasn't a happy marriage?'

'You could say that.'

'You don't seem greatly upset by her death.'

'I'm not shedding tears, if that's what you mean.'

'You were glad to be rid of her?'

Scott gave a shrug. 'She asked for it, didn't she?'

'I don't know, Mr Scott. That's why I'm asking you.'

'Well, take it from me. She did.'

There was a pause. Tench said nothing.

'Look, Chief Inspector, it was a marriage of convenience, no more than that. She was pregnant. I hadn't known her for long, but I felt I had a responsibility. It was only after she lost the child that I found out what she was really like.'

'And what was she really like?'

'She was a bitch, a promiscuous bitch. I'd

60

already begun to take steps to divorce her.'

'Then it was very convenient for you that she died.'

'I'm not denying that.'

'Did you kill her?'

Scott glared. 'No, of course I bloody didn't.' He glanced at his watch. 'Now is that the lot? Because as far as I'm concerned, you're just wasting my time.'

5.

Tench made no comment. He simply sat back and slid the file across to Gregg.

Unlike McKenzie, Andrew Gregg had always been ambitious, if discreetly so; and again unlike McKenzie, he cherished the notion that he was a man of some refinement. To him, the concept of style was important, and his initial approach to witnesses, and indeed to suspects, was always in consequence one of polite inquiry; and this, in some quarters, created the impression that he was most unlikely to be anything more than gentle, well-mannered and mildly ineffectual.

But those who inadvertently jumped to this conclusion were deceiving themselves. As they later discovered, to their considerable cost, Gregg could, on occasion, be intimidating, caustic and utterly relentless in pursuit of the evidence he was determined to acquire; and his promotion from sergeant to detective inspector three months before had merely served to convince him that his methods were correct.

He turned three sheets in the file, and then turned them back. 'You seem,' he said, 'to be an honest, plain-spoken man, Mr Scott.'

'I try to be, yes.'

'Then I'm sure you'd want us to track down the man who murdered your wife in such a brutal fashion.'

'Of course I would. That goes without saying.'

'Then bear with us, sir. All we're trying to do is to build up a picture of what might have happened.'

Scott gave a sigh. 'But it's nothing to do with me. I haven't the faintest idea what happened.'

'That still doesn't mean that you can't be of help.'

'I don't see how.'

'Then let me explain, sir. You lived with your wife for more than a year. You must have known her far better than we can ever hope to do. And we need to understand her. Details that you think are quite irrelevant may be of considerable value to us. Like pieces of a jigsaw, they may help us to build up the picture we need.'

Scott shrugged his shoulders. 'Fair enough. Fire away.'

'When was the last time you saw her?'

'Friday morning. She was still in bed when I

left to open up the shop.'

'You don't live over the shop?'

'No, we're in Priory Court. The shop's in the main street . . . When I closed the place for lunch and got back home, she'd gone.'

'Gone in what sense?'

'Walked out. Left me. Packed a couple of suitcases, and just disappeared.'

'Did she leave a note?'

'No.'

'You were surprised then to find her gone?'

'Not in the slightest.'

'Why not?'

'She told me the night before.'

'She told you on the Thursday night that she was leaving on the Friday?'

'Yes, it was no surprise. It had been coming for months.'

'But you went out to work as usual on the Friday morning? Didn't you try to stop her?'

'Why should I do that? I was better off without her.'

'Had you quarrelled on Thursday night?'

'We had a row, yes. We had one every night. It was the usual thing.'

'What was it about?'

'More or less everything. When was she going to pull her weight at the shop? When was she going to stop wasting my money? When was she going to stop sleeping around? The top and bottom of it was we were quite incompatible.'

'What started it that night?'

'She'd stayed out the night before.'

'Where?'

Scott shrugged again. 'Don't ask me. It must have been with some man. It usually was. She was emptying my bank account. I told her I was going to put a stop on her cheques.'

'And?'

'She told me what she thought of me. Accused me of every crime under the sun, and said she was off. She wasn't going to put up with my nagging any more.'

'And what did you say?'

'I told her it was the best idea she'd come up with for months. I'd be happy to see her go.'

'And she went.'

'She went,' Scott said, 'and bloody good riddance. It'll be a long time before I get married again.'

6.

Gregg turned to another sheet in the file. 'Did you know she'd gone to stay with her sister?'

'No.'

'But you guessed she might have done.'

'It was always a possibility.'

'So you followed her.'

Scott stared at him. 'Why the hell should I do that?'

'Are you saying you didn't?'

'Of course I damned well didn't. As far as I

was concerned she was out of my life. That was just what I wanted.'

'It didn't bother you that she might have gone off with another man?'

'Why should it? She'd already had a string of men. There was bound to be another one sooner or later. She couldn't keep her hands off them.'

'You say she'd had a string of them. Did you know their names?'

'Some. Not all.'

'Does the name Edward Bolton ring any bells?'

'Not even a tinkle. If he was the one she was found with, she probably picked him up in some pub. That was the sort of thing she usually did.'

'Where were you, Mr Scott, between six o'clock on Saturday evening and six thirty on Sunday morning?'

There was a sigh of impatience. 'Look, Inspector, if you think I spent the night chasing round Norfolk trying to find a woman I was glad to see the back of, then you'd better think again . . .'

'Just answer the question, please, Mr Scott. Where were you between those times?'

'I closed the shop at five thirty. From there I walked back to Priory Court. Then I spent the rest of the evening and night at home.'

'On your own?'

'On my own. It was a relief to think that at

last she'd upped and gone. I opened a bottle of Glenfiddich and spent the evening bringing the shop accounts up to date. I went to bed about eleven, and slept until seven on Sunday morning.'

'You didn't see or communicate with anyone?'

'No. Why should I? If I'd known I was going to be suspected of murder, I'd have driven into Norwich, booked in at the Maid's Head and had room service running around half the night. As it was, I didn't bother. I passed a diligent evening, and slept the sleep of the innocent.'

'So there's no one who can corroborate what you say.'

'No one at all. You'll just have to take my word.'

'And what if we're not prepared to do that, Mr Scott?'

Scott shrugged again. 'Then it's just too bad. I can't do anything about it.'

Gregg raised his eyebrows. 'You tell us you were glad to be rid of your wife. You knew she'd walked out. You suspected she'd gone to stay with her sister. You knew very well she'd be meeting another man. You claim to have spent the night she was murdered completely on your own at Priory Court. You haven't one single witness to confirm your account, and you expect us to accept what you say as the truth? That's expecting a very great deal, Mr

Scott.'

'You mean you don't believe me.'

'Why should we?' said Gregg. 'You had the motive to kill her. You had the opportunity, and you've no satisfactory alibi for the time of her death.'

Scott pushed back his chair for the second time and, standing, slammed it back against the table. 'I've had enough of this nonsense,' he said. 'I've told you what happened. If you're not prepared to believe me, then that's not my fault. I'm off back to Binham.'

'Sit down, Mr Scott.'

'You said I was free to leave. Right then. I'm leaving.'

'Sit down.' This time it was Tench who spoke, quietly and yet with a crisp authority.

There was a moment's hesitation. Scott glared at him.

'I still have something to say, Mr Scott. If you're anxious to leave, then I suggest you pull out that chair and sit down.'

The chair scraped across the floor.

'Thank you,' said Tench. 'Now listen, and listen very carefully. You must appreciate our position. Inspector Gregg is quite right. We've no means of knowing whether your statement is true or false. We know nothing about you and, that being so, you can hardly expect us to take you on trust. Before we do that, we need to make further inquiries . . . For the moment, Mr Scott, you're free to go, but we may need to see you again very soon, so be prepared to make yourself available, and that means whenever we happen to do so . . . I trust you'll not be travelling very far from Binham.'

Scott breathed deeply. 'I'm an antiques dealer. You know that, Chief Inspector. I get around to sales. I've arranged to attend one tomorrow in Cambridge. You mean I shouldn't go?'

Tench gave a nod. 'That's precisely what I mean.'

'Well, if that's an order . . .'

The Chief Inspector was terse. 'It is, Mr Scott. If you want us to trust you, then stay close to Binham.'

7.

They watched as a police car pulled out of the compound, taking him back to the antiques shop. Tench swept up the file. 'So, Andy,' he said, 'what's your opinion of our friend Mr Scott?'

'As a possible suspect?'

'As our only suspect.'

'Forget him, sir,' said Gregg. 'He's a bit bolshie, yes, but his tale was convincing enough. I believed him.'

'You think he really did spend the whole night in Binham?'

'If he didn't, he's a better liar than I think he is.'

'Jealousy can be a powerful motive,' said Tench.

'Yes, sir, it can, but that's the whole point. He showed no sign of being jealous. I got the impression that he'd just given up completely on his wife. As he said, she'd gone, and good riddance to bad rubbish. Let her go and plague someone else for a change. And if what he said was true, and he's already taking steps to divorce her, why would he want to kill her? If she's had a string of men, he's good grounds for divorce, apart from all the other charges he levelled against her . . . No, sir, he's not the one. We'll have to look elsewhere.' He paused. 'Unless, of course . . .'

'What?'

'Unless, sir, you think he was telling us a pack of lies.'

Tench gave a sigh. 'That's the trouble,' he said. 'I don't. I'm with you all the way; but we'll need to do some checking. That's your job, Andy. Find out who his solicitor is, and his bank, and talk to them both. And do a bit of nosing round Binham. Let's be sure he's in the clear before we strike him off the list. If you turn up two or three times at his shop, he'll be more than eager to get you off his back. It might persuade him to be a little more helpful, don't you think?'

Gregg seemed doubtful. 'It might, sir,' he said.

'Then I'll leave him to you. I'm off to

Burnham, so ring up Lock and tell him I'm on my way. Let's see what the rest of the team have dredged up. If we're looking for someone else, then we need a fresh lead. Until we find one we're just thrashing around in the dark.'

8.

The first reports he heard provided no lead at all. Detective Constables Rayner and Spurgeon, conducting a house-to-house in Burnham Northgate, had drawn a complete blank. No one in the village, so it seemed, had noticed anything unusual happening around the church late on Saturday night or early Sunday morning. As in most Norfolk villages, once the light had begun to fade, they'd closed their cottage doors, drawn their curtains and left the rest of the world to fend for itself. As Rayner drily remarked, a whole Panzer division could have driven through the Burnhams and no one would have seen them.

*   *   *

It was left to Sue Gradwell to provide the single spark of illumination.

WDC Susan Jane Gradwell, the only woman on Tench's team, was young, intelligent and self-possessed, and she was also frustrated.

When she'd joined the CID a couple of

years before, she'd imagined herself as a kind of pioneer, bringing something to a totally masculine squad that had hitherto been lacking; solving the odd intractable case by a typical flash of woman's intuition; appraised as an asset in the fight against crime, and possessing a talent unique in itself that no one would possibly dare to misappropriate.

But it hadn't turned out to be quite like that. It was true she'd been regarded as something unique, but her singularity had been that of the only sex object within easy vision: a slip of a girl, first to be ogled and then dismissed as a mere strip of frippery to be tacked on the fringe of a squad of complacently self-sufficient men.

She'd spent most of her time proving her male associates' all too plausible thesis that the most mundane, petty and boring tasks were purposely designed to be done by women. She'd held the hands of bereaved wives and mothers, tended weeping sisters and calmed bewildered children. She'd returned victims' clothes to grieving relations, answered the phone in the CID room, typed out innumerable statements from suspects, and done little else but run errands for those who refused to bother themselves with the routine chores; and when, at last, more out of boredom than anything else, she'd decided it was time to use her own initiative, she'd been left battered and bound on an airfield runway, lucky to escape death at the hands of a man who'd revealed himself as a multiple killer.

For a few days, lying in a hospital bed, she'd been a heroine, if a misguided one; but, once back with the squad, nothing seemed to have changed. All the men she worked with, McKenzie, Gregg and Lock, Ellison, Rayner and Spurgeon, even the Chief himself, if not misogynistic, still clung to the belief that God had designed women to do this and men to do that, and this was always the most tedious, uninspiring and unproductive.

Since then, it was true, she'd detected in one of them, Constable Bob Ellison, something strangely appealing that marked him out from the rest of his colleagues and awakened inside her from time to time feelings that, for the sake of survival in a masculine world, she was determined to hold in check. But, apart from that, her job had remained as tedious and uninspiring as it always had been. She might just as well have stayed with the uniformed branch.

Not that her smouldering dissatisfaction was visible that afternoon. Standing demurely alongside Rayner and Spurgeon, her fair hair swept back and pinned in a pleat, her eyebrows delicately pencilled, her upper lip very much the Cupid's bow, she knew that for once she had the advantage, and as Tench turned towards her, she was ready to make the most of it.

72

'Sue,' he said. 'What about you? Anything to report?'

She nodded. 'One thing, sir, yes. It might be important. I took over the phone from Constable Lock. There was a call.'

'Who from?'

'A man, sir. I don't know his name.'

'You asked him?'

'Yes, but he wouldn't tell me.'

'What did he have to say?'

'He wanted to speak to whoever was in charge of the murders at Burnham Northgate. I said DCI Tench, but I told him you weren't immediately available and I didn't know where you were.'

'And what did he say to that?'

'He said he thought he must have seen the murderer, but he wasn't going to speak to anyone but you, so I asked him where he was phoning from. He said he was in a phone box at Stanhoe.'

'Where's that?'

'It's about four miles south of here, sir, on the road to Great Bircham, so I told him to stay there, I'd be down in ten minutes.'

'And did he?'

'He took some persuading, and I didn't know whether I'd find him there or not, but yes, sir, he was there.'

'Go on.'

'Well, he wouldn't tell me anything. Said he had to see you. So I told him there was only

73

one way to do that. He'd have to come back here with me.'

'And did he?'

'Yes, sir. After a long argument.'

'And where is he now?'

'In the stock room, sir. Constable Ellison's with him.'

'And he said that he'd actually seen the murderer?'

'Thought he must have done, sir.'

Tench pushed back his chair. 'Then we'd better go and have a little chat with him,' he said. 'Hadn't we, Sue?'

9.

The stock room at Burnham Northgate was like most other stock rooms attached to church halls: a clutter of stacked chairs and tables, cups, saucers and plates, and dust-ridden piles of long-discarded hymn books. In the centre, with barely any space to pass round it, was a single trestle table, and seated at it was a tall, slim young man with Brylcreemed hair and a pencil-line moustache.

Tench dismissed Ellison, wrestled with two chairs, one for himself and the other for Sue Gradwell, wound his six-foot frame into the insufficient gap between table and chair, took from his pocket first a notebook, then a pen, and favoured the man with what he hoped was a winning smile. 'Good afternoon, sir,' he said.

74

'I understand from Detective Constable Gradwell that you've something to tell me.'

The young man looked him up and down. 'That depends,' he said.

'On what, sir?'

'It depends on who you are.'

Tench took a deep breath. 'My name is Tench. Detective Chief Inspector Tench. I'm in charge of the investigations here at Burnham Northgate.'

'Have you any means of identification?'

Tench produced his warrant card and slid it across the table. The man studied it carefully and then pushed it back.

'Now, sir,' said Tench. 'You know my name. Would you care to tell me yours?'

'Is that necessary?'

'Yes, I'm afraid it is. If we're to take a statement from you, we must know who you are.'

The young man inclined his head. 'Very well then,' he said. 'If you have to know, then I suppose I must tell you. My name is Truscott, Francis Webb Truscott. I'm a flight lieutenant in the RAF, stationed at North Creake.'

'And what is it you have to tell us, Flight Lieutenant?'

'I think I may have seen the man who committed this crime.'

'Where, sir, and when?'

'In the churchyard here at about quarter to two last Sunday morning.'

'And what exactly did you see?'

'Nothing at first, but I heard the sound of a car.'

'And where were you at this time?'

'I was in my own car. It was parked in the band of trees at the edge of the churchyard.'

'Go on, sir,' said Tench.

'I was just about to switch on my sidelights, but I didn't, because the car slowed down, the driver switched off his own lights, turned into the trees and parked about fifty yards from where I was. I didn't particularly want to be seen at that time, so I stayed where I was and watched. The view I had was restricted by the trunks of the trees, but from the passenger seat I could see through a gap. It wasn't a car, but a van. The driver got out and opened the doors at the back. Then he lifted out what looked to me like a wheelbarrow, loaded on to it something heavy—it seemed like a sack—and wheeled it away through the trees towards the churchyard.'

'Was it a barrow?'

Truscott nodded. 'Yes, I saw it again after that, and decided it was.'

'You stayed in the car?'

Another nod. 'Yes, I was a bit intrigued by that time. There wasn't much of a chance that he'd spot my car—it was black, without lights—so I waited and went on watching. After about five minutes, he came back through the trees, trundling the barrow,

76

opened the van doors again, tossed something inside, loaded up another sack, and made off again towards the churchyard.'

'You waited?'

'Yes, I did. The whole affair seemed a bit fishy to me: a van without lights, and a chap toting sacks into a graveyard at two o'clock in the morning. So I thought, if he was going to be away for another five minutes, I'd take a closer look. I gave him time to get clear, then took a stroll towards the van. It wasn't a very big one, and at that time of night it was difficult to see the colour. It could have been dark blue, black or even dark green, and I couldn't tell the make—I'm no expert on vans—but I did make a note of the registration number.'

Tench was impassive. 'What was it, sir?' he said.

'It was a Norwich number,' said Truscott. 'CL4658.'

10.

Tench made a note. 'We'll get it checked, sir . . . What happened after that?'

'Well, I must have spent longer by the van than I thought, or else he did the second trip quicker than the first, because I heard him coming back and had to do a quick scarper. I hadn't enough time, even so, to get back to the car. I was still about ten yards short, so I dropped to the ground and hoped he wouldn't see me. He opened the van doors again, put the barrow back inside, and took out a spade. Then he closed the doors—he was always careful to do that—and set off again through the trees.'

'With the spade?'

'Oh, yes, he was carrying the spade.'

'And how long was he away the third time?'

Truscott shook his head. 'That I can't tell you. He'd only just disappeared, when a lorry came past with its headlights blazing. It lit up both our cars, so I thought it was best not to tempt fate any further. I backed out of the trees and drove off at speed through the village and back to North Creake. I didn't switch on the lights till I was clear of the church.'

'Did you see any name on the side of the van?'

'No, it was just coloured dark and anonymous.'

'And you didn't get a chance to look inside the back?'

'No, I was just about to do that when I heard him coming back.'

'Can you describe the man?'

Truscott shrugged. 'Only vaguely. It was dark and I couldn't make out his face. He wasn't very tall. I'd say he was around five-seven or five-eight. Seemed fairly thick-set. Gave the impression of a man of some strength. He didn't have any trouble manhandling the sacks. But there was one thing I remember. He had a pronounced limp.'

'Which leg?'

'The left. It was quite distinctive. He walked as if that leg was shorter than the other.'

Tench nodded slowly. 'Well, thank you, Flight Lieutenant. From what you've told us, we shouldn't have any difficulty in tracing the man.' He paused. 'But there are a couple of questions that we'd still like to ask.'

Truscott looked uneasy. 'What are they?' he said.

Tench slid the notebook across to Sue Gradwell. She looked up at Truscott and frowned. 'You saw all this, sir, early on Sunday morning. It's now late on Tuesday. Why have you taken so long to come forward and tell us?'

'I didn't see the report of the murders till I read this morning's paper, and I couldn't get away from the base till early this afternoon.'

'But surely, sir, what you saw was highly suspicious. It was two o'clock in the morning. A man carrying sacks and a spade into a graveyard. Wasn't it your duty to report such an incident?'

Truscott shifted uncomfortably. 'I thought about it, yes, but I decided to wait. It might have been nothing. I didn't want to look foolish. It was only this morning when I read about the murders that I put two and two together.'

Sue Gradwell raised her delicately pencilled eyebrows. 'And that was the only reason?'

'No, perhaps not, but it's the only one I'm prepared to offer.'

'You told us you were parked in the band of trees for a particular reason. You didn't want to be seen. Why was that?'

Truscott glanced at Tench. 'Do I have to answer that question?' he asked.

'We can't force you to answer anything, sir.' Tench was smooth, still impassive. 'You've come here of your own accord to help us with this case. It might be wise, nonetheless, if you chose to answer.'

'And why should I do that?'

'Quite simply, sir, for your own protection. You say you were at the churchyard here at Burnham Northgate early last Sunday morning, and you saw a man acting in a very strange manner. Some few hours later two bodies were found not more than a hundred yards from where you were parked. That means that, by your own admission, you were close to a scene of murder at a very vital time, and all we have is your unsupported word that what you've told us is true.'

Truscott stared at him in disbelief. 'And that makes me a suspect?'

'It makes it important, sir, that we know why you were there at that particular time, especially since you didn't want to be seen.'

'I was visiting someone.'

'Who?'

'I'm afraid I can't tell you that, Chief Inspector.'

'Was it a woman?'

'A lady, Chief Inspector, of unimpeachable character.'

'You had an assignation with this lady?'

'Yes.'

'Where were you meeting her?'

'I was visiting her house.'

'And did you do that?'

'I did,' said Truscott. 'Not that I think it's any business of yours.'

'And will she support your statement?'

'I wouldn't ask her to.'

'Is there anyone else who would?'

'No, Chief Inspector. No one else knew where I was that night, and as far as I can tell no one else saw me. I sincerely hope they didn't.'

'I'm to assume that the lady's married?'

'Assume what you like. I'm not prepared to say any more than I have.'

'You're not prepared to tell us the lady's name?'

Truscott was tight-lipped. 'No, sir, I'm not. Now can I ask a question?'

'Of course.'

'Is it your intention to charge me with murder?'

Tench gave a smile. 'There's no question of

81

that, sir. None whatsoever. You've been very helpful. We'll follow up your information. Thank you very much.'

'You don't want to ask me anything else?'

'Not at the present, sir, no. Once we've traced the van, we may need you to take a look at it. I presume we'll be able to find you at North Creake airfield.'

Truscott nodded. 'You will.' He placed his hands on the table and pushed himself up. 'Then, if that's all,' he said, 'I'll leave. Perhaps Detective Constable Gradwell will be good enough to run me back to Stanhoe. I've an assignation there with a very old motorbike. It's parked in a friend's garden. And no, Chief Inspector, there's no need to ask. This friend's not a woman.'

11.

At half-past six that evening Tench called his team together for a briefing on the case.

By that time the church hall at Burnham Northgate had been transformed from its initially bleak and deserted state into what appeared, at least, to be a hive of activity. Half a dozen trestle tables, folded and stacked in a corner of the room, had been pulled out, erected and spaced around the floor. Four of them held boxes of files, and were manned by a clutch of constables imported from Norwich. The other two had been pushed together to

82

accommodate Desmond Lock, his two telephones and a miscellaneous collection of local directories held firmly in place by two heavy bookends embossed with the faces of Sherlock Holmes and Watson: personal treasures which had graced a whole succession of incident rooms in widely separated parts of Norfolk.

The normally blank walls had been likewise transformed by half a dozen panels holding maps of the area, photographs of the sites at Holkham Gap and Northgate churchyard, and detailed shots of the bodies, the clothing discovered in the pine woods, and the marks on the ground.

Tench positioned himself between Lock's special chair—the only one with arm rests—and the panels on the wall; and, picking up a ruler, placed its tip on the blown-up print of the bodies. 'It's time,' he said, 'for a run-down on what we know and what we've still got to learn.'

He tapped the photograph. 'Two bodies,' he said, 'the first of a man, the second of a woman, laid out on a churchyard grave in such a manner as to simulate an act of sex, and pinned beneath a tombstone felled to fall on top of them.' He paused for a moment. 'We believe the man to be Edward Bolton, aged thirty-four, unmarried, a sergeant in the Royal Army Service Corps stationed at Munchen-Gladbach. He arrived in England a week yesterday on a fortnight's embarkation leave prior to posting to the Suez Canal Zone, and travelled direct to Norwich to stay with his only brother, Terence, who lives on Earlham Road. He left there last Saturday. Booking a taxi from Excelsior Cars, a firm in the city, he had himself driven to Brancaster Staithe. This is confirmed by the taxi driver, a man named Wilfred Coates. At Brancaster Staithe he booked into a bed-and-breakfast, a place called Creek Cottage on the edge of the marsh, run by a Mr and Mrs Jelf. The booking was for a week in a single room, and he paid in advance in cash. He then got the taxi to take him to Wells, where he hired a white Ford Consul convertible, registration number CL9547, from Joseph Scanlon, the part-proprietor of Two Furlong Autos located on Mill Road. Dismissing the taxi, he drove the convertible back to Creek Cottage, spent the afternoon in his room and left about six o'clock, telling Jelf that he might not be back that evening. His movements for the next few hours are uncertain, but we believe he may have been drinking later that evening in the Queens Hotel at Holkham. All we know for sure is this: that yesterday morning the barman at the Queens reported the car as abandoned outside the pub, Bolton's bloodstained clothes were discovered in the woods at Holkham Gap, and his body, together with that of the woman, was found here at Burnham

Northgate.'

Another pause. 'Now to the woman. All the evidence we have indicates that she was one Tamara Scott, aged twenty-five, living with her husband, Robert Stratton Scott, at 7 Priory Court in the village of Binham. Robert Scott is an antiques dealer there, with a shop in the main street. Their marriage, it appears, was acrimonious and on the point of total failure, and Scott had already taken steps to institute divorce proceedings. Quarrels between them were frequent, and last Friday morning Mrs Scott packed two suitcases, walked out of the house and sought refuge with her sister, a Miss Erica Westaway of Bridge Street in Stiffkey. At about seven o'clock on Saturday evening she left her sister's house, saying that she needed to find a bit of life and intended to catch a bus into Wells. She didn't return that night or the following one, and her sister reported her as missing at nine o'clock yesterday morning. Her movements on Saturday evening, like those of Bolton, remain uncertain, but her clothes, like his, were found at Holkham Gap, and her body, with his, in the churchyard here. It seems likely, therefore, that somewhere en route to Holkham, or maybe even in Holkham itself, the two of them happened to meet, and it seems moreover to have been a chance meeting since there isn't any evidence that they knew one another before last Saturday.'

He tapped another pair of photographs with

the ruler. 'These are blown-up prints of two recent snapshots of Bolton and Mrs Scott. There are copies here on the table. Take one of each away with you when you leave tonight. You're going to need them to show around tomorrow.'

12.

He swept up a handful of files from the table. 'We already have a number of reports,' he said, 'that provide us with certain valuable facts. Dr Ledward's autopsies on the two bodies reveal that the victims died almost simultaneously sometime between eleven o'clock on Saturday night and half-past one the following morning, and that death was caused in each case by a series of massive blows to the head and face delivered in what he called a frenzied attack. Both of the victims had been struck some twenty or thirty times, and since flakes of rust were found in the wounds, it seems likely that the weapon was made of iron, though Dr Ledward stresses that it wasn't a hammer. He also concludes from the evidence of hypostasis that Bolton and Mrs Scott weren't killed where they were found, but moved to the churchyard sometime after death. There was no sexual interference with either of the bodies, but there were signs in both cases that intercourse had occurred just before death, and semen from Bolton was found in Mrs Scott. Both victims had eaten nothing for five or six hours prior to their deaths beyond apparently sharing a packet of chips, and both had drunk the alcoholic equivalent of three pints of beer. In the woman's case this was in gin and limes.

'Dr Ledward, unfortunately, wasn't able to give us a great deal of help in identifying the assailant, beyond saying that he was right-handed, but he did find a number of hairs adhering to Bolton's fingers and passed them to Ted Merrick at the lab. Now, as you may or may not know, there's a lot of nonsense talked about human hair. Most people think that when the lab gets hold of a single hair they can build up a profile of the person concerned. They seem to think it offers some kind of blueprint. The truth is that it doesn't unless it has sufficient follicle or root cells attached, and in this case there were none. Because of that, Merrick was unable to tell us much beyond the basic facts that the hair wasn't Bolton's, nor was it Mrs Scott's; it was from the head of a fair-haired man probably aged between twenty-five and thirty-five. He did make the point that the hair had been cut off, almost certainly by a pair of scissors, and he concluded from this that the man had had a haircut shortly before the attack took place, and in the interval had not washed his hair. This could possibly provide us with a valuable clue, and the colour of the hair almost certainly rules out Robert Stratton Scott, Mrs

Scott's husband, as a likely suspect, since his hair is dark.'

He looked across at Gregg. 'Andy,' he said, 'you made some inquiries about Robert Scott, didn't you?'

'Yes, sir.' Gregg nodded.

'And they seemed to confirm everything he told us?'

'That's right, sir, yes. I traced his firm of solicitors, Havelocks in Norwich. They said that he consulted them a fortnight ago and instructed them to begin divorce proceedings against Mrs Scott. I haven't yet been able to contact his bank, the Midland, because they'd already closed for the day, but Mrs Scott left a cheque book in her sister's house at Stiffkey, and the used stubs confirm that in the last two months she'd drawn nearly six hundred pounds from the joint account she shared with her husband.'

'So, taken with Merrick's evidence, you think we can strike him off the list as a suspect?'

'I think so, sir, yes. We'd just be wasting our time.'

Tench, in his turn, nodded. 'That's my opinion too, and it means that we have to start looking for someone else, and before we can hope to make any headway we need more information. At the outset we made the obvious assumption that the killer had mutilated the faces of the victims to make identification difficult, but in view of Ledward's autopsy report. I feel more and more inclined to discard that theory. Nor do I believe it was a random killing—a random killer would have left the bodies where they were, in the pine woods at Holkham—and it's clear that the motive couldn't have been robbery, since nothing was taken from either Bolton's wallet or Mrs Scott's handbag. So, if we discount those three theories: calculated mutilation, random killing and robbery with violence, what are we left with? This was a frenzied attack and that suggests rage. It can also suggest hate. Now I could well be wrong, but such evidence as we have seems to indicate to me that the murderer knew at least one of the victims, had some reason for hatred and was coldly determined to exact his revenge. That means that he set out to track them down, followed them on Saturday night, waited till they were in a particularly vulnerable position and then beat them to death. And assuming that to be true, there are certain things that we need to know, and we need to know them quickly.

'We need to know everything we can possibly dredge up about Bolton's past life and that of Mrs Scott, particularly where they were born, where they were brought up and where they lived. We need to know where they went on Saturday night, from the time Mrs Scott left her sister's house and Bolton his lodgings to the time they were killed at Holkham Gap.'

He pulled out a chair and sat down. 'Now, thanks to Sue Gradwell, we may well just have a vital lead . . . Sue,' he said, 'perhaps you'll tell the team what Flight Lieutenant Truscott had to say for himself.'

13.

She recounted the story slowly and methodically, savouring every moment of her time in the spotlight. Tench didn't interrupt. He simply waited till she'd finished, then addressed the whole team. 'Truscott's evidence,' he said, 'is confirmed to some extent by Sergeant Lester and the scene-of-crime squad. Heavy rain, as you know, broke over the Burnhams at half-past two on Sunday morning and lasted for all of a couple of hours. This, in conjunction with the trampling of the ground around the grave, made it almost impossible to discern any footprints, and the squad discovered only one of sufficient clarity to prove of any use. This was in a patch of recently seeded ground sheltered by the trees—the mark of what appeared to be a wellington boot—but it was some considerable distance from the grave and well outside any line that the killer might have used. Because of that, we're assuming, for the moment, that it may have no connection with the crime. However, Lester's men did find something else: a quite distinct track of beaten ground underneath the trees, running from the point where Truscott said that the van was parked, and emerging in the general direction of the grave. The ground, of course, is covered by a carpet of fallen leaves, and no footprints were visible, but the leaves had been scuffed, and at one particular point there was an indentation which could have been made by the wheel of a barrow.'

He paused again and gave a little shrug. 'Unfortunately,' he said, 'though Truscott impressed us as telling the truth, we'd be foolish to take what he said as gospel without checking further. This for two reasons. First, because his story lacks confirmation. He admits that he kept his movements a secret. No one knew where he was going, nobody saw him, and he refused point blank to reveal the name of the woman he was meeting. Second, because Constable Lock checked the registration number he gave for the van.' He nodded towards Lock. 'Your turn, Des.'

'The number's false,' said Lock. 'It isn't a van. It's a car, a white Morris Minor, and the registered owner's a Miss Ada Vellacott of Shotley Road, Chelmondiston in Suffolk.'

'And that, ' said Tench, 'means one of three things. Either the van that Truscott saw was carrying false plates, or it was stolen, or, quite simply, he made the number up. And if he did, then that invalidates the whole of his story and puts him at the top of any suspect list.'

McKenzie dropped a tab end on the floor of the hall and ground it out with his foot. 'You listened to Truscott,' he said. 'What's your opinion?'

'If I had to make a guess, I'd say he was genuine.'

McKenzie drove his hands deep in his pockets. 'But that's not enough.'

'No,' said Tench, 'it isn't. That's why we need to make further checks. We need to know more about Flight Lieutenant Truscott, just as we need to know more about Bolton and Mrs Scott. He must have been visiting a woman who lives somewhere in Burnham Northgate, and Norfolk villages being what they are, someone around here must know who she is. And even more important, we have to track down this lorry. It was driven past the scene at about two o'clock, travelling from north to south, and that means it must have gone through the village. We need to find the driver. If he saw two vehicles parked in the trees, then that'll corroborate one part at least of Truscott's account.'

He shuffled the files together and pushed them aside. 'Now,' he said, 'let's turn to tomorrow. This is what we do . . .'

*   *   *

He detailed their various assignments.

92

Ellison was to interview Terence Bolton and build up a picture of Bolton's background, and Sue Gradwell was to do the same for Mrs Scott with the help of her sister, Erica Westaway. Gregg was to make discreet inquiries at the base at North Creake and find out what he could about Francis Truscott, while Rayner, working with Constable Barnes, was to do a house-to-house in Burnham Northgate in the hope that someone would know something about the lorry and also cast some light on the identity of Truscott's lady friend. Desmond Lock, with the phone at his disposal, was to assist and supplement their inquiries by compiling a series of pertinent lists: lists of small dark vans registered in the area and any reported as stolen within the past week; lists of farmers, hauliers and any other businesses owning lorries which were out on the road in the small hours of Sunday morning; and a list of men's hairdressers within a radius of twenty miles from Holkham, to be passed to Detective Constable Spurgeon, whose job would be to check which of them, if any, had cut the killer's hair.

'We can only act,' said Tench, 'on the evidence we have, and that means including Truscott's until such time as we prove it to be false. So we're looking for a strong thick-set man aged between twenty-five and thirty-five, about five foot eight, who limps with his left leg and has fair hair that's recently been cut.

There'll be a couple of constables manning the phones with Lock, so if you find any traces report them right away to the incident room. If there's anything requiring immediate action, he'll know where to find me.'

He turned towards McKenzie. 'Mac,' he said, 'you'll be with me. It's our job to follow the victims' trails, and find out where they went on Saturday night.' He looked round the squad. 'Right. Any questions?'

'One, sir,' said Gregg. 'Have we got a date for the inquests?'

'Yes, next Monday. Provisionally.'

'You'll be asking for an adjournment?'

'If we have to, yes. Let's hope it won't be needed . . . Anything else?'

No one spoke.

'Right then,' he said. 'In the morning there'll be a front-page spread in the *EDP* appealing for information. You know what you have to do. Debriefing here at the same time tomorrow. Let's see if we can't crack this case on our own before we find ourselves sidelined and swamped by the Met.'

14.

He watched the team disperse, and then, stacking a dozen files on the table beside him, read through them carefully one by one, absorbing all the available evidence and making notes as he proceeded. As he closed the last of them and pushed it aside, he heard, from outside, the unmistakable sound of Lubbock's Morgan three-wheeler, followed by the sight of Lubbock himself, pipe firmly between his teeth and, like some mythical dragon, trailing clouds of smoke.

'Evening, laddie,' he said.

Tench leaned back. 'What the devil are you doing here?' he asked. 'I thought you were back at Cley.'

'On my way,' Lubbock said. He pulled out a chair, extracted a box of matches from his pocket, struck one, and applied it to his pipe. Another cloud of smoke rolled up towards the rafters. 'Thought I'd make a little detour and see if you were here. It's a good thing I did.'

'Is it?'

'Of course it is, laddie. What I have to say may be vital, you know that. So how's the case going?'

'It's progressing.'

'That's no answer. Have you unearthed any clues to the killer?'

'A few.'

'Then give me a run-down. Let's see how we stand.'

Tench took a deep breath and paraphrased the evidence.

'Well, that's something,' said Lubbock. 'At least you've got a description of the man, if it's only tentative.'

'Oh, we've got a description, for what it's

95

worth. But we still don't know who he is or where he might be.'

'Of course you don't.' His old Chief bit hard on his pipe stem. 'That's because you're asking yourself the wrong questions.'

'You think so?'

'Yes, I'm sure of it, laddie.'

Tench raised his eyebrows. 'And you're going to tell me the right ones, are you?'

'I'm always willing to help. That's what I'm here for.'

'Then tell me. What are the wrong questions I'm asking myself?'

'You're asking who the man is and where he is. That's just a waste of time.'

'And what should I be asking?'

'You should be asking yourself not who or where, but why?'

'But I need to find the who before I can ask the why. I can't hope to find the motive until I've found the killer.'

Lubbock looked at his pipe with some dissatisfaction, and knocked it out in a waste bin under the table. 'I don't mean why in the sense of why did he kill. There's another why of more immediate importance.'

'Which is?'

'Why did he choose the churchyard here at Burnham Northgate?'

'The Chief Super mentioned that, or something very similar.'

'Then the Chief Super's right.' Lubbock

96

brought out his pouch and began to fill his pipe. 'Look, laddie,' he said, 'this is nothing to do with witchcraft—it's not like the business at Taddenham last year—but there's an element of ritual about this murder. Whoever it was who killed these two people, he brought the bodies here and laid them out neatly on a grave in the churchyard. There are churches a good deal closer to Holkham Gap, the one in Holkham Park and St Clement's at Burnham Overy, so the question is why did he choose Burnham Northgate?'

'And what's your answer?'

'I haven't one, yet. But I'm pretty sure of one thing. In some way or other, the churchyard here held a peculiar significance for this man, and it wasn't the particular grave that he chose. I made a note of the inscription on the stone. It was the grave of a man called Isaac Thober, who died almost ninety years ago at the age of eighty-two. So I made a few inquiries. He lived all his life in the village, and died quite peacefully, apparently of old age. Nothing suspicious, so perhaps our man simply chose that stone because it was old and already on a tilt. It was easier to topple. There isn't any other obvious reason.'

Tench frowned. 'Are there any legends about Burnham Northgate?'

'There are legends, laddie, everywhere in Norfolk. It's a county of more than a million acres with seven hundred villages: places that were, until recently, nothing more than small, isolated communities. People lived there and died, and only rarely travelled beyond the village bounds. Among such communities legends proliferate, but the strange thing is that, among all the many thousands of tales that abound, I've never heard one connected with Burnham Northgate.'

'And you should know,' said Tench.

'I should. I've lived in Norfolk all my life.'

'Then you've no idea of the answer to this conundrum?'

'No, I haven't,' said Lubbock, 'but sooner or later I'll find it for sure, and if you'll take my advice you'll search for it too. I'm quite convinced of one thing. The significance of this place holds the key to the man's identity. Find the one, and you'll find the other. So, if I were you, I'd take another look at Burnham Northgate's churchyard. There's a secret hidden somewhere inside its walls, and it's a secret you need to fathom if you're going to solve this case.'

15.

It was half an hour later that Tench, braking to a halt by the churchyard gate, stepped out of the car, walked across to the wall, and stood for a moment staring at the scatter of graves around the church. By then the sun was low in the sky, and the stones were casting ever-lengthening shadows across the grass. The canvas shelter that for three days had hidden Isaac Thober's grave had been folded away and, apart from those round the belt of trees where Lester's men, on their hands and knees, were still picking their way through the carpet of leaves, the tapes had been removed. Burnham Northgate churchyard had, so it seemed, all but returned to the peace and quiet that had reigned on Sunday morning, when Lubbock, on his way to the village, had pushed open the gate and stumped up the slope.

Tench, in his turn, unlatched the gate and climbed up the gently rising ground till he reached Thober's grave. The stone still lay flat and the soil around it was heavily scuffed, but that was the only sign that, almost seventy-two hours before, this was where two battered bodies had lain, stretched out in a parody of consummated passion.

Turning away, he wandered round the churchyard, peering at the stones. Many were now in shadow, and it was difficult to read the letters incised on the older ones, but, determined to persevere, he continued to wander in and out of the plots till the rapidly fading light made it impossible to read any more.

As far as he could tell, no Boltons lay underneath the ground at Burnham Northgate, nor were there any Westaways or even any Scotts. Whatever the secret was that lay beneath the turf, it was clearly unwilling to divulge itself that evening.

He straightened up, eased his back and looked at the rapidly darkening sky. Then he gave a little shrug, turned away down the slope and, starting up his car, drove back through the village and took the road to Norwich.

Detective Chief Inspector Michael Bruce Tench had had enough for one day of bodies and blood and the stench of death.

All he wanted to do was go home and forget them.

IV

FRESH FRUIT

ABEL (kneeling): Oh, brother, pray!
Jehovah's wroth with thee.
CAIN: Why so?
ABEL: Thy fruits are scattered on the earth.
CAIN: From earth they came, to earth let
them return;
Their seed will bear fresh fruit there ere the
summer.

Lord Byron: *Cain*

1.

The task of tracking Bolton's bibulous progress through the pubs of Wells and Holkham, when he himself was condemned to stay dry, was one that held little appeal for McKenzie. So when, at ten o'clock the following morning, he pushed open the door of the Queens Hotel at Holkham, and found himself facing an empty bar and a multitude of bottles, his mood was no better than it had been the previous day.

He scowled at the bell and thumped it viciously half a dozen times.

Not that he expected an immediate response. He was quite prepared to thump it again, ram it down on the bar and, if all else failed, to kick open every door in the Queens. What he wasn't prepared for was the sudden appearance of a tall thin man with a long thin face, dark sleeked-back hair, an immaculate white shirt, a black bow tie and widely projecting ears, who leaned forward, rested both hands on the bar and addressed him with a cheerful, yet businesslike precision. 'Yes, sir?' he said. 'What can I do to help you?'

McKenzie blinked at this unexpected vision. 'You the landlord?' he asked.

The man frowned and scratched his head. 'I think so,' he said. 'I was last night, and as far as I remember I still was this morning.' He frowned again. 'Yes,' he said. 'Come to think of it, I must be. Allow me to introduce myself. Peter John Rushbrook. Licensed to sell alcohol, but not at this time on a midsummer morning, so what else can I do to help?'

McKenzie produced his card. 'Detective Sergeant McKenzie, Norwich CID.'

Rushbrook studied it. 'Ah, yes,' he said, 'the fuzz. Licensed to make inquiries. You're here about the murders . . . Right then, Sergeant. Ask and it shall be given you. Rest assured, I'm all ears.'

McKenzie bit back the obvious pertinent comment. He reached in his pocket, brought out two photographs and laid them on the bar. 'Edward Bolton,' he said, 'and Tamara Scott. Have you ever heard of them or seen them before?'

Rushbrook rested both elbows on the bar and peered at the photographs. 'No,' he said, 'Sergeant. Can't say that I have. Are they suspects?'

'Victims.' The answer was curt. Once on the trail, McKenzie wasn't one for beating round bushes. 'We believe they were drinking here on Saturday night, but we need confirmation. So who was on the bar?'

'Ah . . . well . . . now . . . that's a very good question.' Rushbrook scratched his head again. 'Busy night, Saturday. Should have been me, but I wasn't here. Finals night, too. There'd be more than one serving.'

'Finals night?'

'Final of the North Norfolk darts competition. Queens against The Fisherman's Rest from Cromer. Joss was in charge. Said the bar was packed solid, so one of the girls must have helped him. Trouble is, I've no idea which . . . Hang on a tick. I'll have to go and fetch him.'

He vanished through the door at the back of the bar, and left McKenzie facing hundreds of bottles, scores of empty glasses and another large poster showing a man tipping ale down his throat from a grossly enlarged tankard.

The sergeant ran a tongue across his dry lips. Then he turned away, walked across to a window and stared for a change at a brindled Siamese cat that was lapping up the last of a saucer of milk. Once finished, it sprang on the bonnet of a black Morris Minor, cleaned its whiskers and spat at him.

'Bloody hell,' he said. 'Not you as well, cat.'

The whole world seemed to be conspiring against him.

Even the moggies.

2.

Mike Tench, on the other hand, had the feeling that for once, on this bright Wednesday morning, the world might be with him.

This despite the fact that at that precise moment he was standing in the office of

Norfolk Coastal Services on the quayside at Wells, holding up his card to a surly man with a ticket machine, who clearly resented being dragged off his bus to face questions from a representative of the law.

'Tench,' he said. 'Detective Chief Inspector . . . Your name's Walter Craske?'

'Aye.' The man nodded. 'Has bin thirty year.'

'You were the conductor on the seven-fifteen bus from Stiffkey to Wells on Saturday night?'

Another nod. 'Aye.'

Tench laid two photographs on the supervisor's desk, and then moved one of them an inch to the left. 'D'you remember seeing this woman get on the bus?'

Craske placed his ticket machine on the desk and peered at the picture. Then he nodded a third time. 'Aye. Tha's right. She were waitin' at Lion . . . So wha'?'

'Lion?'

'Red Lion. There be three stops i' Stiffkey. Church, Post Office an' arter tha', Lion. Tha's where she were waitin'.'

'Take another look. You're sure it was her?'

Craske straightened up. He seemed almost affronted. 'D'ye think I be shanny?' he said. 'Couldn' miss her, not that one. Bonny mawther she were. Dressed ter kill anorl. Showin' half her tits. Ye'll not be seein' many like her aroun' Stiffkey.'

'Then you'll know where she got off.'

106

'Aye. Same place they all do. Buttlands, o' course.'

The Buttlands, the traditional centre of Wells, was a spacious green fringed by trees and Georgian houses where, many years before, the bowmen of England had practised their skills. From its open northern end, narrow streets led down to the quay, and it also boasted, at its southern extremity, the old Crown hotel, a tavern of some repute.

It was Tench's turn to nod. 'Did you see where she went?'

Craske, for some reason, was suddenly suspicious. He reverted to type. 'What d'ye want ter know tha' fer?'

'Just making inquiries, Mr Craske, nothing more. Where did she go?'

'She weren' doin' nothin' wrong. Jus' lookin' fer a good time mebbe, tha' were all.'

'I'm sure she was, yes.'

'Then why all this squit about where she were goin'?'

Tench gave a sigh. 'Simply because she was murdered, Mr Craske.'

'Murdered?'

'Yes, she's dead. Very dead, Mr Craske. Somebody killed her. So where did she go when she got off your bus?'

Craske stared at him blankly. 'You mean she were one o' they two as were . . . ?'

'Yes.'

'So she's dead?'

'Yes, she is . . . Now where did she go?'

'Well, bugger me!' said Craske. 'Tha's a fair rummun. On my bloody bus!'

'You're wasting my time, police time, Mr Craske . . . Where did she go?'

'Ent on'y one place as she'd be mekkin' fer, ent there?'

'Is there?'

'Aye.'

'And where would that be?'

'Why, Crown o' course.'

'And did she?'

'Did she wha'?'

'Make for the Crown?'

'Said so, didn't I?'

'Did you see her go inside?'

'Aye.'

'Still on her own?'

'Aye.'

'Thank you, Mr Craske.' Tench paused . . . 'And you?'

Craske looked blank again. 'Me?'

'That's right, you.'

'What about me?'

'Where did *you* go?'

'Back on th'bus ter Cromer.'

'And after that?'

'Home. Where else would I bloody go? It were end o' shift, weren' it?'

'You're sure about that?'

'Course I'm bloody sure.'

'You live in Cromer?'

108

'Aye.'

'Are you sure you didn't go back to Wells, Mr Craske? Back to the Crown?'

'Now look here . . .'

'No,' said Tench. 'You look, Mr Craske. I ask the questions, you give the answers. Did you go back to Wells?'

'No, I damn well didn'.'

Tench gave a nod. He slid the other photograph an inch to the left. 'D'you know what that is?'

'Aye.' Craske was sour. 'It's a bloody car, ent it?'

'It's a white Ford Consul convertible, Mr Craske. Did you see it parked anywhere on the Buttlands?'

'No.'

'You're positive?'

Craske's answer was scathing. 'D'ye think I ent knowin' a bee from a bull's arse? Course I'm bloody positive. Sticks out like a bare prick, car like that do. Ye'll not be seein' many o' they aroun' Wells. We ent th'sort o folk as breeds 'em in Norfolk. Got more bloody sense.' He picked up his ticket machine from the desk. 'Now,' he said, 'you got any more squit ter be askin? Cos if you ent, I got work ter be doin'.'

'Back to Cromer, Mr Craske?'

'If I ever bloody get there.'

'Oh, you will, Mr Craske.' Tench was smooth as mellow wine. 'I'm quite sure you will.'

109

3.

As he waited for Rushbrook to return with Joss the barman, McKenzie continued to glower at the cat; it was infinitely preferable, he found, to glowering at beer pumps, lines of full bottles and empty glasses. But Joss, it seemed, was proving elusive. Minutes passed by and each of them added at least a degree to his rising temperature. By the time the landlord swept back into the bar, with Joss ambling lazily along in his wake, McKenzie's temper was visibly fraying round the edges.

Nor did the sight of the barman do much to banish his mounting frustration. A dwarf-like man with a pendulous paunch and a pair of thick glasses that betokened myopia, he inspired little confidence as being likely to prove a reliable witness. McKenzie took one look at him and decided that, even if he was tall enough to see across the bar, he could hardly be expected to locate a dartboard, let alone remember the faces of two complete strangers sitting somewhere in a crowded, smoke-screened room.

Rushbrook waved a hand. 'This is Joss,' he said cheerfully. He thrust the two photographs under the barman's nose. 'Did you see these two people on Saturday night?'

Joss peered at them. Then he took off his glasses, laid them on the bar, switched on the bar lights, and looked at them again. 'No,' he said.

'No?'

'Never seen 'em,' said Joss.

McKenzie gave him a glare that would have shrivelled most barmen into their socks. 'Well, their car was parked outside. They must have ordered some drinks. So take another look.'

Joss ignored him completely. He shuffled the photographs together and handed them to Rushbrook. 'Told him once,' he said, 'an' I ent tellin' him twice. I ent never set eyes on 'em. It ent me. It's Meg as he needs ter to be askin'.'

McKenzie glared again, but this time at Rushbrook. 'Who the hell's Meg?'

'Meg Rooney. She was the girl who was on duty with him.'

Joss nodded in confirmation. 'She were flittin' roun' the room, a-tekkin' the orders. All I were doin' was gettin' the drinks.'

McKenzie closed his eyes and took a deep breath. He gripped the edge of the bar. 'Then where is she?' he said.

'Reckon she be at 'om. Ent on duty terday.'

'So where does she live?'

Joss turned to the landlord. 'Worram way, ent it?'

'Rose Cottage, Warham,' Rushbrook said. 'It's on the other side of Wells.'

*　　*　　*

111

It was roughly four miles from the Queens Hotel to Warham, and McKenzie covered it in precisely five and a half minutes. The fact that he took another five to locate Rose Cottage, and only found it after knocking on three separate doors, failed to improve his temper, though the sight of Meg Rooney, a slim, full-busted girl with a visible cleavage, did much to restore his lost equilibrium.

He summoned up what he hoped was a winning smile. 'Morning, Meg,' he said.

'Do I know you?' She stared at him, hands on hips.

'Detective Sergeant McKenzie. All the way from Norwich.' He flashed his card.

'Never heard of him,' she said.

McKenzie was unabashed. 'Come on, Meg,' he said. 'Take a good look. Two years ago. The Black Dog at Morston. You were working there, weren't you?'

'And what if I was?'

'You remember Moses Shelton?'

'That drunken old soak. Don't link his name with mine.' She narrowed her eyes. 'You did though, didn't you? Came asking questions. Cheeky sod you were. Wanted to know if I'd taken a walk with him after closing time.'

'And you gave me a mouthful.'

'I should think so too. Me? Walk out with Moses Shelton? I'd sooner take a walk with a two-legged pig.' She looked him up and down. 'My, my,' she said. 'You've put on some

112

weight.'

'Muscle,' McKenzie told her.

'Oh, yeah?' She laughed. 'First time I've heard of muscle below the belt . . . So what d'you want this time?'

McKenzie reached in his pocket. 'I've some pictures to show you.'

'Don't tell me you've taken to selling filthy postcards.'

'Not yet,' he said. 'Aren't you going to ask me in?'

4.

It was half-past midday when his snarling old Norton turned off the coast road north of Burnham Market, threaded its way down the narrow lane that led to the foreshore at Overy Staithe, and rolled to a halt by Tench's police car.

Hauling the motorbike on to its rest, the sergeant opened the car door and lapsed with a grunt into the passenger seat.

After the lean six years of the war, Overy Staithe was beginning to resume its normal summer traffic. Half a dozen yachts were moored in the channel, and yet another two were drawn up on the hard, but Tench, staring out across the marshes to the sea, seemed to be rapt in a world of his own.

'You know, Mac,' he said, 'if we'd lived just a couple of hundred years ago and walked

113

down here from Northgate over the fields, we might have seen Nelson standing on this spot, watching the merchantmen putting out to sea.'

McKenzie was no dreamer. 'Well, he'd find it a bit different if he came back today,' he commented drily. 'More to the point, what would he have done if he'd cut through the churchyard and found two of his pals pinned under a gravestone?'

Tench smiled and shook his head. 'We'll never know, will we?'

'Maybe not,' McKenzie said, 'but I'll tell you one thing for sure. He wouldn't have gone chasing round half the pubs in Norfolk with his tongue hanging out, like I've been doing.'

'A policeman's lot, Mac . . .'

'It's a thirsty one. Yes, you don't need to tell me.'

'The question is, was it worth it?'

'For you or for me?'

'For both of us.'

'Well now,' McKenzie said. 'that all depends.'

'On what exactly?'

'On whether my vocal cords can stand the strain of telling you. At the moment my tongue's like a swollen chunk of desiccated meat and my throat's like a bucket of sand's been chucked down it.'

Tench leaned forward and started up the car. 'Oh, what the hell,' he said. 'Let's find a pub and I'll buy you a pint.'

'Now that,' McKenzie said, 'reminds me of a

114

story. Exactly where was it that Nelson turned a blind eye?'

*   *   *

'Copenhagen,' said Tench as he set down a pint in front of his sergeant and a half for himself.

'Copenhagen what?'

'That's the place where Nelson turned a blind eye. So let's get down to business. What did you find out?'

'You first,' McKenzie said. 'Give me time to recover.' He took two gulps and emptied half the glass.

'Okay,' said Tench. 'If that's the way you want it. Tamara Scott. She caught the seven-fifteen bus from Stiffkey to Wells, got off at the Buttlands and went into the Crown. That must have been just after eight o'clock. The bus had a five-minute stop in Wells and had to drive round the Green to reach the main road, so I asked both the driver and conductor whether they'd seen Bolton's car parked anywhere on the Buttlands. They hadn't.'

'Well, they could hardly have missed it,' McKenzie said.

'They made a point of telling me that,' said Tench, 'in no uncertain terms, but I knocked on a few doors close to the Crown, and found an old boy who lives in a flat on one of the top floors. He remembered seeing it parked by the

115

Green about quarter-past eight, and it was still there, he said, half an hour later.'

McKenzie killed off the rest of his pint at a single gulp. 'That fits,' he said. 'They ordered drinks at the Queens just after nine o'clock, so Bolton must have picked her up at the Crown and then driven straight to Holkham.'

'Who told you that?'

'The barmaid,' McKenzie said. 'The delectable Meg Rooney, an old friend of mine. She entertained me in the privacy of her two-up-and-down.'

'Did she now?'

'She did, and for both of us it was worth it.'

'I've no doubt it was.'

'Both of us means you and me,' McKenzie said stiffly. 'It doesn't mean me and her. Why does everyone always think the worst of me, never the best?'

'Put it down to long experience, Mac,' said Tench.

'You want visual proof of my devotion to duty?'

'Why not? Let's brighten up the day.'

'Right then.' McKenzie reached deep in an inside pocket, produced a fan of photographs and laid them out on the table. 'Take a look at those.'

'What are they?'

'They were taken inside the Queens on Saturday night by Meg Rooney's brother. It was the final of the North Norfolk darts competition—the Queens against The Fisherman's Rest from Cromer. Look at them closely. You may find a couple of faces we know.'

5.

Tench took his time. He examined each in turn, then produced his own photographs of Bolton and Mrs Scott and laid them side by side against McKenzie's prints.

At last he nodded. 'Looks like them,' he said.

'Of course it's them,' McKenzie said. 'Who else could it be? They parked the car outside, and found a corner table close to the dartboard. Meg took their order. A pint of beer for him and a gin and lime for her. That tallies with Ledward's autopsy report. And there's one of those prints that shows the table quite clearly. You can see the two glasses. Everything fits . . . Now take another look. Does anything else strike you?'

Tench leaned forward again and peered at the prints. 'They don't seem to be very interested in the darts match,' he said.

'Good. That's Point One . . . But there's another, Point Two.'

'Then you'll have to point it out.'

McKenzie tut-tutted. 'Everyone in those prints is intent on the match. They're all looking at the players, except for three people.

117

Our friends, the murder victims, are intent on each other. They're not bothered a toss about the dartboard, the players or anybody else. And then there's this chap.' He placed a nicotine-stained fingertip on one of the prints. 'He's sitting on the opposite side of the dartboard, but he's not looking up at it. He's staring straight at them. It's the same in all the pictures. They're sat there, gazing into one another's eyes, and he's watching them. He never moves. Never shifts his gaze from them . . . And I'd be willing to take a bet that when they get up and go, he'll get up and follow them, all the way down to Holkham Gap and into the woods.'

'You think he's our killer.'

'Don't you?'

Tench gave a shrug. 'Well, even if he's watching them, that doesn't mean he's going to follow them out and beat them to death. He could have been interested in them for any number of reasons.'

'Such as?'

'Might have thought he'd met one of them somewhere before and was trying to puzzle out just where it was. Might have been wondering why they'd chosen to sit so close to the dartboard if they weren't even bothered about what was going on.'

'Look at him, Mike. Look at the expression on his face. He's not wondering about anything. He's watching them, watching them

118

like a hawk.'

'Well, suppose he is. Did this barmaid of yours know him?'

'No. Nor did anyone else at the Queens.'

'What time did they leave—Bolton and Mrs Scott?'

'That's the trouble. Nobody saw them. Closing time was normally half-past ten, but the pub had an extension to eleven o'clock because of the final, and since the Queens won the match, the celebrations went on for another twenty minutes after the last drinks were served. Then the whole crowd left more or less at the same time. Meg was busy collecting glasses and she didn't see them leave, or the chap who was watching them, so we don't know whether he followed them out or not. The one thing she's sure of is that all three were still there when last drinks were called.'

'And no one saw whether this chap of yours limped?'

'None of those I asked.'

'That's a pity,' said Tench.

'I could try tracing those who were close to him on the photographs.'

'No.' Tench shook his head. 'I'll do that. You get down to The Fisherman's Rest at Cromer. See if anyone there knows him. Track down the members of the darts team and talk to them. Take one of the prints with you. I'll get the rest to the lab and have them blown up.

Which one d'you want?'

'This.' McKenzie took one and stuffed it in his pocket.

'You know this place of course, The Fisherman's Rest?'

'That's the sort of question that riles me,' McKenzie said. 'How long have we been working together?'

'Oh, must be six years.'

'And have you ever known a pub that I couldn't remember?'

Tench grinned. 'No,' he said, 'but I still haven't altogether given up hope. There must be one you don't remember, somewhere in Norfolk, and one of these days I'll find it.'

'Well, not today, Michael,' McKenzie said. 'The Fisherman's Rest is a poky little pub with a snug and a horseshoe bar. It's close to the church, on one of those narrow streets that lead down to the sea. The licensee's an old fisherman, Jennis Algar. Has a fetish for chamber pots. Collects them and hangs them on hooks from the ceiling. Goes round the sales and picks them up for next to nothing. Must have about fifty slung around the bar. And he serves a good brew. From what I've been told, the urinals are well patronized. All you need to do is take a look at the ceiling and you begin to feel the urge. It's a good selling gimmick, because once you've paid a visit you're ready for another pint . . . It's a good place for pubs is Cromer. There's the Anchor, the Lifeboat, the old Cod and Lobster . . .'

'Say no more, Mac,' said Tench. 'I believe you. Just give my regards to the chamber pots. And don't burn up the road to get there before closing.'

'As if I would,' McKenzie said. 'You know me. I'm a stickler for regulations. I've hardly ever broken a rule in my life.'

6.

For all they uncovered in the next three hours, both of them might just as well have spent the afternoon in a very different fashion: Mike Tench in his car on the foreshore at Burnham Avery dreaming of Nelson, and McKenzie in blissfully drinking a barrel dry at The Fisherman's Rest.

No one, it seemed, who'd been present at the Queens on Saturday night had ever before set eyes on the man who'd shown such an interest in the two murder victims, and it was left to the other members of Tench's team to achieve what little progress the day still had to offer.

And not without their inevitable share of frustrations.

*   *   *

Bob Ellison, whose job was to interview Bolton's brother and learn as much as he could about the family background, was in the very best of summer morning spirits as he wound his way through the Norwich traffic to Earlham Road. He was, he felt, going to have an easy day. All he had to do was talk to Terence Bolton and get him, in his turn, to talk about Edward. That was simple enough.

The Bolton house was small and Edwardian. Two grey stone steps led to the front door, which was painted dark green with an old brass knocker that had probably been there since the place was built.

Ellison gave it two raps. There was no response, nor did a further couple elicit any sound from inside. He tried the next door house on the right with a similar result, and it was only at the third attempt, next door on the left, that a short, emaciated, bald-headed man told him that it was no bloody good him knocking at Bolton's, Terry was at work, and if he wanted him urgent he'd best go and ask at Pegasus Coaches.

'Does a bit o' drivin' for 'em,' the man said. 'In his spare time like. Said as he was doin' a bit for 'em today, though God knows where he's gone.'

Pegasus Coaches, it appeared, ran excursions to various points of interest in Norfolk. They had a garage close by, on the Dereham Road.

'He'll have tekken a coach out from there,' the bald-headed man said. 'Reckon they'll be tellin' you whereabouts he be.'

They did. He'd taken a party of pensioners out for the day to Cromer.

Ellison, while always a courteous young man, was blessed with a fund of steely determination. He wasn't going to be thwarted by a busload of greybeards. Searching out the nearest telephone box, he rang the incident room and told Lock that he was spending a day by the sea. Then, returning to the car, he executed a faultless three-point turn and set off for Cromer.

*　　*　　*

It was an hour and a half later that he ran Bolton to earth at last in a seaside car park, sitting behind the wheel of an empty coach, consuming a packet of marmalade sandwiches and a bottle of beer.

Terry Bolton was broad and phlegmatic with a mass of unruly russet-coloured hair and a pair of sinewy forearms patterned with freckles. He looked up as Ellison pulled back the door of the coach and clambered inside. 'Morning,' he said.

'Good morning, sir.' Ellison came to rest on the nearest seat. 'Am I speaking to Terence Bolton?'

A nod. 'Reckon so, yes.'

Ellison showed his card. 'Detective Constable Ellison. I'm from Norwich, Mr

Bolton. I'm one of the team investigating your brother's death.'

'Long way from home then, aren't you?' Bolton said.

'That's true, sir, yes. But it was important I found you.'

Bolton took another sandwich from a tin labelled 'Macintosh's Toffee-de-Luxe', bit off a sizeable portion and chewed. 'Why?' he asked through a mouthful of bread and marmalade.

'We need to know as much as you can tell us about your brother.'

'He's dead.'

Ellison forced a smile. 'Yes, sir, I know.'

'Then what's the point of wanting to know things about him? You'd be better off finding the bugger that did him in.'

'That's what we're trying to do, Mr Bolton.'

'Not making a very good job of it then, are you? He's been dead for four days.'

'We are making progress, sir.'

Bolton took another bite at his sandwich. 'Can't say I've noticed a deal. Not so far.'

'Murder investigations take time, Mr Bolton. Time and a lot of help. That's why we need yours.'

'Can't see what knowing about Ted's got to do with it.' Bolton tipped back the bottle and took a swig of his beer. Then he gave a shrug. 'All right,' he said. 'What d'you want to know?'

'Start at the beginning, sir. Where was he born?'

'In Norwich. We both were.'

'Whereabouts in Norwich?'

'Tipworth Street. Down by the cemetery'

'What number?'

'25 . . . Does it matter?'

'Every single detail may matter, Mr Bolton.'

Bolton looked at his watch. 'Well, you'd best get a move on,' he said. 'Another half-hour and we're due off to Sheringham. At the rate you're going, Ted won't have left school.'

7.

Driving back to Burnham Northgate to make his report, Ellison wondered whether he hadn't been wasting his time. According to Terry Bolton, his brother had led an utterly blameless life. Born and brought up in Norwich, he'd attended two local schools. An average, yet always a well-behaved pupil, he had, on leaving, taken a job as a motor mechanic at Thankerton's Garage on Nash Street, where he'd worked for six years; but his ambition had always been to join the army, and in 1938, at the age of twenty, he'd volunteered for the Army Service Corps to train as a driver. Posted first to Catterick and then to Colchester, he'd moved into France with the British Expeditionary Force early in 1940, and been evacuated from St Malo. For the next couple of years he'd been back in the barracks at Colchester, apart from a brief spell in Norwich in the April and May of 1942 when his unit had been called in to help clear the devastation caused by the two great 'Baedeker' air raids. He'd landed in Normandy in 1944 as part of the support troops and been part of the first British contingent to cross the Rhine at Remagen after the Americans had seized the bridge.

Electing to stay on once the war was over, he had, since then, been at Munchen-Gladbach, serving with the British Army of the Rhine, and it was only the growing unrest in Egypt that had prompted his despatch to the Suez Canal Zone.

He was a good lad, was Ted, so his brother maintained. Never been in any trouble. Always bright and cheerful. Fond of the girls, but not the sort of lad who'd be likely to make an enemy. No, he couldn't think of anyone who'd want to do him harm.

'So you'd better get weaving,' he said, 'and find the chap who did it, because if I find him first I'll wring his bloody neck.'

*   *   *

Nor was there much for Sue Gradwell to report. It was true that her questions hadn't met with the same scepticism as Ellison's had produced, but there was little in what Erica Westaway had to tell her that cast any light on her sister's killing.

It was true that Tammy had been a bit of a wild spirit, and her marriage to Robert Scott had been little less than disastrous, but she wasn't really a bad girl. Yes, she'd had her share of men, but her liaisons had been brief and there hadn't been any, as far as she knew, with men who were married. None of them had been serious, long-lasting relationships.

No, they hadn't lived long in Stiffkey. She and her sister had been born in King's Lynn where their father, a solicitor, had worked for most of his life, but when they were in their teens he'd suffered a near-fatal heart attack and been forced to retire. Looking for somewhere quieter than Lynn, he'd bought the cottage at Stiffkey and settled down there with his wife and two daughters. Then, three years later, when Tammy was sixteen, they'd been travelling home from a holiday in the Lakes when a lorry had burst a tyre on the Al near Wetherby and ploughed into their car. She and Tammy, who were sitting in the back, had escaped with nothing more than cuts and bruises, but both their parents had been killed.

'It was terrible,' she said, 'but more for Tammy than for me. I was already working, articled to a law firm in Sheringham, but she was still at school with very real prospects of getting to university. Luckily for us, Dad left us well off, there was no mortgage to pay on the cottage, and it helped me that I had to take on the responsibility of looking after Tammy. I did my best, but it was a difficult time. She went all to pieces and failed her exams. I think she felt that life was such a lottery that the only thing to do was live for the day and to hell with the future. It just might never come.

'I strained every nerve to help her, but she was quite determined to go her own way, drifting from job to job and from man to man. When she found herself pregnant, I tried to persuade her to get rid of the child. I promised to pay for an abortion, but then Robert offered to marry her, and I think she saw marriage as just another wild experiment she hadn't yet tried.

'I told her that was the worst possible reason for getting herself hitched. She was planning to spend the rest of her life with a man she didn't love and with whom she'd had only a casual relationship. So what? she said. If it didn't work out, they'd get a divorce.

'At that point I think I simply gave up. Perhaps I shouldn't have done, but they married and well, you know the rest of the tale.'

She gave a deep sigh. 'Yes, maybe Tammy wasted her life, but I can't imagine anyone wanting to kill her, not even Robert. He wasn't that kind of man.'

8.

All in all, it was a day of repetitive frustration.

Detective Constable Stephen Spurgeon, searching for the hairdresser who'd cut the killer's hair, spent the day driving from shop to shop within the designated twenty-mile radius of Holkham, only to report at the end of his stint that while many thick-set, fair-haired men between twenty-five and thirty-five had taken a haircut within the past week, none of them had limped, and without further evidence it was virtually impossible to link them with the man that Truscott had seen by the churchyard at Northgate.

Nor did Rayner and Barnes have any better luck. No one in the village could identify the lorry that Truscott had mentioned, and though the inveterate traders of local gossip had been only too willing to whisper their doubts about the purity of some of their female neighbours, none of them had linked their names with anyone who remotely resembled the flight lieutenant.

Even Desmond Lock, constantly on the phone in the incident room compiling his lists, struggled to achieve any positive response. No small dark van registered in the area had been reported as stolen within the past week, and a succession of calls to local farmers and hauliers failed to produce any news of a lorry that might have been driving past Northgate church in the small hours of Sunday.

Striking one name after another from his list, Lock began to feel he was engaged in a fruitless search for some ghostly vehicle that existed only in Truscott's imagination. The chance of finding the one fleck of gold he was seeking seemed to recede with every call that he made.

The last name on his list was an Isaac Eson of Norton Breck Farm, two miles to the west on the coastal road. He dialled the number and a gruff voice repeated it, adding for good measure, 'Ike Eson, Breck Farm.'

Lock was a conscientious young man, determined to pursue his inquiries to the limit. He wasted no time. 'This is Detective Constable Lock,' he said. 'I'm speaking from the incident room at Burnham Northgate.'

'Oh aye.'

'D'you happen to own a lorry, Mr Eson?'

'Aye . . . What's he bin doin this time?'

'Who?'

'Joe Sadler. He's the one as drives it.'

'Oh, he's done nothing wrong, Mr Eson.'

'What then?'

'Did he take the lorry out early last Sunday morning?'

'Depends what's early?'

'About half-past one?'

'Aye, allus does. Teks taters to Fakenham for Sunday mornin' market.'

'Does he go past Northgate church?'

'Reckon so, aye. He'd tek shortest road. Not one fer wastin' his time, Joe ent.'

'Then where can I find him?'

A pause. 'What's the trouble?'

'No trouble, Mr Eson. He may have seen something, and we just want to check.'

'Then ye'd best get down here sharpish.' The farmer was uncompromisingly laconic. 'He's loadin' up now. In another ten minutes he'll be off down to Wells.'

*   *   *

Lock was there in five. He found Sadler, a tall, stringy young man, leaning against the mudguard of an old, dilapidated Chevrolet lorry, smoking a cigarette and watching two other men heaving sacks of potatoes on to the bed of the truck.

The conversation was brief.

Aye, that were right. He'd bin passin' Northgate church, reckoned it were round about quarter to two. Aye, there were two on 'em, a car and a van, both parked on the verge. Course he was sure. Road swung a bit when it got close to the church, an' headlights moved over 'em slow enough to see. He'd wondered what the hell they were a-doin' of stuck by the church at that time in a mornin', but he'd had to get taters to Fakenham by two an' he were runnin' a mite late, so he'd just driven on. No, he hadn't seen what the number plate was on the van. What the hell did Lock think he was? A golden bloody eagle?

Lock had no such illusion, so he didn't feel

131

deprived. He drove back to Burnham Northgate in a happier frame of mind than most of Tench's team. At least he hadn't wasted the whole of the day.

9.

Gregg, on the other hand, found it difficult to decide whether his own day, patiently devoted to Flight Lieutenant Truscott, had been anything more than a profitless exercise. Driving to North Creake airfield that morning, he'd been hoping to uncover some damning indictment of the man's reliability, but all his inquiries had merely served to prove that Truscott's reputation was utterly stainless. His commanding officer was quite categorical. He would, he said, have no hesitation in accepting Truscott's word as the truth. He was a thoroughly competent, dependable officer with a record that was second to none at the base. Whatever the evidence was that he'd volunteered to the police, there was no reason at all to deem it unreliable.

Gregg wasn't prepared to leave it at that. Hazarding a guess that Truscott wasn't a teetotaller and was therefore more than likely to frequent a local pub, he made a tour of those around North and South Creake, and then drove straight to the Hoste Arms in Burnham Market.

The Hoste Arms, a seventeenth-century

132

coaching inn named after Sir William Hoste, one of Nelson's captains, was the oldest and most exclusive hotel in the area: just the kind of place, he argued to himself, that a flight lieutenant in the RAF might choose as his local watering hole. So, having drawn a blank at a good half-dozen less distinguished taverns, he approached the imposing façade of the Hoste with a feeling that here he might well strike lucky.

He wasn't disappointed. 'Frank Truscott,' said the barman. 'Yes, he's a regular. Pops in most evenings. Doesn't stay, though. Takes a nip of Scotch and he's off some place else.' He tapped the side of his nose. 'Better things to do with his time, I reckon. Good sort of chap, though. Always cheerful. Honest with it, too. Undercharged him the other week, and he tossed his change back. "Can't have the Hoste going bankrupt, Fred, can we?" That was what he said.'

'Does he ever bring a lady friend with him?' Gregg asked.

Fred gave a shrug. 'Never seen one,' he said, 'but I reckon he must have one stowed away somewhere. He doesn't spend his evenings drinking, that's for sure.'

Gregg probed a bit further. 'Never happened to mention her name, has he?'

'Never mentioned her at all.' Fred gave a regretful sigh. 'Like to meet her though. Just out of curiosity. Enjoys his nip of Scotch, so she must be quite something.'

Flight Lieutenant Truscott, so it appeared, was not merely competent, dependable and trustworthy. He was also a man of exemplary discretion.

*   *   *

Reporting this to Tench at the briefing that evening, Gregg found himself sounding almost apologetic. 'Never heard a single word against him, sir,' he said. 'Looks like everything he told us could well be the truth.'

Tench merely nodded. 'Well, fair enough,' he said. 'It fits in with the lorry driver's statement to Lock. We have to accept it, and that at least means we're making some progress. We've a description of the man, and probably also a photograph of him. All we have to do now is find out who he is and then track him down.'

He turned to the rest of the team and held up a clutch of prints. 'These,' he said, 'are photographs taken at the Queens at Holkham on Saturday night. They show a square-jawed, thickset, clean-shaven man, with what looks to be short fair hair, intently watching our two murder victims, Bolton and Scott. I want everyone out tomorrow, armed with one of these. We need to identify this man as soon as possible. You'll be detailed to work in specific areas, apart, that is, from Steve Spurgeon.

134

He'll be doing another round of the barbers' shops he visited today. If we're right in our assumptions, this could be the man who followed our two victims out of the Queens and down into the pine woods. Someone must know him, so show the prints around. Let's see if we can't put a name to the bastard and nail him down fast. And remember. According to Truscott, he limps.'

10.

All taken in all, it was a difficult day for Tench and his team, that Wednesday of the Rionero Case.

Most of its members, Ellison and Sue Gradwell, Rayner and Spurgeon, and to some extent Gregg, left the incident room that evening wondering whether the hours they'd spent trailing round Norfolk had made any contribution to the progress of the case. Only Lock and McKenzie felt any degree of satisfaction, and even McKenzie's buoyant mood, in the Adam and Eve that night, could well have been fuelled by the sight of a pint of good Norfolk ale in front of him on the bar, and its taste and that of the subsequent pints as they slid down his throat.

Even Tench, for all his display of optimism, had his doubts about what had really been achieved. They had, it was true, confirmed Truscott's tale of a van being parked on the edge of Northgate churchyard, and they'd found nothing at all to invalidate his evidence, but they had, at the same time, found nothing to support his account of a limping man armed with sacks and a spade. Nor, it seemed, were they ever likely to do so. And though the photographs taken by Meg Rooney's brother had given them a new lead which they had to follow up, he admitted to himself that they were acting on a hunch and nothing more than that. The man by the dartboard, who seemed to be watching Bolton and Mrs Scott, might well have had murder on his mind, but he might just as well have had other, more innocent reasons for his interest. Who could possibly read a man's intentions from nothing more substantial than a black-and-white print shot from a distance in a smoke-filled room?

Left on his own that evening in the church hall at Northgate, he spread out the photographs and studied each in turn. Then he gave a mental shrug. It was all conjecture. The square-jawed, thick-set, clean-shaven figure (was his hair fair or was it no more than a trick of the light?) could be their man, but the odds were just as short that he mightn't have any connection with the case.

Were they about to spend another day chasing shadows, with nothing to show for their labours at the end? He simply didn't know, but the doubts crowded round him.

He sat for a moment staring at the prints,

then he swept them all together and dropped them in a drawer. It wasn't often nowadays that he deliberately sought out his old Chief's company, but he needed to talk.

Slamming the drawer shut, he locked up the hall and drove down to Cley.

* * *

But if he thought that Lubbock would be ready to offer reassurance, he was wrong.

'So you've got a description of this man,' he said, 'and now you've got a picture of someone who might or might not be him, but you still haven't the foggiest idea who he is or where you can find him. You're not much further advanced than you were at this time yesterday, are you, laddie?'

Tench took a deep breath. 'Not much, I suppose.'

'And why? Because in spite of what I said, you still persist in asking all the wrong questions. I've already told you what to do. The key to this case is in the churchyard at Burnham Northgate. That's the place to look. Somewhere within the walls of that little patch of ground there's something that has a connection with the killer. That's what's going to lead you to him, not a picture of someone who may not be him at all.'

'And you don't know what it is any more than I do.'

'No, I don't,' Lubbock said.

'I've examined every gravestone. There isn't a sign that any Boltons or Westaways or Scotts are buried there.'

'True enough, but you know what they say here in Norfolk, laddie. "That dunt signify." This man you're looking for isn't a Bolton. He isn't a Scott and he isn't a Westawav. He's someone with an entirely different name.'

'And we don't know what it is.'

'No, we don't. Not yet. But, given time, we will.'

'Then, out of your great wisdom, what d'you suggest we do?'

'We wait,' said Lubbock. 'Be patient and wait. As I've told you before, most cases solve themselves if you give them the time. We haven't heard the last of this man with the limp. He'll show himself again. There's nothing as sure as that. And when he does, he'll hand us the key to this case, and we'll turn it in the lock. It's as simple as that.'

11.

He was right, in a sense.

At twenty past five the following morning, the phone at Tench's bedside shattered his sleep.

It was the Duty Sergeant on the line. 'Message from Constable Barnes, sir,' he said. 'He's found another body.'

Tench gave a groan. 'Did he say where?'

'Burnham Northgate churchyard. That's what he said, sir.'

'Hell's bells! Not again!'

'Looks like it, sir.' For such an early hour the sergeant was quite unbecomingly cheerful. 'Who was it said that lightning never strikes twice?'

V

THE FATAL KEY

The fatal key,
Sad instrument of all our woe.
John Milton: *Paradise Lost*

1.

There were times when Mike Tench detested his job.

The sun was already a brilliant blaze in the wide Norfolk sky as he drove towards the coast, and twisting and turning between the flatness of the fields, he asked himself with some ferocity why the devil he'd decided to bypass the rest of his time at Cambridge and chosen to train as a detective. If he'd had any common sense, he could have been wandering along the Backs, gazing idly across the river to the pinnacles of King's, instead of dashing hell for leather without any breakfast to gaze at blood and death in a nondescript graveyard.

It clung to him, that angry sense of regret, all the way to the Burnhams, and it was only when he reached Northgate church and Will Barnes flagged him down that duty once again thrust aside all the thoughts of what might have been.

He pushed open the car door. 'Where is it, Constable?' he asked.

'The other side, sir,' said Barnes. 'First grave by the gate. Looks as if our killer's got a thing about this churchyard.'

'One or two?'

'One, sir, this time.'

'Man or woman?'

'It's a man, sir, but it's difficult to tell who he is.'

Tench took a deep breath. 'Right, he said. 'Get in.'

*   *   *

He'd gazed at many bodies, shot, knifed, poisoned or bludgeoned into pulp, but he'd never looked down at one laid out in this deliberately peculiar fashion.

The stone stood, erect, by the churchyard wall, adjacent to the gate that Lubbock had pushed open the previous Sunday.

It marked the grave of a husband and wife, Silas and Gertrude Etherleigh who, having reached the ripe old age of ninety-three, had died within days of each other back in the March of 1897.

The man lay as he might have lain in a coffin, his feet together and his head towards the stone; but his hands, instead of being clasped or pressed together in prayer, were covering his face as if his last conscious act had been to hide from his eyes something that was far too terrible to see.

He was quite clearly dead, cold and rigid as the stone.

And more than that, he was naked.

Tench turned away. 'Get the place screened and taped off,' he said, 'and this time tape off the whole of the churchyard. No one's to step

144

inside without permission from me. And that includes the Rector. Everyone's to use the other gate. That's the only way in. If we're going to catch the bastard who's responsible for this, the last thing we want is for half of Burnham Northgate to be tramping around. Get started now. As soon as the scene-of-crime squad arrive, they'll take over . . . Oh, and by the way. Chief Superintendent Hastings is on his way down, so if you see him, send him round here to me.'

2.

The Chief Super parted the canvas screens, stepped inside and looked down.

'What do we know, Mike?' he asked.

'So far,' said Tench, 'only the little that Ledward could tell us. He died somewhere between ten o'clock and midnight last night. A single heavy blow to the back of the head. It shattered his skull.'

'You've no idea who he is?'

'No, sir, and at the moment we haven't much chance of telling. His hands are hiding his face and he's as stiff as a board. Rigor's fully established. If we wanted to see his face, we'd have to break his arms, and we daren't do that. We'll have to wait until Ledward gets him on the slab and relaxes the muscles.'

The Chief Super nodded. 'We're looking at the same killer?'

'Well, the pattern's the same. He was murdered somewhere else, then brought here and laid out with his hands deliberately placed across his face. There seems to be something of a ritual about it, as there was about the other.'

'Then it could still be a random killing. We might very well have a madman out on the loose.'

'We might,' said Tench, 'but I don't think we have. I'm pretty sure that the other murder was planned. One of the victims was quite deliberately targeted. The killer was someone who knew either Bolton or Mrs Scott, and was determined to be rid of whichever one it was.'

'A grudge killing?'

'That's my feeling, sir, yes. And bearing in mind the similarities—same place, same pattern, same kind of ritual—I'd say there's an obvious connection between the two.'

'Then which of the first two victims was the target?'

'I'm not certain, sir, yet. We still don't know enough about them, but if I had to make a guess, I'd say it was Bolton.'

'But that's just a guess?'

'That's all it can be, sir, at this stage, I'm afraid.'

'He was a soldier, wasn't he? You think there's something somewhere in his army career . . . ?'

'It's possible, sir, yes.'

'Then you need to know all the details.'

'We've already got a rough outline, sir, from his brother, and we're in touch with his CO at Munchen-Gladbach. We're hoping for more from him.'

'The War Office?'

'Yes, we could contact them officially, but the wheels of government turn far too slowly. We need quick results.'

'Then what about that chap you know in the Archives Section? He's turned up trumps a couple of times before.'

'Jeremy Clyde?'

'That's the chap.'

'It's already in hand, sir. I phoned him this morning.'

'You're sending someone down?'

'Yes, sir. Gregg's already on his way. Clyde's met him before. He went down last year on the Medford case.'

Hastings stared at the body and took a deep breath. 'We could have done without this, Mike,' he said. 'The powers that be aren't going to like it one bit . . . You've had no luck as yet with the man in the photographs?'

'No, but someone must know him. Apart from Gregg, all the rest of the team are out asking around, and I've sent a print to Ransome. It'll be splashed on the *EDP*'s front page tomorrow.'

'Well,'—the Chief Super shrugged—'there's little more you can do except pray for a slice of luck.' He paused. 'By the way, who found the body? Don't tell me it was Lubbock.'

Tench mustered a smile. 'No, sir, not this time. A fisherman from Northgate cycling home.'

'You've spoken to him?'

'Yes, sir. Nothing suspicious. He was on board ship all night, waiting to cross the bar into Wells.'

'Then all you can do is press on and hope, but as you say, Mike, we need a break and we need it fast if I'm to keep the wolves at bay.' He parted the screens again and stepped outside. 'If there's any development, let me know right away. As soon as the Chief Constable gets wind of this, the phone on my desk won't just ring, that's for sure. It'll explode like that bomb we dropped on Hiroshima. And if his breakfast egg didn't come up to scratch, it'll be left to the Met to pick a way through the rubble.'

3.

The compartment was dusty, the windows were edged with grime, and the engine seemed to be labouring under the misapprehension that it was pulling a slow train from Cromer to Wells, but Andrew Gregg was oblivious to all such minor irritations. He was sleeping soundly.

148

When, five years before, Lubbock had instructed his young assistant, Mike Tench, to travel up to London to make contact with a Mr Jeremy Clyde at the War Office in Whitehall, Tench, then no more than a trainee sergeant, had viewed the prospect with some trepidation, and Lubbock, in his briefing, had done little to allay his fears.

'It won't be easy,' he'd said, 'to get hold of the facts we need, you can rest assured of that. These faceless wonders who sit behind desks in their Whitehall offices are trained to be clams. This chap Clyde's going to quote you rules and regulations that make it impossible to reveal a damned thing. You'll just have to be patient, laddie, patient and persistent. That's why I'm sending you and not Sergeant McKenzie. I need someone with tact and diplomatic skills to do a bit of persuading. So get away home and have an early night. It's your job tomorrow to try and prise open the tightest pair of lips in the whole of England.'

Tench had gone away, but he hadn't slept well, nor had he even dozed on the train next morning. Ready to feel overawed by the corridors of power, he was determined not to show it, and spent the journey to London, wide awake, thinking his way around every awkward situation he might possibly encounter.

Lubbock's prudence and his own had paid ample dividends. He'd managed to prise the facts from a tight-lipped Mr Clyde, so many of them indeed that that same evening he'd taken the wildly quixotic step, in that terrible winter of 1947, of driving out to Cley in his unheated car across the icebound roads just to brief the Chief Inspector on what he'd discovered.

It had been well worth the journey. 'You've done well, laddie,' Lubbock had said. 'At least we've now got a starting point. We can begin to ask questions with some degree of knowledge.'

*　　*　　*

That was probably why, when four years later, as Detective Chief Inspector, he'd found himself face to face with a similar situation, he'd copied Lubbock to the letter, and sent his young sergeant, Andrew Gregg, rather than McKenzie, to put the questions to Clyde.

And he had, like Lubbock, been amply rewarded, despite the fact that Gregg was certainly no Tench.

Discreetly ambitious, confident in his own abilities and eternally optimistic, Gregg had been a good deal more relaxed in his approach to the problem. This was the kind of assignment he was prepared to enjoy. All he had to do was ask a few questions, get the right answers, and after that make a leisurely journey back to Norwich.

He'd been fast asleep before the train reached Cambridge, and he hadn't wakened

150

up till it drew to a halt in Victoria station.

*   *   *

It was therefore not surprising that, despatched to London a second time to see Mr Clyde, he was, that Thursday morning, soundly asleep only ten minutes after the train left Norwich. The prospect of entering the corridors of power wasn't one to disturb Andrew Gregg's equanimity, and the prospect of failure never entered his head.

Whatever it was that was more than a little shady in Edward Bolton's army career, it wasn't going to remain in the shadows for long, once he reached London and renewed his acquaintance with Mr Jeremy Clyde.

4.

Tench wasn't asleep. Standing by the slab in Ledward's laboratory, gazing down at the naked body, he was very wide awake.

'Well, Chief Inspector? Have you seen enough?' Ledward was impatient. 'Can I make a start?'

'Not yet, Doctor. I want him photographed,' Tench said.

'And just how long will that take?'

'Half an hour at the most.'

'It's necessary?'

'In this case, sir, yes.'

151

Ledward gave a shrug. 'Well, it's your choice,' he said. 'You'll just have to wait a bit longer for results.'

'That's regrettable,' said Tench, 'but it's unavoidable. I need prints of the man, and I need them as soon as possible. That's more important . . . I'd like to use your phone.'

The doctor was all apparent sweetness. 'Oh, do help yourself, Chief Inspector,' he said. 'I'd be the last person to stand in the way of the police, even if it means disrupting the whole of my morning schedule.'

5.

McKenzie was not merely wide awake, he was hot and frustrated.

Tramping round the narrow streets of Wells-next-the-Sea wasn't his ideal way of spending a summer morning, especially when all he had to do was go from shop to shop armed with a photograph, repeating the same bloody stupid question time and time again.

He was convinced that the question was stupid for the simple reason that he was equally convinced that the man in the photograph didn't live in Wells, had never lived in Wells, and furthermore had never even taken it into his head to visit the place.

He had, he felt, good reason to be so convinced. Since parking his pride and joy on the Buttlands that morning, he had, he

152

reckoned, asked that same bloody question at least a thousand times and received an equal number of negative responses. Nobody knew the man, nobody had ever seen him, and he might just as well have been a lifelong resident of Muck who'd never once set foot outside his God-forsaken island.

He mopped his forehead, took a deep breath and looked up at his next shop. 'William Drinkwater' the sign read, as if in guilty denial of its owner's trade, 'Licensed to sell alcohol'. McKenzie groaned. Not an off-licence. No, not that. Fate couldn't be so cruel. The sun was beating down, his armpits were wet, his throat felt as rough as a sheet of sandpaper, and he was suddenly face to face with a window full of bottles. It was more than any reasonable man could endure.

For a moment he was minded to give the place a miss, then some flash of wild determination, such as drove his Highland ancestors forward at Culloden, propelled him across the threshold.

It was perhaps unfortunate that that same threshold was bounded by an inch-high step made of stone, and even more unfortunate that, intent on nothing more than blinding himself to every bottle in sight, he also blinded himself to the step.

The result was catastrophic. Plunging helplessly forward, his fourteen stones hit a five-foot high stack of crates like a battering

153

ram, scattering their contents, twelve bottles of beer in each, across the stone floor, where six of them shattered, discharging a river of foaming ale towards the shop counter.

McKenzie's oath was that of a trooper, not a clansman. He heaved himself up and surveyed the wreckage.

That was when he was seized by yet another conviction.

It wasn't his day.

6.

Gregg had little doubt that it was going to be his day.

Everything was the same as it had been on his visit twelve months before: a visit that had proved to be both smooth and productive.

Clyde was still in the same room, which would have consumed the floor-space of his small modern flat on the outskirts of Norwich, and he still wore the same type of pin-striped suit with the light blue fleck, the same spotless white shirt and navyblue tie that seemed to be his trademark.

And his room was still the same. It contained a highly polished mahogany desk, half a dozen tall metal filing cabinets, two high-backed leather-seated chairs and nothing else beyond a carpet of thick Axminster pile.

Nor had Clyde himself changed. Not much older than Gregg, languid, but keen-eyed and trained to be cautious, he did exactly what he'd done on that previous visit. Seated behind the desk, he waved a hand towards the vacant chair, then swivelled round to one of the cabinets, extracted a file, laid it on the desk and placed a paperweight on top of it.

'I gather,' he said, 'from Chief Inspector Tench that you have now been promoted.'

'That's right, sir.'

'You are now Inspector Gregg?'

Gregg nodded. 'I am, sir.'

'Then, since I've never had the pleasure of meeting an Inspector Gregg, and you might, unknown to me, possess a twin brother, perhaps we should go through the usual formalities. You have some means of identification?'

Gregg produced his card and handed it across the desk. Clyde studied it carefully and handed it back. 'That seems quite satisfactory, Inspector,' he said. 'Permit me to offer my belated congratulations.'

'Thank you, sir.'

Clyde gave a barely perceptible nod. 'Now, to business,' he said. 'I was asked by Chief Inspector Tench to trace the army records of one Edward Bolton, a sergeant in the Royal Army Service Corps, now serving in the British Army of the Rhine at Munchen-Gladbach. Is that correct?'

'Correct, sir, yes.'

'And I presume that, as on previous

155

occasions when the Chief Inspector has requested similar details from me, he hoped to find some . . . irregularity, shall we say?'

'I think that was the general idea, sir, yes.'

There was another barely perceptible nod from Clyde. He reached forward, lifted the paperweight, slid the file from underneath it, and glanced through the handful of sheets inside. 'Then I'm afraid,' he said, 'that on this occasion the Chief Inspector may well be disappointed. I can see nothing here that could possibly be classed as such.'

'No, sir?'

'No. Sergeant Bolton's conduct appears to have been exemplary. There is nothing in this file that casts any kind of shadow on his army service.'

Gregg frowned. 'You're certain, sir?'

Clyde looked down his nose. 'Are you doubting my ability to read, Inspector?'

'No, sir. It isn't that.' Gregg was apologetic.

'But you find what I say difficult to believe?'

'We did expect . . .'

'Then it seems, Inspector, that your joint expectations were somewhat wide of the mark. There is nothing—I repeat, nothing—in this man's army service that could possibly be construed as culpable. Rather the reverse. He was decorated for bravery in June '44. Awarded an MM.'

'Does it say why?'

'I'm afraid not, Inspector, but it must have

156

been during the Normandy landings.' He held out the file. 'Here, read for yourself.'

Gregg read, then he looked up and gave a shrug of resignation. 'Then it seems we were wrong.'

'It would appear so,' said Clyde. 'Please tender my commiserations to Chief Inspector Tench . . . Oh, yes, and keep the file. I hardly think it contains material that, by any stretch of imagination, could be classed as top secret.'

7.

If McKenzie was hot and frustrated trudging from shop to shop, he wasn't on his own. So were the other members of Tench's team. Detective Constable Stephen Spurgeon, trailing round the same succession of scattered barbers' shops that he'd visited the day before, was finding the day particularly irritating. Time and time again, he'd felt that he might be on the edge of a breakthrough, only to be left with his hopes unfulfilled. By midday he'd called at twenty-three shops, shown the same photograph, asked the same question, and the net result of his labours was that fifteen barbers were ready to swear that they'd never in their lives set eyes on the man, five had thought they might have, but couldn't be sure, and three, after much cogitation, had said yes, they were more or less certain he'd paid them a visit, but they didn't know who he was, and the last time they'd seen him was more than a month before.

That was why, promptly at ten past twelve, Spurgeon parked his car on the quayside at Blakeney, took out his notebook, ran a line through all twenty-three different names, stared at the muddy channel twisting out through the marshes, leaned back in his seat, closed his eyes against the sun and, quite unintentionally, dozed off to sleep.

*   *   *

He woke with a start ten minutes later to find a cherrywood stick pointing at him through the open window of the car, and beyond it the craggy, unmistakable face of ex-Detective Chief Inspector John Spencer Lubbock. Then he heard Lubbock's equally unmistakable voice. 'Sleeping on duty, lad? Not the sort of thing to bring credit to the force.'

Spurgeon blinked and then, all contrition, heaved himself up. 'Sorry, sir,' he said. 'Must just have dropped off.'

'Then be thankful I saw you, not Chief Inspector Tench.' Lubbock peered at him closely. 'Had a hard morning, lad? Is that the trouble?'

'A bit of one, sir, yes.'

'Still trying to put a name to that chap in the photograph?'

'Trying to, sir.'

'But not with much success.'

'No, sir. None.'

'Where've you been looking?'

'Every barber's shop, sir, within twenty miles.'

Lubbock tut-tutted. 'Then no wonder you haven't made any headway, laddie. You're in the wrong place.'

Spurgeon blinked again. 'Am I, sir?'

'Of course you are. You'll never put a name to the chap around here. This isn't his stamping ground.'

'It isn't?'

'No, it isn't.'

'Then where should I be looking?'

'Norwich, laddie. Norwich. That's the place to look. You might just as well be sledging around the North Pole as trying to find him here.'

Spurgeon was doubtful. 'You think so, sir?'

'I'm certain.'

'But the Chief's never mentioned Norwich at all.'

'Oh, he will,' said Lubbock. 'You wait and see . . . By the way, where is the Chief Inspector? Any idea?'

Spurgeon shook his head. 'Not seen him today, sir. There wasn't a briefing. He wanted us all out on the road early this morning, so we didn't report in.'

Lubbock fumbled in his pocket and dragged out a folded sheet of paper. 'Well,' he said, 'when you see him, give him that, will you? And tell him I've a hunch that the name he's trying to find may be somewhere on that list.'

8.

It was at half-past twelve that McKenzie, as instructed, rang the incident room from a phone box in Wells and spoke to Desmond Lock. 'Anything moving at your end, Des?' he asked.

'Plenty,' said Lock. 'We've had another murder in the churchyard here at Northgate, and the Chief wants you back in Norwich ek dum.'

It was thirty-one miles from Wells to Norwich, but McKenzie, by cranking the Norton up to a sweet sixty on the road beyond Fakenham, covered the distance in not much over three-quarters of an hour. By half-past one he was climbing the stairs to the DCI's office.

Tench met him half-way. 'Back down again, Mac,' he said.

'Right. So what's the panic?'

'No panic, but I need you to take a look at something.'

'Something like what?'

'A body,' said Tench. 'We've got an appointment with your friend and mine, Dr Reginald Ledward.'

160

Ledward folded back the sheet that covered the body, revealing the face.

'Take a close look, Mac—a close look,' said Tench.

McKenzie peered down, then he frowned, stood back, walked round to the other side of the slab and repeated the process.

'What d'you think?' said Tench.

McKenzie scratched his head. 'Well, it looks like him, but I wouldn't be prepared to swear that it is.'

'He's got fair hair.'

'Yes, that's true.'

'And it's cut short.'

'Yes, I can see that, too.'

'He's thick-set, five foot eight and a half and, according to Dr Ledward, aged between thirty and thirty-five.'

'All noted,' McKenzie said, 'but what about the limp?'

Tench turned to the doctor. 'Tell Sergeant McKenzie, sir, what you told me.'

Ledward folded back the other end of the sheet, and raised the left leg. 'This one,' he said, 'is a good two inches shorter than the right. At some time in the past he must have suffered a serious injury which caused a compound fracture of the shin bone with considerable complications. A metal plate's been inserted to strengthen the bone and hold the two parts together. The damage to the leg was so extensive that he's lucky he was able to walk at all. Many surgeons would simply have advised amputation.'

McKenzie frowned again. 'Is it possible to tell, sir, just when the metal plate was inserted?'

Ledward half-smiled in a tired sort of way like a weary teacher attempting to explain to a backward child. 'No, not precisely, Sergeant; he said. 'I'm a doctor, not a member of the Magic Circle. I can only give you a rough estimate, but I'd say that whoever performed the operation did so round about ten years ago.'

'1942?'

'Yes, Sergeant, that's right. Ten from fifty-two does leave forty-two. I learned that way back in elementary school.'

McKenzie ignored him. He turned back to Tench. 'So where do we stand now?' he asked.

'It all tots up, doesn't it?'

'It seems to, yes.'

'But you're still not convinced?'

'I'm a cautious sort of bloke. My old man drank himself to death on Glenfiddich. I never touch the stuff.'

'Well, there's still one thing that can clinch it . . . Dr Ledward's sent a sample of hair to the lab.'

'So we go and see Ted Merrick.'

'We go and see Ted Merrick,' said Tench,

'so let's go.'

*   *   *

Merrick set two microscopes side by side and placed a slide under each. 'Have a look at these,' he said.

'You first, Mac,' said Tench.

McKenzie bent down and studied each in turn, then he straightened up and made way for Tench.

'The one on the left,' Merrick said, 'was found by Dr Ledward adhering to Bolton's right middle finger. The one on the right's been taken from the head of your latest victim.'

Tench made a point of looking twice at each, then he, too, straightened up. 'I'm no expert,' he said, 'but to me they both look exactly the same. What about you, Mac?'

McKenzie gave a shrug. 'They just look like a couple of hairy centipedes to me. They seem to be the same. That's all I can say.'

'They are the same,' Merrick said. 'The hair on Bolton's finger'—he tapped the microscope on the left—'is identical in every respect to this'—he tapped the one on the right—'that was cut from the second victim's head this morning.'

Tench glanced at McKenzie. McKenzie turned to Merrick. 'Well done, lad,' he said. 'You've just killed off our one and only

163

suspect, and we don't even know his name.'

The young analyst looked puzzled. 'You mean . . . ?'

Tench laid a hand on his shoulder. 'Don't try to work it out, Ted,' he advised. 'If you do, you'll be lost in the same maze as we are.'

'And it's one of those,' McKenzie said, 'with hedges twenty feet high . . . smothered in bloody great thorns.'

9.

Back in his office, Tench put a call through to Lock at Burnham Northgate. 'Des,' he said, 'there's a change of plan. There won't be any briefing at the incident room tonight. Everyone's to report back to me here in Norwich. And tomorrow morning I want them all here promptly at eight.'

'Right, sir,' said Lock.

'And if Lester rings in, pass me any messages.'

'Will do, sir.'

'Good. I take it that no one's reported back yet.'

'Not so far, sir, no.'

'Well, you know what to do. Sergeant McKenzie's already here with me, so as soon as they're all on the way, lock the place up and report back yourself.'

'Aye, aye, sir. Is that all?'

'Yes, Des, that's the lot.'

He rang off, pushed the phone aside, locked the office door and spread a series of files across the desk top. 'Pull up a chair, Mac,' he said. 'We've got some thinking to do. Even if Merrick doesn't need to work things out, we do, and fast. Today's events have turned the case upside down. We've got to find a way out of this maze before tomorrow morning, so let's get down to it and lay out the facts.'

'That's the easy part,' McKenzie said. 'The problem's trying to work out what the hell they mean.'

'Then let's do the easy part first,' said Tench. 'We've been probing a double murder. We know that the victims spent Saturday evening in the Queens Hotel at Holkham, and we assume that from there they walked down the road to the Gap and into the pine woods, where somebody savagely beat them to death and then laid out their bodies in Northgate churchyard, four miles to the west. We also suspect that a man was watching them in the Queens, that he followed them down to the woods, and that he was the one who committed the murders . . . We've got photographs of this man. We know what he looks like, but we don't know who he is, and up to the present moment no one within twenty miles of the murder scene has offered a positive identification.'

Tench paused and looked up. 'That's the first lot of facts. Agreed, Mac?'

165

'Agreed.'

'Good. Let's move on. We now find that this man has himself been murdered, and his body laid out in much the same fashion at the very same location; and all the available evidence seems to prove that he did indeed kill the first two victims. In other words, the murderer has himself been murdered. We still don't know who he is, and, apart from that, we're now faced with the task of finding a second killer. Right?'

'Right.' McKenzie nodded.

'So . . . questions. Who is he? Why did he murder Bolton and Mrs Scott? Why did he choose to lay them out in Northgate churchyard? And now, in addition, two further questions to complicate the issue. Who killed him and why?'

'You want me to guess?'

'No, Mac, I don't. We can all of us guess, but guessing isn't going to get us very far. That's why the last question's probably the most difficult of all to answer. Which path do we take to get out of the maze?'

McKenzie lit a cigarette, leaned back and blew a smoke ring. 'Start at the beginning,' he said. 'Take the first and most obvious path, and only think again if it leads to a brick wall.'

'And which path would that be?'

'The one that leads straight to the man's identity.'

'You mean the first step to take is to find

out who he is?'

'If you want my opinion, yes, that's what I'd do.'

'You think we should follow the path we're already on?'

'Yes. Stick to it. Keep right on to the end of the road. It's an old Scots adage.'

'But it's led us nowhere so far.'

'Maybe it hasn't, but it's still the path to take.'

'But why, Mac? Why?'

'You don't need me to tell you.'

'Perhaps not, but I want to hear it . . . from you.'

'All right . . . Because who always comes before why and how.'

'You sound just like Lubbock.'

'That's because I learnt a lot from him . . . just as you did.'

'Fair enough. Carry on.'

'When you're trying to solve a murder, you look for motive and opportunity. We've got a man here who's both killer and victim, but we haven't the faintest idea who he is. To discover his motive and what moved his killer, we need to know his name. Without it, we haven't a cat in hell's chance of finding out just why he murdered Bolton or why someone else chose to do the same to him.'

'The old order never changeth?'

'If you like to put it that way . . . It's just common sense.'

167

'So the first item on the list is still the same: who is he?'

'Always was. Always will be. We've just got to keep on searching.'

'Right. Then let's think a bit further. Ransome's promised us a front-page spread in the *EDP* tomorrow morning. Everyone in East Anglia'll be able to see his photograph.'

'That's not enough. We can't afford to sit and wait. If we haven't found him so far, there can only be one possible reason for that . . . We haven't looked in the right place.'

'And the right place is . . . where?'

'You know that already, so let's stop playing games.'

'It's a big place, Mac. We'll need the whole of the team and half the local force.'

'Then get them,' McKenzie said. 'We may only need them for a couple of hours. If we can track the man down, the disruption'll be worth it.'

10.

The Chief Super leaned on the window jamb and stared out across the city. 'You think he was living here, Mike?'

'I don't know, sir,' said Tench. 'It's a gamble, but one that we think's worth taking. He doesn't seem to be known by anyone within twenty miles of the Burnhams, and there may be a possible connection with here.'

168

'What kind of a connection?'

'Well, that's also a bit of a gamble, sir. We're assuming there must have been some previous contact between him and Bolton: something that engendered a desire for revenge, and led to Bolton's murder. And we know three things for sure. Bolton was born in Norwich, at 25 Tipworth Street, close to the cemetery, and lived there until he went into the army; his brother still lives on Earlham Road and works as a mechanic at Pegasus Coaches; and Bolton stayed with him for the last five days that preceded his death.'

Hastings nodded thoughtfully. He waved a hand at the rooftops. 'It's a big place, Mike, and we can't afford to let this business drag on for days. If we're going to do a check quickly, you'll need a bigger team.'

'Yes, sir, I know, but given the men to target, say, a dozen of the likely areas, we could perhaps get it done swiftly enough.'

'How many men would you need?'

'A couple of hundred.'

'For how long?'

'With that sort of force, two hours at the most.'

'Well, we can't take them all from the city, that's for sure. We'll have to bring them in from all over Norfolk . . . When d'you want to start?'

'First thing tomorrow morning, sir. I'm briefing the team at eight.'

169

'What about today's search?'

'I'm not hopeful, sir. No one's rung in so far. It looks as if we've simply drawn another blank.'

Hastings sat down and pulled the phone towards him. 'Then I'd better start making arrangements,' he said.

* * *

Tench was right not to hope. As the members of his team reported back, one by one, to the incident room, their results were depressingly negative. Among the thousands of people who, at their insistence, had studied the photograph, none had provided a sufficiently positive identification to make the lead worth pursuing. The man they so desperately wanted to name remained as elusively anonymous as ever, and by the time that Gregg arrived back from London, Tench had already resigned himself to the fact that this particular summer's day, for all its bright promise, had proved to be utterly unproductive.

The look in Gregg's eyes, as he produced Clyde's file and laid it on the table, merely served to confirm his fears.

'No luck, Andy?' he said.

'Not a sausage, sir,' said Gregg. 'Mr Clyde's commiserations, but Sergeant Bolton's as clean as a whistle. Exemplary conduct. He even got a couple of commendations for bravery.'

*　　*　　*

The last to report was Spurgeon who, with time on his hands, had gone back to question customer, at three of his barbers' shops. 'No, sir,' he said. 'Nothing that's really worth following up . . . But I did meet Mr Lubbock when I was down in Blakeney.'

'Lubbock? What was he doing there?'

'No idea, sir,' said Spurgeon, 'but he gave me this and said it was for you.'

Tench opened the folded paper, and spread it on the table. It contained a list of two dozen names in alphabetical order:

Allen	Brett	Carslaw	Craven
Edwards	Foskett	Grant	Hudson
Jakes	Jones	Monement	Okelbie
Pollard	Pulvertoft	Reddaway	Ross
Sanders	Schwartz	Smith	Symondes
Turner	Vincent	Warner	Young

Two of the names, Carslaw and Jakes, were scored underneath with a single line, and another two, Grant and Reddaway, with thick double lines.

Tench stared at them. 'Did he give you any message?'

'Yes, sir.' Spurgeon nodded. 'Said he had a hunch that the name you were trying to find might be somewhere on that list.'

171

'He didn't say why?'

'No, sir.'

'Did you read it?'

'Thought I'd better, sir, but none of the names rings any kind of bell . . . If you ask me, sir, it all seems a bit cryptic.'

Tench frowned at the list. 'Mr Lubbock's always cryptic. Deliberately so, Steve. He works to an agenda that serves his own purpose.'

'And what's that, sir?'

'He wants me to get in touch with him, put him in the picture. He doesn't like to think that he's being neglected.'

'Are you going to get in touch with him?'

Tench placed an ashtray on top of the list. 'I haven't much alternative, have I, Steve?' he said.

11.

Once Spurgeon had left, he dragged the phone towards him, lifted the receiver, gave the operator Lubbock's number and asked to be connected. All he got in response was the tone that told him the line was engaged.

He swore, rang off, and five minutes later repeated the process. The result was the same.

He rang twice again in the next half-hour. The line was still engaged.

Slamming the receiver down on its hook, and deploying a number of sanguinary

172

adjectives to describe his old Chief, he stuffed the list in his pocket, seethed his way to the car park and, ignoring the designated speeds within the city, took the shortest route that would lead him to Cley.

*　　*　　*

Slowed down by a couple of crawling farm tractors on the road beyond Holt, he was still in no mood for a quiet cup of coffee when, almost an hour later, he wrenched the car to a halt in front of Lubbock's cottage on the Green below the church.

He didn't bother to knock. Flinging the door open, he marched straight into the parlour where his old Chief, lounging in his chair, pipe between his teeth, was contentedly blowing clouds of smoke toward the rafters. Beside him, on a little side-table, was the phone. The receiver was off its hook.

Tench pointed at it, accusingly. 'Your receiver's off,' he said.

Lubbock glanced to one side, and frowned. 'So it is,' he said. 'Now how did that happen?'

'You know damned well how it happened,' Tench was still seething. 'You send me an incomprehensible list, and then force me to waste hours that I can't afford to waste, driving all the way down here from Norwich just to see you.'

Lubbock was unperturbed. He waved the

stem of his pipe. 'Sit down and relax, laddie,' he said. 'The coffee's almost ready.'

'I haven't the time to be sitting around drinking cups of goddamned coffee.' Tench dragged the list from his pocket and tossed it towards him. 'So you'd better explain what that is and quick. Otherwise I'm on my way.'

Lubbock watched the folded sheet of paper flutter to the floor. He still didn't stir. 'You're in no fit state to drive anywhere,' he said, 'so do as I say. Sit down and relax. What you need is a good strong cup of Umzinto coffee to steady your nerves. After that, we can talk.'

Tench stared at him and laughed. 'Oh, what the hell?' he said. 'If I've got this far, I may as well waste another couple of hours. He flung himself down in the second armchair. 'Go on. Get the coffee. But I hope you've got a bloody good reason for getting me all the way down here from Norwich. If you haven't, I'll be tempted to take that stinking pipe of yours and snap it across my knee.'

Lubbock heaved himself up and stretched. 'Remember what I've always told you, laddie,' he said. 'If you give them the time, cases of murder can often solve themselves. The dead aren't impatient. So why should we, the living, try to be what they're not? Just let the case simmer and listen to one or two words of experience. If I've read things correctly, every minute you're so reluctant to spend with me tonight could well save you ten when you get on the road tomorrow. So lie back, close your eyes and let the peace of Umzinto wrap itself round you. A few yards from here there's a church that's survived for seven hundred years. Your couple of hours is but a speck in its life. Contemplate that. Dream of its patient stones, and let the world slip away . . . I'll rouse you once I bring in the coffee.'

12.

It was half an hour later that Tench drained the last of his coffee and Lubbock poured himself a third cup of tea. 'So, laddie,' he said, 'you've got one dead killer and another on the loose.'

Tench gave a nod. 'That about sums it up, but we haven't much chance of tracing the loose one till we know who the dead one is. We've scoured every place within twenty miles of the Burnhams, but no one seems to know him. Which brings us to that enigmatic list of yours. What the hell does it mean?'

Lubbock reached for his pouch and methodically filled his pipe. 'It means that I've been trying to solve the problem that faced us at the very beginning of this case. Why should a man beat two people to death, and then move them four miles and lay them out neatly in the churchyard at Burnham Northgate? He could have left them where he killled them, in the pine woods at Holkham. Or, if he'd wanted

175

just any old churchyard, there were plenty nearby: St Withburga's at Holkham, St Nicholas' at Wells, or even St Clement's at Burnham Overy. They were all of them closer than Burnham Northgate. But no. He deliberately chose to drop them at Northgate, and the question was why?'

He struck a match and applied the flame to his pipe. Billows of smoke rolled away to the rafters. 'The only conclusion I could reach,' he said, 'was that this particular churchyard held some significance both for him and for one or other of the victims, and that such significance must be related in some way to one of the graves. Because of that I took a little stroll round the place, examining the gravestones, listing all the names of people buried there, and noting their dates of death; but the trouble was, as you discovered for yourself, that no Boltons, Westaways or Scotts appeared among them.'

He paused. 'That,' he said, 'could mean only one thing—that the name we were looking for wasn't directly connected to the victims, but rather to the killer.'

'And,' said Tench, 'we didn't know what his name was, and we still don't know.'

'True enough, laddie. That was the missing link. But when you told me last night that Bolton had been born and brought up in Norwich, at Tipworth Street between the Earlham and Dereham Roads, I decided that the only thing to do was to work on a hunch. From what you'd told me about both Bolton and Mrs Scott, it seemed to me that the fatal association at the root of this case, the one that had driven this unknown man to murder, was more likely to have been between him and Bolton, rather than between him and the woman. Somewhere, at some time or other in the past, he and Bolton must have crossed swords, and that being so, there was more than a faint chance that they'd known one another in earlier days in Norwich.'

He paused again, laid down his pipe and unfolded the sheet of paper. 'I spent this morning,' he said, 'in Norwich, asked a few questions and enlisted a bit of help from some people I know. Tipworth Street, in the years before the war, was a street of some twenty-six houses, two of which had been knocked together to form a social club. I managed to get a look at the electoral register for 1938, and this is a list of the twenty-four families living in the street at that particular time. I compared it with the list of names I found on the gravestones at Burnham Northgate, and the four that I've underlined—Carslaw, Jakes, Reddaway and Grant—appeared in both places . . .'

'And the double underlines?'

Lubbock raised a hand. 'Patience, laddie, patience. One of the first things I taught you was to listen and learn, so listen and you'll

177

learn . . . I then took a step further and checked the dates of death that appeared on the gravestones. Wilfred Carslaw died in 1898, and Elizabeth Jakes in 1916, but the other two were more recent—Harriet Reddaway in 1939, and Catherine Agnes Grant in 1942. Now it's only a hunch, but let me spell it out. Two women, whose names correspond with the families living in Tipworth Street in 1938, died during the war years and were buried in Burnham Northgate churchyard. Both of them were young. Harriet Reddaway was twenty-six, Catherine Agnes Grant no more than twenty-three, so I'm suggesting—and it can't be any more than just a suggestion—that our unknown killer could, like Bolton, have been living in Tipworth Street, and that one of those two graves may prove to be significant. Something drew this man to this particular churchyard, and what could provide a more powerful inducement than the grave of a much-cherished wife or sister?'

Tench was thoughtful. 'Fair enough,' he said, 'but all this presupposes three things: that the man did in fact live in Tipworth Street, that he knew Edward Bolton, and that there was some rift between them that ran deep enough to leave Bolton dead.'

'If they lived in the same street, laddie, then it has to be odds on that they knew one another. All I can tell you is that the Reddaways lived at 22 Tipworth Street and the

178

Grants at 13. You'll just have to do some checking, and that won't be easy.'

'Surely there must be someone still living there who knew them.'

Lubbock reached for his pipe and struck another match. 'Correction, laddie,' he said. 'There must certainly be someone still living who knew them, but they won't still be living in Tipworth Street.'

'Why not?'

'For one very good reason. It isn't there any more. It was so badly damaged in the wartime bombing that they bulldozed the lot. There aren't any houses where Tipworth Street stood. Just a rubble-strewn bomb site, partially cleared. So, laddie,' he said through a haze of tobacco smoke, 'if you want to track down the folk who once lived there—those who survived the blitz—you'll have a devil of a job, because God knows where they are.'

13.

As he drove back to Norwich through the gathering dusk, Tench wondered whether his evening excursion to Cley had been anything more than three wasted hours of valuable time. Lubbock's theory was feasible enough, it was true, but, as he'd told his old Chief, it was dependent on a set of unverified facts. Before it could begin to have any relevance, they had to prove that this still unnamed killer had at

179

some time lived in the same street as Bolton, and had known him well enough to develop a hatred for the man which had led him to murder; and that in itself seemed improbable enough, given Bolton's exemplary army record and his brother's assertion that Ted was a good lad and not the sort likely to make any enemies.

And apart from that, before they could start to check whether he had in fact ever lived in Tipworth Street, they had to know his name, so what Lubbock had told him was, immediately, quite irrelevant. The first essential step was still what it had been when he set out for Cley—to put a name to the man, and to do it within the time span that Hastings had allowed him.

If they couldn't do that, and do it inside the designated couple of hours, then everything else would have to be put on hold. The identity of the man that Ted Merrick had linked to the murders of Bolton and Tamara Scott had to be proved. That was the prime requisite. His name, as Lubbock himself had admitted, was the first of the missing links. Only when they had it could the case move forward with any hope of success.

Much would therefore depend on the way that he deployed his extended forces the following morning, and as he turned into the drive of his house at Cringleford, he already had a map of Norwich spread out in his mind.

Detective Chief Inspector Tench was prepared to work late and then rise with the dawn. Everything depended on a word, a man's name.

As he pulled the car to a halt, agnostic as he was, he breathed a little prayer and crossed his fingers on the wheel. Give me a name, he begged. Just a name. That's all I need.

VI

THE MISSING LINK

Look in my face. My name is Used-to-was;
I am also called Played-out and Done-to-death.

Henry Duff Traill: *After Dilettante Concetti*

Whatever the obscure deity was to whom Tench addressed his prayer, his plea was answered with some celerity.

By six o'clock next morning, copies of the *Eastern Daily Press* were on sale on the streets of Norwich, bearing on the front page a blow-up of one of the photographs taken in the bar of thc Queens Hotel at Holkham, accompanied by a banner headline, 'WHO IS THIS MAN?'

By half-past eight the CID team with its host of helpers was deployed around the city, armed with the same photograph and asking the same question.

But the deity ignored them all and spurned every copy of the *Eastern Daily Press*, choosing instead to use as its agent a man who should never have been in Norwich at all, but treating himself to a leisurely breakfast in his semi-detached at Chelmsford.

Nick Treffry was a sales representative for Essex Comestibles based in Chelmsford. Responsible for publicizing Comestibles' products throughout the whole of East Anglia, he'd set out on Wednesday morning for a two-day sales drive to spread the news of Sunnybrek, his firm's new foray into the world of breakfast cereals. His crusade was intended to take in Ipswich, Norwich and Boston,

Lincoln, Peterborough and Cambridge, returning to Chelmsford on Thursday night, since Friday was the day when he was due to start a fortnight's holiday in his native Cornwall.

He had, in consequence, been considerably miffed when, early on Wednesday afternoon, his ageing car, due for replacement by Essex Comestibles six months before, had died underneath him near the centre of Norwich. Tramping to the nearest garage, a small and apparently one-man concern, he'd had it towed in, only to be told by the somewhat morose proprietor that the work would take at least twenty-four hours, and the car wouldn't therefore be ready for collection till the following afternoon.

Because of that, Mr Treffry had been forced to spend Wednesday night at a far from salubrious local hotel, an experience that did little to sweeten his temper.

It was tested still further when, at four o'clock on Thursday, arriving at the garage to collect the car, he'd discovered the place closed and securely locked, with no one in the immediate neighbourhood available to tell him precisely where it was that the proprietor lived.

It was, in consequence, hardly surprising that at half-past nine that Friday morning Constable 'Wally' Walters was despatched to investigate a reported disturbance at Thankerton's Garage, located on Nash Steet close to the junction of Earlham Road and Chancellor Lane.

*   *   *

Constable Walters was a man of some eminence. Standing six foot eight and weighing eighteen and a half stone, all of it solid muscle, he had for some years been Eastern Counties weightlifting champion. Arriving on the scene, he found an irate young man swearing blue murder and attempting to break down the sheet-metal doors that fronted the garage.

Walters seized him round the waist, lifted him clear, set him down on his feet, turned him round and towered over him. 'What's your name, lad?' he said.

'What the hell does that matter?'

'Name,' Walters said.

'Treffry. Nick Treffry. I'll kill the bugger when I find him.'

'Calm down, lad.' The constable led him aside. 'Now tell me. What's the trouble?'

'Trouble? I'm supposed to be on my way to Sennen.'

'And where would that be?'

'Four hundred bloody miles away. That's bloody where.'

'Then why aren't you?'

'Why aren't I what?'

'On your way to wherever it happens to be.'

The young man stared at him in sheer

187

exasperation. 'Because he's got my bloody car. That's bloody why.'

Walters chose to be deliberately obtuse. 'You mean he's borrowed it?'

'No, he bloody well hasn't. It's in for repairs.'

'So what's the problem?'

'He's not here.'

Walters frowned. 'I think you'd better spell it out slowly, lad. Start at the beginning.'

Treffry took a deep breath and, step by step, as if explaining a simple mathematical process to a backward child, laid bare the facts of his desperate situation. 'The car's locked inside,' he said, 'Thankerton's not here and I'm bloody well stranded.'

'He told you to collect it yesterday afternoon?'

'Yes, he did.'

'But he wasn't here.'

'No, and he's not here this morning.'

'Have you tried round the back?'

'There's no way round the back.'

Walters stroked his chin. 'There must be a back entrance somewhere,' he said. 'Let's go and take a look.'

2.

There was indeed a back entrance, but it consisted of nothing but a small wooden door at the end of a narrow alleyway between two rows of houses, and the only other feature in the solid brick wall at the rear of the garage was an even smaller double-light window a good six feet above the level of the ground.

'There's a light on,' said Treffry. 'If he's working in there, why the devil didn't he answer?'

'Perhaps he didn't want to be disturbed,' said Walters. 'It is his garage after all. He can please himself.'

'It won't be his for much longer if he doesn't please his customers.' Treffry was in no mood to offer absolution. 'If he's deliberately trying to dodge me, I'll give him bloody Thankerton. He'll get no thanks from me.'

Walters pressed his nose against the window. 'This car of yours,' he said. 'What's the registration?'

'HJ5897. It's a Chelmsford number. Why? Can you see it?'

'Looks like he's still working on it,' said Walters. 'There's a mat underneath it. Tools scattered around . . . No sign of him though. Must be taking a break.'

'A break!' Treffry was close to spontaneous combustion. 'Hell's bells! He's had that car for all but two bloody days. What the devil does he think he's playing at?'

Walters frowned and stepped back. 'I don't know, lad,' he said, 'but I think we'd best find out.'

He raised a large fist and rapped on the

189

door. There was no response from inside.

'Mr Thankerton!' he shouted. 'Police! Open up!' There was still no sound.

He turned the knob and pushed, and the door swung open.

'Where is he?' said Treffry. He stared at the car, the mat, the tools littering the concrete floor. 'Just let me find him,' he said savagely. 'I'll strangle the bugger. I swear I will.'

Then he paused. 'What's that on the bonnet?' he said. 'He's spilled something on it. Looks to be like paint . . . Good God, the man's incompetent! He's spattered red paint all over the bonnet.'

He tried to move closer, but Walters held him back. 'Stay here, lad,' he said. 'It's my job to find him.'

He walked across to the car, peered down at the bonnet, then ran a finger across one of the stains and sniffed. 'It's not paint, lad,' he said. 'Reckon you'd best book a seat on the train. You'll not be getting this car back for a week.'

3.

It was quarter-past ten when Mike Tench received the call. At ten twenty-five he pulled his car to a halt on the garage forecourt, where Walters, an unmistakable figure, was waiting with Treffry and another uniformed constable.

'This is Constable Hicks, sir,' he said. 'Nash Street's on his regular beat. He knows a lot

190

about the area, and about Thankerton's. And this is Mr Treffry, who raised the alarm.'

Tench nodded and shook their hands. 'Glad to meet you,' he said. 'I'll need to speak to you both . . . Perhaps for the moment, Constable'—this to Hicks—'you'll give Mr Treffry a seat in the car.'

He'd already worked with Walters and had a healthy respect not merely for his strength, but also his judgement. He took him aside. 'So, what's the score, Wally?' he said. 'You think there's been a murder?'

'I wouldn't go so far as to say that, sir, not for certain,'—Walters, for all his size, never lifted a weight without due calculation—'but all the signs point to some kind of violence, and the man's been missing since Wednesday afternoon.'

Tench nodded again. 'Then we'd better take a look,' he said. 'You lead the way.'

*   *   *

They stood by the car.

'Blood, sir,' said Walters. 'The front doors of the place were locked, but the back one wasn't. Mr Treffry brought his car in for repair on Wednesday afternoon. According to what he says, it was a pretty big job and he needed it done quickly, but the garage man was on his own. He does have two apprentices working for him but, according to Hicks, one was on

191

holiday and the other had been whipped into hospital on Monday with acute appendicitis . . . The light was on in here this morning, so it looks to me as if he decided to work late on Treffry's car and closed the front doors . . .'

'And while he was underneath the car, someone crept in at the back and took him by surprise.'

'Looks that way, sir, doesn't it?'

'It's as good a theory as any on the visible evidence, but the question is—who? . . . You didn't know this man Thankerton?'

'It wasn't Thankerton, sir. He's dead. That's what Hicks says. Died during the war, and the garage changed hands. Since then it's been owned and run by a chap called Grant.'

Tench seized on the name. 'Grant?'

'Yes, sir. Joe Grant.'

'Have you ever met him?'

Walters shook his head. 'No, sir. It's not my beat.'

'How long's Hicks been around?'

'Must be five or six years, sir. If you want to know about Grant, he's the one to see.'

'Then I think I'd better have a talk with him,' said Tench. 'Send him in, Wally, will you? And have a chat with Treffry. Take the weight off your feet.'

* * *

Hicks was broad and stolid.

'Joe Grant,' said Tench. 'How well did you know him?'

'Well enough, sir. Had a word with him most days.'

Tench produced a photograph. 'Is that the man?'

Hicks looked down at it and nodded. 'Yes, sir,' he said. 'That's him.'

'Tell me about him. He owns this place?'

'Yes, sir.'

'How long has he owned it?'

'Ever since old Thankerton died, so he told me.'

'And when was that?'

'Back in '44, sir. Joe said it was the week of the Normandy landings.'

'And when Thankerton died, he bought it ... Wasn't he in the services?'

'For a short time, sir, yes, but he was invalided out. Never told me what happened, but he walked with a limp.'

'D'you know what made him buy the place?'

'Well, he'd worked here for years, sir. Ever since he left school. And he had the money to do it. From what folk tell me, his wife died young and left him a tidy packet ... And I think he enjoys the job, sir. He's a good mechanic. It's due to him that my old banger still keeps running.'

'When did you last see him?'

'Wednesday morning, sir. Round about eleven. He was working on a Morris Minor.

Said he had to have it ready by two o'clock. That was when he told me Jimmy Castle was in hospital.'

'You didn't see him yesterday?'

'No, sir,' said Hicks. 'There was a break-in at Jefferson's the jewellers on Tite Street. Had to spend most of the day over there.'

'But you'd have expected him to be open?'

'Never closes, sir, this place.' Hicks was firm. 'Save on Sundays, that is. And even then you'll find him here, more often than not. Lives for his work, does Joe. If the garage wasn't open, I'd be wondering why.'

'D'you know where he lives?'

'Yes, sir, Newton St Faith. I don't know the exact address, but Jimmy Castle can tell you.'

*　　　*　　　*

Tench glanced at his watch. It showed ten to eleven. He picked up the phone and rang through to Lock. 'Des,' he said. 'Call off the hunt and get everyone back. We've tracked down our man.'

4.

According to Hicks, Jimmy Castle had been taken to the Norfolk and Norwich, and was recuperating there from a burst appendix. Twenty minutes later, after threading his way through the city traffic, Tench found him on his own in a small side ward.

A slim young man, reflective and slow of speech, it took him some time to digest the news. 'Mr Grant? You mean he's dead?'

'I'm afraid so,' said Tench.

'But he can't be, surely. It doesn't make sense.'

'You don't know anyone who might have wanted to harm him?'

Castle looked blank. 'No, sir. Why should they?'

'That's what I'm trying to find out,' said Tench. 'There was no one who could have had a grudge against him?'

'Not as far as I know.'

'What sort of a man was he?'

Castle pondered the question. 'He was quiet,' he said, 'got on with his work, never said very much. He wasn't the type of man you ever really got to know, but he helped me a lot. I learned a lot from him.'

'A good employer?'

'Oh, yes.'

'I'm told that he lived at Newton St Faith.'

'That's right, sir. Grove Cottage . . . You know Lawrence Bell, the writer?'

'I've met him,' said Tench.

'Well, he lives next door.'

'Does he now? That's interesting. Have you read any of his books?'

The young man nodded. 'Most of them. He's good . . . I've never seen him about

195

though.'

'He must be a busy man.'

'Yes, I suppose so.'

Tench didn't commit himself any further. 'Mr Grant,' he said. 'Did he own a van?'

'Yes, sir, an old Ford.'

'What colour?'

'Dark blue.'

'D'you remember the registration number?'

'Could hardly forget it, sir. Saw it every day . . . MP6248.'

Tench frowned. 'That's a London number.'

'Yes, sir. The van was pre-war. I think Mr Grant picked it up at a sale.'

'Where did he keep it?'

'In the garage, sir.'

'Thankerton's?'

'That's right, sir, yes. It was always parked there.'

'Well, it's not there now. When did you last see it?'

'Must have been Saturday, sir. I haven't been able to get to the garage since then.'

'Did he have a car, too?'

'Yes, sir. Used it to drive in from Newton St Faith. A Lancia Aprilia, EBJ398. That was pre-war too, but he always kept it in tip-top condition.'

'He had a garage at the cottage?'

'Yes, sir. I think he had it built on.'

'And when he was working at Thankerton's. Where did you keep it then?'

196

'Usually drove up the alleyway and parked it at the back, sir.'

'Never inside the garage?'

Castle shook his head. 'No, sir. The steel doors at the front only opened from inside, so he always came in at the back.' He looked up at Tench, suddenly worried. 'What's going to happen to the place now, sir? D'you know?'

'You're apprenticed there?'

'Was, sir, yes, till last August. Since then Mr Grant's employed me full time.'

'Well, nothing's going to happen immediately,' said Tench, 'so I wouldn't worry about it. Just concentrate on getting better. The garage'll be closed anyway for the next few days. Forensics'll be going through it with a toothcomb, bagging every speck from the floor, dusting for fingerprints . . . They'll need to take yours for elimination purposes, and those of the other lad who works there with you. What's his name, by the way?'

'Ashton, sir. Fred Ashton.'

'He's still an apprentice?'

'Yes, sir. Only joined us last autumn.'

'I gather he's on holiday.'

'That's right, sir. Spending a week in Scarborough with his girlfriend and her parents. Went last Friday. He's due back tomorrow.'

'Where does he live?'

'Lives with his mum and dad out at Taverham, sir. I'm not sure of the exact

197

address, but it must be in the books.'

Tench gave a nod. 'Well, thanks a lot,' he said. 'You've been a great help. Once you're up and about we may need you to check a few things at the garage. Till then, just look after yourself.' He turned to go, and then paused. 'Oh, there is one thing more. When Mr Grant opened up in a morning, where did he put his car keys?'

'Always dropped them in his back trouser pocket, sir,' said Castle.

'Never hung them on a hook or left them lying around?'

The young man shook his head firmly. 'No, sir, never. Always very careful with his keys was Mr Grant. One day last year he had to leave early, and left me to lock up. But he gave me strict instructions. "On the way home, Jim," he said, "make sure you've got the keys and then give me a ring." And you know what, sir?'

'What?'

'First thing next morning he paid me for the call. It was tuppence I think. He insisted I took it.'

5.

It was only a short step from the Norfolk and Norwich to station headquarters on Bethel Street, but once he'd got a sniff of a worthwhile clue Mike Tench wasn't one for

198

wasting any time. He rang Lock from one of the hospital pay phones. 'What's the situation like with you, Des?' he asked.

'They're still coming in, sir,' said Lock. 'We've got about half the squad back. The rest are on their way.'

'Right. Dismiss all the helpers. Tell our lads to take a break and find themselves some lunch. There'll be a briefing at four o'clock . . . Is Sergeant McKenzie back?'

'Yes, sir. Just arrived.'

'Tell him to meet me at Newton St Faith . . . Grove Cottage. It's next door to Lawrence Bell's place . . . I'll be waiting outside.'

'Grove Cottage. Right, sir.'

'And tell him I don't expect him to flout the Highway Code,' said Tench. 'We've got enough on our plates without bailing him out for trying to do sixty inside the city.'

* * *

Grove Cottage was a small flint-pebble affair with a pantiled roof. It was clearly a couple of hundred years old, and though an effort had been made to match the garage with the dwelling, the two parts of the construction sat uneasily side by side: an incongruity made even more apparent by the presence of McKenzie, astride his red Norton, revving up the engine as if waiting on the line for a starter's flag.

199

When the DCI's car drew up, he switched off and pulled the bike back on its stand.

'Trouble?' inquired Tench.

'She's coughing a bit.'

'She always coughs. And she spits. And when she clears her throat she makes enough noise to wake all the hounds in hell. Apart from that, she stinks. Why don't you get rid of her?'

'Never,' McKenzie said. 'There aren't many like her.'

'You can say that again,' said Tench. 'She reminds me of Lubbock's corroded old pipe. One of these days she'll leave you stranded in the middle of the sticks. It's a wonder you got here at all. It's six long miles from the centre of Norwich.'

McKenzie refused to be drawn any further. 'Which brings us to the point,' he said. 'Just why are we here?'

'Because we've turned up a name.'

'I've gathered that much . . . Grant . . . So who the hell is he?'

'Owner of Thankerton's Garage on Nash Street. That's the place where Ted Bolton worked for a time.'

'And . . . ?'

'This is where he lived, and I've got a shrewd suspicion that when we force the lock on that garage door, we'll find his car inside. I think whoever murdered him, killed him at Thankerton's, stripped him of his clothes and

200

purloined his keys. He then bundled the body in the boot, drove the car to Burnham Northgate, dumped our friend Mr Grant in the graveyard and, driving back here, tucked it safely away out of sight in the garage . . . It's a Lancia Aprilia, silver-grey. The registration number's EBJ398. So, if we find it, don't touch it. That's a job for Forensics.'

'You think the clothes are still inside?'

'Who knows? They could be. But before anyone tries to open up the boot, I want the whole exterior dusted for prints. So we check the car's there, and that's all we do . . . Come on. Let's get to work.'

The garage was secured by a simple padlock. McKenzie snapped it with a tyre lever and flung back the doors. 'You were right,' he said. 'That's it. EBJ398 . . . So what do we do now?'

Tench made no move. 'Leave it where it is,' he said, 'and close the place up again . . . If he had Grant's keys to the car and the garage, he probably had those to the cottage as well . . . It's our plain duty, Mac, to take a look inside . . . How good are you at smashing windows?'

'Degree-trained in the Gorbals many years ago.'

'Right,' said Tench. He gave a jerk of the head. 'Round to the back. And bring that tyre lever with you.'

The cottage was single-storey. There was a scullery, a kitchen, a bathroom and a parlour, and a door from the parlour that, so they presumed, led to a bedroom. The scullery was bare, the kitchen bleak and uninviting, the bathroom no more than a claustrophobic annexe, and the furnishings in the parlour were strictly functional: an old oak table, two chairs, a roll-top desk, and a worm-eaten sideboard that held an ugly gilt clock, a phone and a cabinet radio.

'What are we looking for?' McKenzie asked. He was rummaging through the desk.

'Anything that ties up Grant with Ted Bolton.'

'Well, there's nothing in here. Just a load of old bills and a couple of pencils.'

Tench opened the sideboard drawers, reached inside, felt around and slammed them shut again. 'Nor here,' he said. 'Let's look in the bedroom.'

He turned the doorknob and stepped inside. Then he stopped and stared. 'Mac,' he said quietly, 'come and look at this.'

McKenzie was behind him. 'Jesus Christ!' He breathed. 'What sort of a chap was he, this Grant? A flaming schizo?'

If the rest of the cottage was uncaringly bleak, the bedroom was not. The floor was covered with a rich blue, thick-piled carpet.

The double bed, with its padded headrest was alluring, the pink bedspread folded back to reveal pillows lace-edged and immaculately white, and below them, spread out with precision, a pair of blue pyjamas and a pink silk nightdress. To left and right at the head of the bed were two side tables, each with its cream-shaded lamp on a crocheted doily, and placed in symmetry beside them two small china boxes decorated with roses.

Against the wall to the right was a delicate mahogany dressing-table with a central mirror and a matching stool upholstered in pink, and laid out on top, as if in precisely calculated positions, were a jewel box, a glass-faced stand edged in gilt that held a pair of china-backed brushes and combs, and a wide array of cosmetics.

To the left, on the opposite side of the bed, was a linen chest, similarly upholstered, and draped with a pink tasselled cloth, and every available space on the walls, from the frieze to the white-painted skirting-board, was covered with photographs, ebony-framed, all, it appeared, of the same very beautiful dark-haired woman.

McKenzie stared around. 'Well, one thing's for sure,' he said. 'No woman lives here. None that I know would live within a mile of that desolate kitchen, so who the hell is she?'

'I rather think,' said Tench, 'that her name may be Catherine. Catherine Agnes Grant.

She's buried in the churchyard at Burnham Northgate.'

'His wife?'

'Was his wife. She's been dead for ten years.'

'Then this is what? A shrine?'

'Looks like it,' said Tench.

McKenzie breathed deeply. 'Poor sod,' he said.

7.

'He was a murderer, Mac. He killed a man and a woman. Beat their faces to pulp.'

'But he must have had feelings.'

'Feelings can be dangerous. In his case they were lethal. He murdered Ted Bolton.'

'But why?'

'That's what we need to find out. What we've needed to find out ever since Lubbock turned up the bodies. Now we know who he is, we can start to find out.'

McKenzie stared at the bed. 'Could Bolton have had it away with his wife?'

'Then why all this? If Grant's wife betrayed him, I can't see him turning this room into a shrine.'

'You're sure there's a connection between him and Bolton?'

'There must be,' said Tench. 'All the evidence points to it. Bolton lived in Tipworth Street, and so did a family called Grant. We know he and Grant worked together at

Thankerton's . . .'

'But we've found nothing here to prove the link between them. There's no sign that he and Bolton ever knew one another.'

'Perhaps we haven't searched everywhere.'

'Where else is there to search?'

'I'm not sure. Not yet, Mac. But look at that bed. It hasn't been slept in for years. So where did Grant sleep? And where did he keep his clothes? There must be another room.'

'Then where the hell is it?'

'Must be somewhere.' Tench glanced up and around, then swivelled on his feet and pointed to the ceiling. 'Up there, Mac,' he said. 'Look! There must be a loft.'

Above and behind them, not immediately visible to anyone entering the room, there was a trapdoor in the ceiling, and from it a cord ran down to a cleat in the wall. Tench unwound it and pulled. The trap was hinged. It sprung open and a folding ladder came down within reach. He grabbed the bottom rung and extended it to the full. 'Come on, Mac,' he said, setting foot on the ladder. 'Let's take a look upstairs.'

*　　　*　　　*

The loft was in darkness, but feeling around he located two switches. He pressed the first without result, but when he pressed the second a dim forty-watt bulb suspended from the rafters sprung into light.

The space it revealed was small but planked underfoot. All it contained was a camp bed and three drawers laid out next to one another on the floor. On one side of the bed stood an old wooden chest and on the other a four-bar electric fire. The fire was connected to the first of the switches, and on the chest was an alarm clock and beside it a small brass ashtray.

McKenzie threw back the lid of the chest and peered inside. 'Empty,' he announced.

'Well, this is where he slept'—Tench was riffling through the drawers—'and where he stored his clothes.'

'And that's about all.' McKenzie kicked the chest in disgust. 'If you ask me,' he said, 'this Grant wasn't merely an obsessive schizo, he was a masochist into the bargain. Would anyone in their senses choose to sleep in this hole when they've a cosy little nest like that down below? No, Mike, there can only be one explanation. The man was a raving lunatic.'

'But one who loved his wife, ran a successful business, was a first-rate mechanic and a caring employer.'

'So you say.'

'So the evidence tells us, Mac.'

'It makes no bloody sense.'

'No, it doesn't,' said Tench, 'but there must be an answer and we've got to find it. Down the ladder, Mac! We've got to look elsewhere.'

'There is nowhere else.'

'I think perhaps there may be.'

'Where then?'

'Next door . . . I think it's time we paid a visit to an old friend and helper of mine, Lawrence Bell. He might just know something about his neighbour that provides us with a clue.'

8.

It was Lubbock who'd first introduced him to Lawrence Bell.

He and Lawrence had been schoolboys together: Lawrence the high-flier, the brilliant scholar; he, John Lubbock, the determined plodding mediocrity. He'd always sought Lawrence's help, cribbed his homework, petitioned him for necessary explanations, all of which had been provided without a touch of irritation. Despite or perhaps because of Lubbock's dependence on him, they'd remained firm friends.

Then their paths had diverged. Lawrence, predictably, had won a scholarship to Oxford, while he, for his part, had joined the police; and while he'd struggled for years, rising slowly through the ranks, Lawrence had climbed more swiftly. With a teaching post at Greshams, he'd written in whatever spare time he'd had, till the runaway success of his Norfolk murder mysteries had given him a solid financial independence. Then he'd shut himself away in this quiet little cottage to concentrate on his own brand of mayhem and murder; and ever since then, Lubbock, while probing away at the messiness of death, had constantly sought out Lawrence to tap his expertise, while his friend had sat in front of a battered old Remington tapping out words that spelled all the horrors he'd preferred to imagine.

Over the years he'd had the cottage extended, taking in part of the wilderness of scrub that had lain at the back, and providing himself with a spacious room that was a study, a library, and a place of relaxation all rolled into one.

It had been in that spacious room, four years before, that Lubbock had first introduced him to Bell. 'This is Lawrence,' he'd said. 'If I need any abstruse local information, I always come to him. He knows more about Norfolk than any man living. He put us on to that legend about Elsdon Hall, and told us about those smugglers' tunnels that led us to do that search up at Breckmarsh Mill. He hasn't often let me down.'

He hadn't let them down on that occasion either, and since his old Chief's retirement Tench had himself continued to seek out Lawrence whenever he'd been faced with a peculiar problem that even Lubbock's local expertise had been unable to solve. Over the next three years he'd paid, at the very least, half a dozen visits to Newton St Faith, and in the course of them the world of Lawrence's spacious study had become as familiar to him as the back of his own hand.

It was a world that combined both neatness and confusion: the long wall of books, immaculately shelved; the two deep armchairs drawn up beside the fireplace; the heavy, broad-topped desk by the latticed window; the typewriter rising like a great black rock from a white sea of paper; sheets tossed here and there in utter abandon, bearing no resemblance to the mathematical precision with which Lawrence constructed his intricate plots.

More than once he'd run his finger along the shelves, tracing one by one the hundreds of books on Norfolk that seemed to cover every aspect of life in the county: its history, its legends, its buildings, its roads, its trade and its landscape; and the long rows of detective stories, first editions, reprints and green-backed Penguins, all with the name of Lawrence Bell, all of them set in some part of Norfolk: *The Mannington Murders*, *The Gressenhall Affair*, *The Itteringham Mystery*, and perhaps twenty others to the end of the shelf.

And more and more in the last twelve months, plagued by what had seemed to be intractable cases, and reluctant to seek out Lubbock at Cley, he'd found his thoughts turning to Newton St Faith, like the master of a ship seeking port in a storm; and on each occasion when he'd raised the brass knocker and rapped three times, Lawrence had appeared, a tall, gaunt man with a mop of ginger hair, wearing his usual brightly coloured shirt, his wildly contrasting tie, and the same pair of old disreputable flannels; and each time he'd raised a couple of bushy ginger eyebrows as if in sheer surprise at receiving such a visit, and greeted him with the same inevitable questions. 'More trouble, Mike?' he'd said. 'So what's the problem now that our old friend the Wizard of Cley can't solve? How is he, by the way? Still stumping the shingle with his cherrywood stick?'

9.

That morning, as befitted a man who was a wordsmith by profession, he varied the phraseology. 'So, Mike,' he said, 'how is the old wizard? Still stumping around on his stick before dawn?'

'Too fast and too far at times,' replied Tench.

'Still playing the Sherlock? Trying to solve your cases?'

'Never stops, Lawrence. And never will, you know that. If the grim reaper ever took a swipe at his legs, he'd still be trying to solve them out of a wheelchair.'

'So what's today's question that even his knowledge of Norfolk can't answer?'

'One that's a bit too localized even for Lubbock, but it's right up your street.'

Lawrence, who was wearing a brilliant yellow shirt, a flame-coloured tie, but the same old flannels that even a half-blind tramp would have cast aside, looked at him askance. 'You mean it's way off his normal beat?'

'Something like that, yes.'

Lawrence paused before he spoke. 'Do I scent Burnham Northgate?'

'There is a connection, Lawrence, yes, but the problem's not there. It's here, on the spot, in Newton St Faith.'

'Ah.' Lawrence nodded. 'Carry on then. What is it?'

'What d'you know about Grant?'

'Grant?'

'Joe Grant. The one who lives at Grove Cottage.'

'Oh, him.' Lawrence gave a shrug. 'Not much, I'm afraid.'

'You don't sound impressed.'

'I don't know enough about him to have anything more than a mere impression. He's been here what? Eight years? Nine? And we haven't spoken to one another more than half a dozen times . . Anyway, what's his connection with Burnham Northgate? It's thirty miles from here.'

Tench was guarded. 'It's just that we think

one of his cars was involved . . . We need to know more about him, so anything you can tell us could prove to be vital. You've written enough murder mysteries to know what I mean.'

'Oh. I know what you mean well enough,' Lawrence said. 'The trouble is I don't know enough about Grant, apart from the fact that he runs a garage somewhere in Norwich. Except for passing the time of day—and you can count those occasions on the fingers of a hand—I've never had anything to do with the man. He isn't the type to encourage conversation. I see him coming and going, and that's about all.'

'You said you had an impression.'

'Yes, but that's all it can be.'

'Then what is it?'

Lawrence drew a deep breath. 'He's morose, self-absorbed, seems determined to live in his own little world and resents intrusion. What that little world is, I've no real idea. All I can do is guess, and the conclusions I draw may be wide of the mark.'

'Even so,' said Tench, 'we'd like to know what they are. We need a second opinion about Mr Grant.'

'Well'—Lawrence spoke slowly—'I've come across the same signs before in other men, more than once . . . Something's inhibiting him, and if I had to make a guess I'd say it's self-pity. He thinks the world's dealt him a pretty poor hand, and because of that he's thrown up defences. Something that's happened in his past has left a deep wound, and he's determined to guard against any repetition. It's a case, I'd say, of once bitten, twice shy. Does that make any sense?'

'More than you think, Lawrence. More than you think . . . Anything else?'

'Only that he limps. I've often wondered what part that plays in his attitude.'

McKenzie, for once, had kept very quiet. Now he intervened. 'Would you say he was a bitter man?'

Lawrence pondered the question. 'Yes,' he said, 'I think I would. But then again, I'm only guessing.'

Tench, in his turn, was thoughtful. 'You told us you see him coming and going.'

'I didn't mean always. Only from time to time.'

'Think back to Wednesday Lawrence. Did you see him go out on Wednesday morning?'

Lawrence nodded. 'As a matter of fact, I did. I was fetching in the milk. He left when he usually does, about half-past eight.'

'Did you see him come back?'

'No, but I heard him.'

'What time was that?'

'God only knows. He was late, very late. Must have been sometime in the small hours, I'd say. That Lancia of his makes quite a distinctive sound. It wakened me up. I heard

213

him drive into the garage, and close the garage doors. After that I must have drifted off to sleep again . . . I thought it was strange, because I'd never known him get home as late as that before. He's normally back in the evening by eight o'clock at the latest. Very much a creature of habit is Mr Grant.'

'Did you see him next morning? Yesterday morning?'

'No,' Lawrence said. 'Didn't have the chance. I was away from here well before half-past eight. Needed to do a bit of research in the Breckland, so I drove down to Thetford and stayed overnight. Only got home a couple of hours ago.'

'Is there anyone else who might have heard him on Wednesday night?'

'I wouldn't think so,' Lawrence said. 'We're out on a limb at this end of the village, and he made his obsession with privacy all too clear from the start. He could be dead for a week before anyone else in St Faith cared to notice. You know, Mike, the lines old Thomas Hoccleve wrote with his quill five hundred years ago are still true today. "Woe be to him that lust to be alone," he wrote, "for if he falle, helpe hath he none." It's not a comforting thought. As it happens, I'm a pretty gregarious type and I've a daughter who calls in to see me every day, but in all the time he's been here I've never known anyone call to see Grant. Frankly, Mike, I don't know what to make of the man, and that's the honest truth. It wouldn't surprise me if he had a few millions tucked away somewhere. You read about folk like that.'

10.

'And if he has,' McKenzie said, when they were back in Grove Cottage, 'then it's ten to one they'll be stitched inside the mattress on that bed.'

'And we're not going to search for them, Mac,' Tench said. 'That's Forensics' job. Leave it to the experts . . . Who's the local bobby at Horsham St Faith?'

'Young lad. Bob Clifford. Hasn't been there long.'

Tench pulled on a pair of rubber gloves and lifted Grant's phone. 'I'll deal with this,' he said. 'Go and get some lunch.'

In the next three-quarters of an hour he made five calls: a brief one to Lock, another that was even briefer to Clifford, and three, somewhat longer, to Chief Superintendent Hastings, to Lubbock at Cley, and to Dave Ransome at the offices of the *Eastern Daily Press*.

By the time he was ready to leave Newton St Faith, Clifford was taping off the cottage and garage; a detachment of Lester's scene-of-crime squad was already on its way; his old Chief had answered, not without interruption, a couple of vital questions; Dave Ransome, in return for a front-page scoop, had promised to feature a further appeal to the public; and he, for his part, had arranged to meet and give Hastings a briefing at half-past three.

And, promptly at four o'clock, he faced his assembled team in the CID room.

*   *   *

'Find a seat,' he said. 'A lot's happened today. It's time for a reassessment.'

There was a scraping of chairs. He looked round the room. 'Last Sunday,' he began, 'when we found the first two bodies at Burnham Northgate, we didn't know quite what to think. They could have been the victims of a robbery; a random killing, or a targeted attack carried out to fulfil some plan of revenge. We didn't even know who the victims were. Nor did we know whether they'd been killed in the immediate vicinity or their bodies ferried in from some more distant place.'

He paused for a moment. 'However,' he said, 'by the end of the day, with the discoveries, first of the car outside the Queens Hotel, and second of the bloodstained clothes in Holkham woods, we were able to rule out a couple of the options. It was clear that this was a local killing, and it hadn't been committed with robbery in mind. It could still have been random, but a number of factors inclined us to the view that one of the victims had been the target of some plan for revenge. A man had been watching them in the Queens Hotel; the attack had been a savage one, indicative of an uncontrollable hatred; the bodies of the victims had been laid out in an almost ritualistic fashion; and the site appeared to have been deliberately chosen—rather than a number of others that were easier of access—implying that the killer, whoever he was, attached some importance to Burnham Northgate churchyard.

'By last night we knew who the victims were, and had gathered enough evidence to assume with some conviction that the man, not the woman, had been the killer's target. But this morning, when a third body was discovered, also in the churchyard, a number of fresh questions presented themselves. Had the same person who killed the first two victims also killed the third? Was the theory of a targeted murder still feasible? Could this possibly, after all, be a random killing, and was there a homicidal maniac on the loose? Or could it be merely a copycat murder—some entirely different person with a grudge of his own reproducing what he knew of the original crime?'

He paused again and looked round the assembled team. 'Since then,' he said, 'we've learned a great deal more. The body found this morning is, according to Dr Ledward, that of a thick-set man, five foot eight and a half tall, aged between thirty and thirty-five. He has fair hair cut close, his left leg is two inches shorter than his right, his physical appearance matches that of the man who was watching the first two victims in the bar of the Queens Hotel, and samples of his hair match those found earlier by Dr Ledward, adhering to the fingers of one of them, Edward Bolton.

'In the face of such evidence, we can only conclude that this man is the killer we've been searching for since Sunday—the one who murdered Edward Bolton and Tamara Scott—and that he, in his turn, has now been murdered. In other words we've solved one killing, only to find ourselves landed with another. Or, to be more precise, we've been presented with one murderer, only to discover that we now have the job of tracking down a second.

'That,' he said, 'may prove to be an even more difficult task, but we are in possession of certain facts which go some way, at least, to confirm our belief that the original killings sprang out of a feud between this man and Edward Bolton.' He nodded towards McKenzie. 'Your turn, Mac,' he said. 'Tell them just where we stand.'

11.

McKenzie, as he could be when loyalty

demanded his full commitment, was businesslike and concise.

He pushed back his chair.

'We now know the identity,' he said, 'of this, the third, victim. He was Joseph Grant, the owner of Thankerton's Garage on Nash Street, who lived at Grove Cottage in Newton St Faith. We believe he was killed in the garage late last night and his body transported in the boot of his own car to the churchyard at Burnham Northgate. The car was found in the garage at his house, and it's already been passed to Forensics for detailed examination.

'Now to come to the point. In the course of the last few days, we've learnt a few things about Bolton and Grant that may be significant. Edward Bolton was born and brought up at 25 Tipworth Street, here in Norwich, and he lived there until he went into the army. A family called Grant also lived in Tipworth Street, at number 13 and, though it's yet to be confirmed, we suspect that Joseph Grant was a member of this family. We know one thing for sure. When he left school, he went to work at Thankerton's and remained there until he was called up for the forces. He didn't serve for very long. He was invalided out, possibly sometime in 1943, and on Thankerton's death the following year, he bought the garage and has owned it ever since. We also know that Bolton worked there too, from 1932, the year he left school, until 1938

219

when he volunteered for the Royal Army Service Corps. It's more than likely, therefore, that they worked side by side.

'There are also other facts which may prove to be significant. According to reports, Grant was something of a loner, a caring employer who ran an efficient business, but who chose to live a hermit-like existence at Newton St Faith, where he seems to have shunned any contact with his neighbours. A morose individual, possibly embittered by some incident in his past, he maintained one room in his cottage as a kind of shrine to the memory of his wife, and it's possible too that she could have been the woman, Catherine Agnes Grant, who died in 1942 and we know lies buried in Burnham Northgate churchyard. If she is, and if Bolton had something to do with her death, then that could well explain why, having killed both him and Mrs Scott, he chose to lay out their bodies in that very place.'

McKenzie pursed his lips. 'Of course,' he went on, 'all this is mere conjecture, but there are other facts which point in the same direction. Catherine Agnes Grant died in 1942. That was the year of the "Baedeker" raids, the heaviest bombing raids suffered by Norwich in the course of the war. It was also the approximate year, according to Dr Ledward's estimate, when Grant sustained such a serious injury to his left leg that a metal plate had to be inserted to strengthen the bone and hold two parts together; and' . . .—he paused—'we know from Bolton's army record that, for a brief spell in the April and May of that year, his unit was posted to Norwich to help clear the devastation caused by the raids.

'So, it is at least possible that Bolton and Grant, born and brought up and living in the same street, knew one another well, went to work together in Thankerton's Garage, and then, separated for a time by their careers in the army, met once again in Norwich in the aftermath of the "Baedeker" raids—and that something then happened, here in the city, which created a serious rift between them; which may have been connected with the death of Grant's wife; and which so embittered Grant that, for years, he nursed a desire for revenge: a desire that festered inside him, turning him into the kind of man he became: morose, withdrawn and now a proven killer.'

12.

Tench looked round the room. 'As Sergeant McKenzie says, much of what we think may be true is nothing but sheer conjecture. It remains to be verified, and our immediate task is to find Grant's killer. We don't know who he is, no weapon has yet been found, and we've no solid evidence to confirm any guess we might make about his motive, but it seems to me that the best chance we have of tracking him down lies in probing the connections between Bolton and Grant, discovering how close they were, whether a rift between them did in fact occur and, if so, what the incident was that caused it.

'We already know much about Edward Bolton, but we need to know more. We need to know all we can about him, about Joseph Grant, and about Catherine Agnes Grant. We need to know, for instance, whether Grant did for certain live in Tipworth Street, whether he attended the same school as Bolton and whether they left at the same time. We need to know how long they worked together at Thankerton's Garage, and exactly when that was. We need to know the precise dates of Grant's army service, when he was called up and when he was discharged, and we need to trace the hospital that dealt with his injury, find out when that was and what circumstance caused it. And we need to know moreover a number of vital facts about Catherine Agnes Grant. Was she, as we believe, Joseph Grant's wife, and if she was when and where did they marry? What was the exact date of her death, what caused it, and why was she buried in Burnham Northgate churchyard? And we need to discover everything we can about the bombing of Tipworth Street, what damage was caused, where Joseph Grant was at that particular time, what precise work Edward Bolton was engaged in, and whether there are any records of an incident which might have involved both him and Grant.

'It's only by checking on all these facts that we can hope to discover just why Bolton and Mrs Scott were murdered, and once we know that, it may give us a lead to track down the killer of Joseph Grant. Some of the facts may be difficult to check: the actual date, for instance, of Catherine Grant's death. It's not recorded on her tombstone, only the year, and the Rector won't know because he wasn't appointed till 1949, so whoever does the checking will have to spend time consulting the parish records. And whoever it is who checks whether Joseph Grant did live in Tipworth Street could find himself up against a similar problem. Grant wouldn't appear on the electoral register until he was twenty-one years old, which would have been sometime round about the outbreak of war. Some electoral rolls may not have survived the bombing and, even if they did, we can't be sure that the register was regularly updated during the war years. In which case it might be necessary to trawl through council records, or trace someone who lived in Tipworth Street at that time: not an easy task, since the inhabitants were either killed or dispersed.

'It's vital, however, that we do trace at least a few of these people if we want to know more about the kind of connection Bolton had with Grant. Bearing this in mind, I've arranged with Dave Ransome to publish an appeal in the

EDP tomorrow asking anyone who lived in Tipworth Street at the time of the bombing to make contact with me. Luckily we already know the whereabouts of one of them, and he may relieve us of any need to check on either council records or electoral rolls.'

He looked across at Ellison. 'Bob,' he said, 'you know where Bolton's brother lives and where he works.'

Ellison nodded. 'Yes, sir.'

'Go with Inspector Gregg and find him. I want him here.'

He turned to Gregg. 'When you find him,' he said, 'Andy, invite him to grace us with his presence at the station. Tell him the DO needs his assistance.'

'And if he doesn't want to come?'

'Arrest him,' said Tench. 'We need to hear what he knows before we start making plans for tomorrow.'

13.

They were back within the hour.

'Any trouble?' asked Tench.

Gregg shook his head. 'No, sir. He was still at work when we found him. Came like a lamb.'

'Where is he now?'

'Down in the interview room, sir. Ellison's with him.'

'What did you make of him?'

'Difficult to say, sir. We didn't have much of a conversation. I simply told him you needed his help, and he came right away.'

'Without even a murmur?'

'Not even a whisper, sir. Just nodded, slung on his jacket and came.'

'Didn't ask whether we'd found the man who murdered his brother?'

'Never spoke a word, sir, all the way back.'

'Strange,' said Tench. 'Well, we'd better go and see if he's still got a tongue. Let's hope he has, for his sake as much as ours.'

* * *

The interview room faced west, and the sun streamed in through the semi-glazed window, falling straight on Bolton's face as he sat at the table, stolid and seemingly quite unperturbed. He'd stripped off his jacket and, still in his dungarees, sat with his sleeves rolled up and his freckled hands flat on the table top.

Tench and Gregg took the opposite seats, while Ellison retreated to a corner, pulled out a chair and armed himself with his notebook.

'Mr Bolton,' said Tench, 'we haven't met before, but I'm the Detective Chief Inspector in charge of the investigation into your brother's death. I've asked you to come here simply because I need your assistance. I trust you'll be willing to offer your help.'

'You haven't found him yet then?'

'Found who, Mr Bolton?'

'The chap as did him in.'

'Murder investigations take time, Mr Bolton. That's why we need your help.'

'Right.' Bolton nodded. 'Let's get on with it then. What else d'you want to know?'

'Both you and your brother were born here in Norwich, at 25 Tipworth Street. Am I correct?'

'Yes.'

'How long did you live there?'

'Up until the bombing.'

'1942 . . . And when were you born?'

'1916.'

'And your brother?'

'A couple o' years later.'

'Then you lived in Tipworth Street for some twenty-six years?'

'Aye. That'd be about right.'

'Did your parents live there too?'

Bolton seemed to hesitate. 'That depends, ' he said.

'Depends on what, Mr Bolton?'

'Depends what you mean.'

'Were you living with your parents in Tipworth Street at the time of the bombing?'

'Not both of 'em, no. Dad died the year after Ted were born.'

'And your mother?'

'She were there, aye.'

'Was the house badly damaged?'

Bolton shrugged. 'Not so bad as some.

Chimney pot through the roof. Lost a few tiles. It were the other end o' the street as got it the worst.'

'The house was still habitable?'

'Aye. She went on living there . . . Till the bulldozers came. Then they moved her out to Cossey. Stayed there till she died.'

'And when was that?'

'Couple o' years back.'

'Was that when you moved on to Earlham Road?'

'That's right. It were easier for work.'

Tench nodded. 'So, at the time of the bombing, she was in Tipworth Street, Ted was in the army . . .

'Aye, down in Colchester.'

'And you? Where were you?'

'In India. Called up in '40. Been out there since June '41.'

The next question came swiftly. 'Did you know a Joseph Grant who lived in Tipworth Street?'

14.

Bolton stared at him. He seemed bewildered. 'Joe Grant? What's he got to do with all this?'

'You did know him then?'

'Course I knew him. He lived at number 13.'

'How well did you know him?'

'Not as well as Ted. He were Ted's best pal. They grew up together.'

'Did they go to the same schools?'

Bolton nodded. 'Dereham Road Junior and the Model Senior Boys'.'

'They were the same age?'

'Aye. Within a couple o' months.'

'Then they'd leave at the same time.'

'Left the same day and both went to work at Thankerton's Garage.'

'When was this exactly?'

'Now you're asking.' Bolton frowned. 'Does it really matter?'

'Believe me, Mr Bolton, it matters a great deal.'

'Well, reckon it were round about 1932.'

'And Ted left there when he joined the army?'

'Had to, hadn't he?'

'That was 1938 . . . Did Grant go on working there?'

'Reckon he must have done. He were still there a month or two afore I joined up.'

'And that was in '40.'

'Aye. July.'

'D'you know when Grant was called up?'

'Not the foggiest, no. Why all this about Grant?'

'I'm just trying to build up a picture of your brother's life when he lived in Tipworth Street, Mr Bolton . . . You said he and Grant were best pals.'

'At that time? Aye, they were.'

Tench paused for a moment. 'D'you mean

by that that later on they weren't?'

'Well, they drifted apart, didn't they? Both in the army. Lost touch with one another.'

'What about on leave? Didn't they see one another then?'

'Never seemed to be on leave both at the same time, and since the end of the war Ted's spent most of his leaves in Germany.'

'But they were here together, weren't they, at the time of the bombing?'

'Ted were here, aye. Don't know about Grant.'

'Did Ted never mention that he'd seen him at all?'

Bolton breathed deeply. 'Look,' he said, 'it's no good asking me anything about the war years. I weren't here, were I? Didn't get back from India till November '45. I were out there four and a half years, and never got a sniff of home leave. And Ted, he were never one for writing any letters.'

'But your mother wrote?'

'Aye. Plenty o' times.'

'But she never mentioned Grant?'

'Why should she? All she were bothered about were me and Ted.'

'After the war then. You must have known Grant had bought Thankerton's place.'

'Heard he had, aye.'

'Didn't you ever see him?'

'Not as I remember.'

'How far's Thankerton's from where you

live now?'

'Quarter of a mile, mebbe.'

'And you're telling me you've never set eyes on Grant?'

'Why should I? No cause to. Never get down Nash Street.'

Tench, in his turn, drew a deep breath. 'You say Ted spent most of his leaves in Germany. Why was that?'

'Had a girl there, didn't he?'

'Didn't he ever come home to see his mother?'

Bolton stroked his chin. 'Well, there were a bit o' trouble there, weren't there?'

'What kind of trouble?'

'He wanted to bring her home, but Ma, she weren't having it. Said she weren't for letting no Jerry set foot in her house.'

'But he came back for the funeral?'

'Right.'

'And he came back last week? Why did he do that?'

'Split up with his fraulein, didn't he?'

'He spent five days here in Norwich. Did he mention Grant then?'

'Just what the hell's all this to-do about Grant?'

'Please, Mr Bolton, just answer the question. Did he mention him?'

'No. Not to me he didn't.'

'Then you've no idea at all why the two of them fell out?'

Bolton frowned. 'Fell out?'

'Yes, Mr Bolton. The evidence we have leads us to believe that some serious rift developed between them.'

'Evidence? What evidence?'

Tench glanced towards Gregg.

'The evidence, sir,' said Gregg, 'that proves beyond doubt that Joseph Grant murdered your brother.'

15.

Bolton laughed. 'Joe Grant? You must be bloody well barmy'

'We don't think so, sir. The evidence is quite conclusive.'

'I don't give a toss if it's cast-iron rigid. You've got the wrong man. Joe Grant? Never. He were Ted's best pal.'

'Nonetheless, sir, it's true. Something must have happened to create a rift between them. A serious rift.'

'And I still say you're wrong. Joe Grant were a quiet lad. Never kill a fly if he could let it out the window. He thought the world of Ted.'

'Worlds can disintegrate suddenly, Mr Bolton. The disillusion that follows can be swift and deadly.'

'Not in their case. They knew each other too well . . . So what's all this evidence you're on about?'

'I'm not at liberty to disclose that at the

231

moment, sir,' said Gregg.

Bolton sat back and studied each of them in turn. 'Typical,' he said. 'That's bloody typical of you lot. You get some hare-brained idea, then refuse to say why. Well, that may be enough for you, but it isn't for me. I still don't believe it.'

'Mr Bolton,' said Tench, 'we've made careful inquiries and we've no doubt at all that last Saturday night Joe Grant trailed your brother and Mrs Scott to the Queens Hotel at Holkham, that he followed them down into the woods and was present at the very spot where they were murdered. We also know that a short time later his van was parked on the edge of Burnham Northgate churchyard, and that he made several journeys into that churchyard armed with a couple of sacks and a spade. The bodies of your brother and Mrs Scott were found there early on Sunday morning . . . Now I've done the best I can to answer your question, so please try and help us probe a bit further . . . Did you know Grant's wife?'

'His what?'

'His wife, Mr Bolton.'

'Never knew he had one . . . So Joe got spliced, did he? When was this?'

'That's one of the things we want to find out.'

Bolton's eyes opened wide, 'Well, if you've got him clapped up in a cell for murder, why the hell ask me? Surely to God he knows when his wedding day were.'

'Unfortunately, Mr Bolton, we can't do that.'

'Why not?'

'Because Mr Grant isn't with us any more. He was found dead yesterday morning in Burnham Northgate churchyard. He'd been murdered.'

Bolton closed his eyes. 'Just give me a moment to work this out,' he said. 'You think Grant did for Ted, and now someone's done for him?'

'That's an accurate summary, yes,' said Tench.

'Then you're pinning a murder on a man who hasn't got a chance to deny it?'

'We've no alternative. The evidence we have is more than sufficient.'

'Hasn't it crossed your tiny minds that someone else might have had it in for both of them?'

'We've considered the possibility.'

'And turned it down?'

'Yes.'

'Care to tell me why?'

'The evidence we have . . .'

'Is more than sufficient.'

'Yes.'

'Well, it isn't for me. Joe Grant never murdered Ted. He just weren't the sort of lad to do anything like that. Someone's trying to frame him.'

'D'you know when he married his wife, Mr Bolton?'

'No, not the faintest bloody idea.'

'He limped very badly. D'you know what caused it?'

'No, I don't. He didn't limp when I knew him.'

'Then tell me. When was the last time you saw him?'

'Reckon it'd be sometime in summer 1940. Just afore I joined up.'

'And you're certain you haven't seen him since then?'

'Told you so, didn't I? If you want to know about him after that time, it's no good asking me.'

Gregg leaned forward. 'You were questioned once before about your brother, weren't you? By Detective Constable Ellison.'

'Him in the corner? Aye. That were down in Cromer.'

'D'you remember what you told him?'

'Told him all he wanted to know about Ted.'

'That wasn't all, was it? You said we'd better find the man who killed him, and quickly, because if you found him first you'd wring his bloody neck.'

'Oh, that. Well,'—Bolton gave a dismissive laugh—'folk say these things. They don't really mean 'em. All I were doing were winding him up.'

234

'But you did make a threat, Mr Bolton, didn't you? So where were you on Wednesday night? Let's say between eight o'clock and six o'clock Thursday morning.'

Bolton stared at him, open-mouthed. 'You're surely not daft enough to think it were me as did for Joe Grant.'

'We need to know where you were.'

'You've gone doolally; both of you. I haven't set eyes on Joe Grant, not for years.'

'Then you won't mind telling us where you were on Wednesday night.'

Bolton breathed audibly. 'All right,' he said. 'I were over at Wessenham.'

'What were you doing there?'

'Staying with a friend.'

'A girlfriend?'

'Aye.'

'What's her name, Mr Bolton?'

'Betty Shooter.'

'And where does she live?'

'Blackbeck Cottage. It's out on the Cawston road.'

'She lives there on her own?'

'Aye, she's a widow.'

'Has she got a job?'

'She's a typist at Norwich Union.'

'You stayed all night at the cottage?'

'Till eight o'clock next morning.'

'And Mrs Shooter will confirm this?'

'Aye. Go and ask her . . . Now is there anything else you want me to tell you?'

235

'I don't think so,' said Tench. 'Not for the moment. And thank you for being so patient, Mr Bolton. I hope we won't need to trouble you again.'

Bolton's chair scraped the floor. 'Me too,' he said, 'but whoever killed Ted, it weren't down to me and it weren't down to Joe, so you'd best start looking for somebody else.'

VII

LIES AND STATISTICS

There are three kinds of lies: lies,
damned lics and statistics.

Mark Twain: *Autobiography*

1.

At half-past eight that same evening, Tench braked his car to a halt in front of Lubbock's cottage.

His old Chief was outside, leaning on the gate, pipe between his teeth, polluting the golden sunshine with blue clouds of smoke. 'Coffee's on,' he said, 'though God only knows why you bathe in that muck. It's death to the brain cells. I suppose I can't persuade you to share a large pot of strong Darjeeling brew?'

'No thanks,' said Tench.

'It retones the mind, firms up the legs, stays the trembling hand.'

'My legs are both firm, my hands don't tremble, and my mind's still as clear as the bells from Cley church.'

'They won't be,' said Lubbock, 'you mark my words. In twenty years' time those Brazilian beans will have done their deadly work. You'll be hobbling around . . .'

'On a cherrywood stick?'

'If you've sufficient strength left to grasp one.'

'I'll risk it. Make the coffee.'

Lubbock sighed. 'Well, you know the old proverb. Reckless in youth, rueful in age.' He opened the gate. 'You'd better come inside before the rot sets in.'

*   *   *

'Then we were right after all,' he said, reaching for the teapot. 'His name was on the list.'

'You were right. I was the one who had the doubts.'

'Well, it was a bit of a gamble, laddie. Luckily it paid dividends . . . So just how much d'you know about this chap Joseph Grant?'

'Quite a lot.' Tench gave him all the details.

'Sounds as if he might fit the bill,' Lubbock said. 'A loner, morose, shunning social contact, nursing a grudge. But there's one thing you said that doesn't fit the pattern. Who was it told you he was Bolton's best friend?'

'Terry Bolton, Ted's brother.'

'Well, he should know, I suppose. And if he's right, then so were you. Something must have happened to break up their friendship. A man doesn't murder his closest friend just on a whim.'

'No, he doesn't,' said Tench, 'and that's the problem. We've still no idea what it was that caused a rift to develop between them.'

'Doesn't the brother know?'

'According to him, he's no idea at all, and that's understandable. He spent the last four years of the war in India.'

'But didn't Ted ever tell him about falling out with Grant?'

'Apparently not. Since he went out to India

240

in 1941, they've hardly seen one another, and he says Ted never even mentioned Joe Grant.'

'That's strange, if they were once so close.'

'But it could fit my pattern. If they'd had a serious quarrel, it's possible he wouldn't want to talk about Grant.'

'That's true, so let's assume there was a quarrel . . . Given that assumption, when d'you think it happened?'

'I'm only guessing'—Tench gave a shrug—'but I think it may have been back in 1942, and sometime during the "Baedeker" raids. We know for sure that Ted Bolton was in Norwich at that time, and I've a hunch that Grant may have been there as well. The trouble is we've so many facts still to check. We don't even know for certain that the woman who's buried in Burnham Northgate churchyard was indeed Joe Grant's wife, and we don't know precisely when it was that she died. But if it was during the "Baedeker" raids, and if she was his wife, then he must have been home on compassionate leave. He'd have been in Tipworth Street and so would Ted Bolton. His mother was still living there.'

'Fair enough,' said Lubbock. 'So?'

'The "Baedeker" raids. When exactly were they?'

'April '42. Monday the 27th and Wednesday the 29th. The Luftwaffe didn't turn up on the 28th.'

'You were in Norwich then, weren't you? So

tell me about them.'

Lubbock relit his pipe and spoke between puffs. 'What d'you want? Statistics? The first raid lasted a couple of hours. The second was shorter—an hour and a quarter. The planes dropped three hundred high-explosive bombs weighing just over a hundred tons. They killed two hundred and fifty people and injured seven hundred. Thousands of houses were either destroyed, or damaged so badly that they had to be bulldozed . . . Isn't that enough?'

'Not quite,' said Tench. 'Tell me what it was like in the city on those two nights.'

'Flaming chaos. Quite literally. The first raid began about an hour before midnight. I was down at the Riverside, stripping off for bed. It was one of those clear moonlit nights, and the first planes that came over dropped parachute flares. What with the moon and the flares, the streets became suddenly bright as day. Then the bombs began to fall, incendiaries and high-explosives. The first fell on rows of terraced houses, tearing them apart. Then the gas mains blew up. The city was a hell of spreading flame, screaming bombs and the roar of cascading bricks, slates and stonework. By dawn most of the streets were choked with debris and quite impassable.'

'And Tipworth Street?'

'I never got anywhere near it,' Lubbock said,

'but everywhere round there received quite a pounding. There were a hell of a lot of UXBs too. The bomb disposal squads were stretched to the limit . . . And if you want more statistics, it was reckoned that by the end of the war, out of all the city's pubs, one hundred and thirty-nine had been either destroyed or damaged.' He paused and blew a smoke ring. 'But none of that's going to help you very much, is it?'

'Not much,' Tench admitted.

'So who was it who murdered this chap Joseph Grant?'

'At the moment we've no idea.'

'Well, you know what we used to say. First of all think close to home. What about Bolton's brother?'

'Terry? We've questioned him. Says he was fast asleep with his girlfriend all night.'

'Have you checked that with her?'

'Not yet, but we will.'

'You'll need to, and fast. Alibis exist to be broken, laddie. I've told you that more than once.' He mused for a moment. 'Talking of pubs,' he said, 'reminds me of something.'

He heaved himself up, made for the pantry, and returned with a bottle. He held it out to Tench. 'One bottle of wine,' he said. 'You brought it from Italy, back in that winter of 1947. Said it was a gift to me from that Italian Professor.'

'Giovanni Visco?'

'That's the chap, yes . . . Well, you know

what I am for wine. I'd much sooner have a good strong pot of tea. I'll never drink it, laddie, not if I live for another thirty years, so you may as well have it. You said it was good. Remember?'

Tench nodded. 'Yes,' he said, 'I do. It was a vintage I'd never tasted before, and I've never seen any since.'

'Then take it,' said Lubbock. 'Broach it tonight, and imagine you're back in that villa of his with the whole Gulf of Naples spread out before you, and the smoking cone of Vesuvius away in the distance. That should bring back some memories. Sooner that than brood over Burnham Northgate and bodies in a graveyard. Forget the case for one night. In the morning things may look very different.'

2.

As he drove back to Norwich, Tench had plenty of time to remember; and remembering, to wonder whether it was merely Lubbock's distaste for wine that had led his old Chief to present him with the bottle.

Giovanni Visco was Professor of English in the Facolta della Letteratura Moderna, the School of Modern Literature, at the University of Naples, but he lived in a villa on the edge of Sorrento, looking out across the Gulf, and it was there that Tench had stayed five years before.

He remembered the evening in question very well. He and Visco had been out for the day to Pirenza, the mountain town where Visco had been born, and before the evening meal the professor uncorked a bottle of wine. 'I think,' he said—his English was accented but grammatically pure—'that this may perhaps be much to your taste. It is called Aglianico— Aglianico del Vulture to give it its proper name. If you go north from Pirenza, you come to the small town of Rionero, and from there the road climbs through magnificent forests to Monte Vulture, an extinct volcano, the twin craters of which are now the lakes of Monticchio. The Aglianico wine is made from grapes that are grown on its eastern slopes. This bottle was a gift from some friends in Rionero. You will, I think, find it quite superb.'

Visco was right. It was indeed superb. A dense red wine, it had a tough, dusty feel and a rich almond taste. They lingered over the bottle long after the meal had finished. The professor lit a cigar. It glowed in the half-light. Then suddenly he said, 'Have you ever heard of the *Lex Talionis*?'

Tench had to rack his brains for a moment before he remembered. 'Yes, it's the law of vengeance. An eye for an eye and a tooth for a tooth.'

'And a life for a life. But it is more than that, my friend.' Visco was sombre. 'It is a cult that runs like a strange disease through the veins of

245

this land. It assumes its own justice, denies the written law. It is a barbarous, bloody and wasteful tradition. It lives by the thrust of a knife in the dark or a shot from out of the shade in the sunshine. These killings, they follow one another with the sureness that night follows day and dawn follows night. The first spawns the second, the second the third, and so they go on. And what can be done? It is like attacking the monster, the hydra that lived in the Lernean marshes. Strike off one head, and two more will spring up to take its place. That is the way that the blood-feud works. Often it is plain who the murderer is. To arrest the man is simple. To convict him impossible.'

'You mean you can't prove it?'

Visco twirled the wineglass between his fingers. 'Here in Southern Italy one can rarely prove anything. That is the second law: an unwritten law like the *Lex Talionis*. But this one does not merely deny the written law; it frustrates justice. It is still one more of the binding and also terrible traditions that exist in this place. We call it *omerta*. Perhaps you know the name.'

'I've heard of it,' Tench said. 'Doesn't it mean manliness: possessing the virtues proper to a man?'

Visco smiled. 'You have much good Italian, my friend,' he said. 'Yes, it means all the most courageous virtues, so the lexicon says. But it is not always safe to put trust in a lexicon. Is

246

that not so? Such virtues here are twisted into vice. *Omerta* more commonly here means silence. It is the conspiratorial silence of the South. People are bred to it. *Omerta* decrees it is a manly thing not to help the police. So, when they happen to find a corpse in the street, no one knows anything, no one sees anything. They smile and they shrug. They say nothing, not a word. It is a matter of honour and also one of caution. They are drugged with caution, these countrymen of mine. To speak would inevitably be to condemn. To condemn a man in a court of law would mean death to the killer. Then the equally terrible *Lex Talionis* would come into play. The family of the killer would be in honour bound to avenge his death. And so the vendetta would raise its ugly head. The first death would mean a second, the second a third, and so it would go on. This is the way things are done in the South. Only two weeks ago, I heard of a boy of thirteen in the town of Afragola, who had shot down the man who had murdered his father six months before he had even been born. His mother had kissed and sucked his father's wounds in the presence of those who came to the funeral. It was a simple matter of honour to do so. It proved to them that her desire for vengeance would never be sated till her husband's killer had himself been killed. The vendetta was sworn. For the boy there was no escape from his fate. As the nearest male relative he was marked down, even before his birth, as the one who must one day avenge his father. It would have been better, in truth, if he had never been born, for shortly, very shortly, he will die in his turn. The knife will come out or the savage lupara that hangs on the wall, and the police will find yet another bloodstained corpse somewhere in the streets.'

Visco drained the last of his wine. 'Here,' he said, 'we simply pass on from one death to the next. But that is the merciless fate of Lucania. That is the South. So remember Pirenza when you rise in a morning, and say a little prayer that its people may one day learn to forget the blood-feud, the silence, and all those relics of the past that sever them from God and make them the slaves of their warped code of honour.

'Save a thought for Pirenza, my friend, and pray for us all.'

*   *   *

They'd talked for another hour as the deep Southern night wrapped itself round the villa and the lights of Naples sprang out across the Gulf.

And the following morning he, Mike Tench, had set off for home, taking with him two bottles of the finest Aglianico, one for himself and the other for Lubbock.

3.

Lubbock's bottle now lay on the seat beside him and, turning on to the Norwich road at Holt, he wondered again just why his old Chief had chosen that evening, after a lapse of five years, to produce it from his pantry like a rabbit from a hat.

Not that he needed to wonder for long. He'd worked with the old boy on so many cases that he'd now reached a point where he could read the man's mind without a great deal of thought. When it came to murder, Lubbock never took a step without due calculation, even if that step appeared to be as casual as merely handing over a bottle of wine. He knew his own county, Norfolk, like the back of his own hand, and it wouldn't have taken much in the way of calculation for him to call up the map that he kept in his mind, and confirm that Wessenham was only three short miles from Newton St Faith.

'Alibis exist to be broken,' he'd said. Then he'd heaved himself up and stumped off to the pantry.

Tench nodded. That was it. He knew Lubbock too well.

*   *   *

Perhaps that was why, a mile or two short of Horsham St Faith, though his luminous watch showed eleven o'clock, he swung off the Norwich road and followed the signs to Wessenham.

It took him some time to locate Blackbeck Cottage. He drove past it once in the darkness and missed it, but he found it at last—a small brick-and-flint affair at the end of a row. None of the windows, there or next door, showed a glimmer of light.

He debated briefly whether to knock on the door, then decided against it. There was nothing to be gained, at that time of night, from rousing Mrs Shooter when she'd just gone to bed.

Turning aside, he started up the car and drove home to Cringleford, but, once in bed himself, he set the alarm for five the next morning.

In another ten minutes he was soundly asleep.

4.

He remembered nothing more till the clock tripped its bell promptly at five and he woke to a dismally wet Norfolk Saturday. The weather was foul, rain streamed down the windows, but he'd decided the night before what he was going to do, and though the sky was still an unrelenting grey, he snatched a scanty breakfast, flung on a waterproof, and set out for Wessenham. At six o'clock he was back outside Betty Shooter's cottage.

There was no sign of life, but the curtains, strangely, were already drawn back, even upstairs at what he assumed was the bedroom window.

He rapped on the door. There was no response from inside.

He took a step back and looked up at the window. Then, clenching his fist, he hammered on the door. There was still no reply.

'Mrs Shooter!' he called. 'Wake up! It's the police!'

There was silence, broken only by the clatter of milk bottles as, somewhere in Wessenham, a milkman made his rounds. Then suddenly, next door, an upstairs window was thrown up and a youngish woman with tousled blonde hair and a yellow-flowered dressing gown leaned out across the sill. 'What's all the racket?' she said. 'It's Saturday.'

'Police, ma'am,' said Tench. He held up his card. 'I need to speak to Mrs Shooter.'

'Well, it won' do no good a-blastin' on the door,' the woman said. 'She ent in.'

'Then where is she?'

'Gawd knows. Packed a bag las' night an' made off in a taxi.'

'What time last night?'

'Round eight, near as not . . . Mebbe half eight.'

'Was anyone with her?'

251

'Nah. Just her an' a suitcase.'

Tench swore beneath his breath. 'D'you know Terry Bolton?'

'Him? Oh, aye. Comes round here a lot.'

'Was he round here last night?'

'If he were, I ent seen him. Could a bin though. Turns up most evenin's reg'lar-like.'

'Was there a name on the taxi?'

'Never saw one. It were black though. Had one o' them hire signs stuck on the top . . . Why d'you want to talk to her?'

'We just need a bit of help, that's all. Mrs . . . ?'

'French. Sally French. An' it's Miss, not Mrs.'

'Well, thank you. Miss French.'

Tench turned towards the car. He was already moving off when she leaned out still further. 'An' if ye're thinkin' she's off an' away with Terry Bolton, then reckon ye could be right.'

But Tench didn't hear what she said. He was speeding away down Wessenham Main Street, making for Norwich, and berating himself for not checking on Betty Shooter as he'd driven down to Cley the evening before.

5.

He stopped at the nearest phone box in the middle of Horsford, and rang McKenzie's flat.

There was a groan on the other end of the

line.

'That you, Mac?'

Another groan. 'Of course it's bloody well me.' He must have glanced at the clock. 'What's all the flap? It's the middle of the bloody night.'

'Are you still in bed?'

'Where else would I damn well be at this time on a Saturday?'

'Then get out of it sharp and get down to HQ.'

A third, and this time an even louder groan. 'What's up? Has something gone up the spout?'

'I'm not sure, yet. I've a shrewd suspicion that our friend Terry Bolton's done a vanishing trick. If he has, then everything's way up the spout. If he hasn't and I find him, I'm bringing him in. You and I need to ask him one or two questions . . . Are your feet on the ground?'

There was a sigh from McKenzie. 'My feet are on the ground.'

'Then get them moving,' said Tench. 'If I do set eyes on Bolton, I'm going to put him on the rack, so see that it's well oiled.'

*   *   *

It was a quarter of an hour later that he pulled up outside the small Edwardian house on Earlham Road, climbed the grey-stone steps

253

and rapped on the old brass knocker.

Not that he was expecting anything but silence. He'd already convinced himself that Bolton too had packed a suitcase and fled, and was probably already on some cross-Channel ferry, seeking a quiet haven somewhere abroad; and it was therefore with a considerable mixture of feelings that he heard the sound of a turning key, saw the door shudder back and Bolton's muscular figure, clad in a vest and trousers, appear on the threshold. 'Oh, it's you,' he said. 'What now?'

'We need to have a further talk, Mr Bolton.'

'At this time in a morning? What the hell for?'

'We need to confirm a few of your previous statements.'

'Can't see why.' Bolton breathed heavily. 'Get on with it then. What d'you want to know?'

'Not here, Mr Bolton.'

'Where then?'

'I need you back at the station.'

'At seven o'clock on a Saturday morning? Are you joking?'

'No.'

'You're not arresting me?'

'No. I'm simply inviting you to help us, Mr Bolton. You say you don't believe Joe Grant killed your brother.'

'Too right I do, aye.'

'Then we need your help to find out who

did . . . Go and put a shirt on, Mr Bolton. I'll wait . . . No.' He raised a hand. 'Inside, if you please. It's a bit wet out here.'

6.

The lights were on in the interview room, but if Tench had hoped they might reveal some trace of apprehension on Bolton's face, he'd deluded himself. There was nothing to signify that the man was in any way perturbed. Lounging in his chair, face to face with both the Chief Inspector and McKenzie, he seemed less interested in them than the corner of the room where Sue Gradwell sat, armed with a notebook and pencil, right leg crossed over left, right toe pointed down and her skirt drawn up to the level of her knee, as she prepared to record every word that he uttered.

Tench wasted no time. 'Mr Bolton,' he said, 'you told us yesterday that you spent Wednesday night in Wessenham at Betty Shooter's cottage.'

Bolton reluctantly switched his gaze from Sue Gradwell's right leg to the Chief Inspector's face. 'Right,' he said. 'So?'

'Did you ever hear of a little girl called Matilda?'

'Not as I remember.'

'That's a pity.'

'Why? Who is she, this Matilda?'

'Not is, Mr Bolton . . . Was . . . She's dead.'

'All right. Who was she then?'

'She was a girl who told dreadful lies.'

'Did she now?'

'Yes.'

'And what's she to do with me?'

'A cautionary tale, Mr Bolton, nothing more. She suffered a terrible fate, did Matilda. When the house caught fire and she called out for help, no one believed her. Poor mite, she was burnt to death.'

'So what?'

'So think before you speak.' Tench looked straight at him. 'I'm asking you again. Where were you between eight o'clock on Wednesday evening and six on Thursday morning?'

'I've told you. In Wessenham.'

'At Blackbeck Cottage?'

'Yes. How many more times?'

'You know Mrs Shooter well?'

'Well enough, aye.'

'Then would you care to tell me exactly where she is?'

'Reckon she's still in bed.'

'At Blackbeck Cottage?'

'Where else would she be? It's Saturday.'

'You're a liar, Mr Bolton, aren't you?' McKenzie said. 'You're spinning us a tale that's just a load of old rope. You know very well where Mrs Shooter is, and it isn't at Wessenham. So think again. Where is she?'

'She allus has a lie-in Saturday morning, an' when she does that she don' answer the door.

Take my word for it, she'll be upstairs in bed.'

'She's not upstairs, downstairs or anywhere in Wessenham. We've checked and we know.'

Bolton gave a shrug. 'Then ye'd best check again, cos that's where she'll be.'

McKenzie glared at him. 'Mr Bolton,' he said, 'I repeat, you're a liar, so just tell me this and stick to the truth for once. What time did you get to Mrs Shooter's cottage on Wednesday evening?'

'It were round about ha' past six.'

'And you were there all night?'

'Said so, didn' I?'

'You never went out?'

'Not till next morning. No cause to go out . . . You satisfied now?'

'No,' McKenzie said, 'I'm not bloody well satisfied . . . Did she tell you she was intending to go away this weekend?'

'No. Course she didn'.'

'Then can you explain why, at half-past eight last night, Mrs Shooter left the cottage in a taxi, and carrying a suitcase?'

7.

Bolton remained as phlegmatic as ever. 'Reckon so, aye.'

'You can?' McKenzie seemed to find even this simple statement hard to believe. 'Then where was she going?'

'Reckon she were off where she allus goes

257

Fridays.'

'And where would that be?'

'Dancing.'

'Dancing?'

'Aye, ballroom dancing. There were a competition on.'

'Where?'

'At the Samson in Tombland . . . Check if you want.'

'Don't worry. I will.' McKenzie was tight-lipped. He paused for a moment. 'You didn't go with her?'

'No.'

'Why was that?'

'She were fixed up already.'

'You mean she had a partner?'

'Right.'

'Who was he?'

'Chap from the office. Allus goes with her.'

'Name?'

'Ricky Thorburn.'

'And what's this Ricky Thorburn got that you haven't got?'

'Simple,' Bolton said. 'He's a dancer. I'm not.'

'So Mrs Shooter went off to the dance on her own . . . With a suitcase?'

'Why not?'

'Why the hell would she need a suitcase?'

'Teks her dress and her shoes. The usual tackle. Allus changes when she gets there.'

McKenzie's eyes were like gimlets. 'And you

258

think that's what happened?'

'Can't be anything else, can it?'

'Oh, I fancy there might be another explanation.' The sergeant was suddenly, dangerously bland. 'D'you want to know what I think happened, Mr Bolton? I think everything you've said is just a load of old rope. I think you murdered Joe Grant, and you've packed Mrs Shooter off to some place where she's out of our way. You arranged for that taxi to pick her up and take her to Norwich station. So where was she going?'

'Look,' said Bolton, 'if ye don' believe me, ye'd best be asking her, not wasting my time . . . Now is there anything else, because I'm booked to drive a bus down to Wells at ten o'clock?'

'Yes, there is, Mr Bolton.' Tench leaned forward. 'There's one important question you still haven't answered.'

There was a deep-drawn sigh. 'Come on then. Let's have it.'

'Where's Mrs Shooter now?'

'I've already answered that. You asking me agen?'

'Exactly that, Mr Bolton.'

'She's where I said she were. If I know Bet Shooter she'll be fast off in bed.'

McKenzie flung himself back in his chair. 'The man's lying,' he said. 'Don't bother asking him anything else. Just lock him up. He wouldn't know the truth if you served it up on

259

a slice of buttered toast.'

Tench seemed for a moment to be pondering the suggestion. He looked straight at Bolton. 'Are you lying?' he asked.

'Course I'm bloody not. He's as mad as a hatter.'

'You're sure Mrs Shooter's at home in Blackbeck Cottage?'

'I'm more than bloody sure. I'm bloody well positive.'

'Then have you got a key?'

'A key to what?'

'The cottage.'

'What if I have?'

'Let's use it,' said Tench. 'If your friend Betty Shooter's in bed as you say; she can tell us precisely the time on Wednesday night when she put her loving arm round you under the sheets.'

8.

Blackbeck Cottage still stood, as it had done, apparently deserted, nor was there any sign of the tousled blonde, Sally French.

Bolton pulled out his key and opened the door, but before he could step inside Tench held him back. 'Upstairs, Mac,' he said. 'Mr Bolton, follow me.'

He led the way down a narrow hall to the parlour, then to the kitchen, and after that the scullery, throwing open each of the doors in

260

turn. Downstairs, at least, there was no Betty Shooter.

Trailing Bolton behind him, He went back through the rooms to the foot of the stairs.

'Is she up there, Mac?' he shouted.

McKenzie's head appeared over the banister rail. 'if she is,' he said, 'she's bloody well invisible.' He clattered down the thinly carpeted stairs. 'She's not in the bathroom and the bed's made up, so if our friend here's managed to tell the truth for once and she always has a lie-in on Saturday morning, then it's pretty clear she never slept here last night.'

Bolton, for once, seemed utterly confounded. 'She must be here,' he said.

'Well, she isn't. I've looked.'

'Everywhere?'

'Under the bed, in the cupboards. Where d'you want me to look?' McKenzie glowered at him. 'Have you killed her and buried her under the floorboards?'

There was silence for a moment. Tench turned to Bolton. 'You were wrong, Mr Bolton. Mrs Shooter's not here. So I'm asking you again. Where is she?'

Bolton shook his head. He seemed to be finding it difficult to believe that she wouldn't suddenly appear in a puff of blue smoke. 'I don't know,' he said fiercely. 'She oughter be here. She never gets up afore ten on a Saturday.'

'Well, if she's still in bed,' McKenzie said,

'then she's sleeping somewhere else.'

Bolton didn't seem to hear him. Furrows of thought were lining his brow. 'You know what?' he said. 'I reckon she's with her mum.'

'And where would that be?' McKenzie was unimpressed.

'Scotland.'

'Scotland? Whereabouts in Scotland?'

Bolton shook his head. 'Don' rightly know for sure. Somewhere in the middle.'

'That's where most people live. Is that the best you can do?'

'Well, I don' know, do I? She never said exactly where.'

'Mr Bolton,' said Tench, 'you say Mrs Shooter may have gone to see her mother. Why would she suddenly decide to do that?'

'She's bin ill.'

'You mean her mother?'

'Aye. That's right. Bet were worried about her. She musta got word she were worse.'

McKenzie fixed him with a glare like a basilisk. 'You know what?' he said. 'There's one thing's plain enough. All you've got in that twisted little mind of yours is a pack of bloody lies. You know damn well where she is, and it isn't in Scotland. You're deliberately obstructing police inquiries, and as far as I'm concerned I'd charge you here and now, and stick you in a cell till you had second thoughts.'

Bolton looked towards Tench. 'I don' know where she is,' he said. 'Honest I don't. And that's telling the truth.'

'Huh!' McKenzie snorted. 'I've heard some tales, but that's the best I've heard this morning . . . Lock the bugger up, and if he doesn't come clean, then charge him with murder.'

'The sergeant thinks I should charge you with murder.' Tench appeared to be deadly serious. 'What do you think, Mr Bolton?'

'He's way off his rocker. I ent done no murder.'

Tench studied him intently. 'You say you're due to drive a bus down to Wells.'

'Aye. Pensioners' outing, though what they're going to do down there all day with the weather like this, God only knows.'

'What time are you due back?'

'Leave there at five o'clock. Back in Norwich six fifteen.'

'And when you get to Wells, where do you park the bus?'

'On the Buttlands . . . Allus park there.'

'You own a car, of course?'

'Course I do, aye.'

'What make?'

'Morris Eight.'

'Registration number?'

'DB. Double nine two nine.'

Tench gave a nod. 'Right,' he said, 'Mr Bolton. For the moment you're free to go. We'll drop you off in Earlham Road, but when you get back from Wells you're to report

263

straight to me at police headquarters . . . Do I
make myself clear?'

'Aye.' Bolton sighed. 'Crystal bloody clear.'

'Good,' said Tench. 'Now lock up the
cottage and give me the key. You'll get it back
this evening once you report to me.'

9.

They watched the door close behind him at
Earlham Road.

'He's lying,' McKenzie said, 'and he's guilty
as sin. Pity you didn't sling him straight in a
cell.'

'We've no evidence, Mac.'

'We've suspicions.'

'We may have, but they're not enough.'
Tench revved up the car and pulled away from
the kerb. 'We need rock-solid proof that his
tale's a pack of lies.'

'From what I've seen of Terry Bolton,
there's about as much chance of him telling
the truth as a snowflake's got of surviving in
hell.'

'We still haven't broken his alibi, Mac.'

'And he's done his best to make bloody sure
that we can't.'

'He may have done, but we don't even know
that for certain . . . Come on. Face the facts.
We've questioned him twice, and his alibi still
holds. What we need is something to hit him
with, hard . . . So what have we got?'

McKenzie reached in his pocket and brought out a plastic bag. 'This,' he said, 'plucked from the bathroom.'

Tench glanced to his left. 'What is it?'

'It's a tube.'

'A tube of what?'

'Shaving cream.' McKenzie held it up like a prize exhibit. 'So unless his little lovebird shaves her legs and her armpits, it's bound to be smothered in our friend Bolton's prints.'

*   *   *

Tench pulled to a halt inside the headquarters compound. 'Right, Mac,' he said. 'How's that death-trap of yours? Still coughing?'

'No.'

'She's cured?'

'Of course she is. Just a minor infection. Bit of dirt in the feed-pipe.'

'She's not likely to choke to death?'

'No, she's as smooth as the proverbial baby's bottom.'

'Then how d'you fancy spending a day by the sea?'

'Not much. It's wet.'

'Then brace yourself to suffer. It's all in the cause of duty . . . Take that tube to the lab, and tell Ted Merrick I want it checked against any prints found at Thankerton's and any that turned up at Newton St Faith. Say it's urgent. If he gets a positive result, I want to know right

265

away . . . Then get over to Pegasus. Make sure Bolton's driving that bus down to Wells, and when he sets off, tail him. Once he drops his pensioners off at the Buttlands, he'll have six hours free to do as he likes. I want to know where he goes, so keep tabs on him . . . Ring me whenever you get the chance, but for God's sake don't lose him.'

'What about breakfast?'

'Grab a bacon sandwich and munch it on the way.'

'I'm allowed to eat, am I?' McKenzie said sourly.

'Oh, I think so,' Tench said. 'But keep a low profile, and if he happens to find his way to a pub, just keep your goggles on, choose a dark corner and treat yourself to a fizzy lemonade.'

'Oh, thanks a million.' McKenzie stared at the rain. 'Didn't someone once say that the cruellest month was April?'

'Yes . . . T.S. Eliot.'

'Well, he was bloody well wrong. It's a wet June in Wells, sitting in a pub with a fizzy lemonade, and watching the barman pull pint after pint of foaming Norfolk ale. Where the hell was he born, this Eliot? Saudi bloody Arabia?'

266

VIII

WET MIST

A dripping June brings all things in tune.
English proverb

1.

There were, McKenzie thought, infinitely better ways to spend Saturday morning than to sit astride a bike amid the drizzling rain in a one-horse Norfolk town way out in the sticks, peering through the mist at the driver of an otherwise empty bus, who appeared to be scoffing a sandwich and taking the odd swig from a bottle of beer.

Not that the Buttlands at Wells, on a normal day, didn't possess an aura of faded grandeur. He acknowledged that much. But today, in the wet, with visibility so poor that he couldn't even catch a comforting glimpse of the Crown, that touch of distinction was far from apparent.

The fact that the pelting rain had eased off to a drizzle had done little to soothe his temper. The drizzle was still wet. It ran off his waterproofs and trickled down his goggles, and the mist that had gathered approaching the coast seemed to be getting thicker with every minute that passed. He felt, indeed, like a live wet fish rolled up in a dirty blanket. The only part of him that was dry was the back of his throat. He was, in other words, soaking wet, thirsty and thoroughly fed up.

Terry Bolton took another long swig from the bottle. He seemed quite content to remain in the bus, and McKenzie was just beginning to wonder whether he intended to stay there till five o'clock, when a small black car with a retractable rain hood appeared through the mist, rounded the bus and drew to a halt in front of it.

It was apparently what Bolton had been waiting for. In another half-minute he was out of the bus and into the passenger seat, and the car was accelerating away round the Buttlands.

McKenzie swore savagely, kick-started the Norton, and the bike, spitting smoke like an unchained dragon, roared off in pursuit.

At the junction with the main road, the car turned right towards Cromer, and set off through the mist at a leisurely pace. Whatever its destination, the driver appeared to be in no great hurry to reach it, and McKenzie, keeping the tail light in view, but wary of approaching too close to rouse suspicion, was forced to slow down to a speed that did little to improve his temper.

Muttering dark imprecations behind his goggles and suppressing his natural urge to swing out, roar past and disappear into the distance, he trailed the car through the narrow twists and turns at Stiffkey, down the slope and through Morston till, at Blakeney, it slowed almost to a stop, took the side road leading down to the quay, and edged its way into a row of parked cars at the side of the Blakeney Hotel.

McKenzie switched off his engine, waited and watched.

For a couple of minutes there was no sign of movement, then the driver's door opened and two trim legs appeared, followed by the rest of a blonde-haired woman in a red blouse and skirt. She stood for a moment waiting for Bolton, then together they sauntered down to the steps, climbed them and vanished inside the hotel.

McKenzie parked his bike at the foot of the steps, took them two at a time, and rammed the revolving doors so hard that they all but catapulted him into the lobby where, stumbling forward, he fetched up abruptly face to face with a tall young man, immaculately dressed in a blazer and flannels.

The youth eyed his dripping waterproofs with some amusement. 'Steady on, old chap,' he said. 'What's all the rush?'

'Have you see a blonde woman in a red blouse and skirt?'

'No.' The youth shook his head. 'Rather wish I had though. Which way did she go?'

'God knows,' McKenzie growled.

'Throw you off the boat, did she?'

McKenzie's reply was withering. He brushed the man aside and made straight for the reception desk, where a prim young woman in glasses was studying a list on a baize-covered board. 'Shop,' he called loudly and thumped on the counter.

She looked him up and down with plain disapproval. 'Yes?' she said sharply.

'Police,' McKenzie said. 'I need to see the register.'

Her expression made it clear that he was hardly a fit person to be seen in the Blakeney. 'Have you some means of identification?' she inquired.

McKenzie struggled beneath his waterproofs and brought out his card. 'Sergeant McKenzie,' he snapped. 'CID, Norwich.'

She peered at the photograph. 'It doesn't look much like you,' she said and reached for the phone.

McKenzie's temper had been tried enough for one morning. He raised his fist and brought it down hard on the desk. 'You've five seconds,' he said. 'If I don't have the register, you're under arrest . . . One . . . two . . . three . . .'

She reluctantly withdrew her hand from the phone. 'Very well,' she said in an icy tone of voice, 'but I shall inform the manager.'

'You can inform Winston bloody Churchill for all I care.' McKenzie thrust out his hand. 'Register!' he demanded. 'And make it double quick or there could be a murder.'

2.

There were two reports on Tench's desk, one

272

from Ledward and the other from Ted Merrick at the lab, but he barely had time to glance at them before the telephone rang, and he heard the Duty Sergeant's voice on the line. 'Chief Super's just arrived, sir. Wants to see you. Says it's urgent.'

He'd half-expected the call. 'Right, Sergeant,' he said. 'Tell him I'm on my way.'

He pushed the reports to one side, retrieved a couple of files from the cabinet beside his desk, made his way down the corridor and knocked on Hastings' door.

The Chief Super was standing at the window staring out at the rain. When he heard the knock, he turned. 'Come in, Mike,' he called.

Tench opened the door. 'You wanted to see me, sir?'

'Yes.' Hastings nodded. 'Sit down.'

Tench sat.

The Chief Super stood and looked at him. 'Define a word for me, will you?'

'If I can, sir, yes.'

'Oh, I'm sure you can, Mike. It must be all too familiar.'

'What is it, sir?'

'The word, Mike, is flannel.'

There was a frown from Tench. 'Flannel?'

'That's what I said.'

'It's a noun describing a kind of woollen fabric.'

'And . . . ?' Hastings said.

273

'And, sir?'

'Yes, it's something else, too. It's a verb, Mike. To flannel. To use words intended to hide one's ignorance, which is all I've been doing so far this morning . . . I've flannelled my way through a crowd of press reporters shooting questions at me; I've flannelled the Chief Constable for ten long minutes to keep him off our backs; and all because I could hardly confess that my Detective Chief Inspector has, for some reason, hidden himself away for thirty-six hours and seen fit to leave me in total ignorance.'

'I must apologize for that, sir.'

Hastings breathed deeply. 'Yes, I think you must. Didn't you see the reporters?'

'Came in by the back way, sir. I always find it's best.'

'And that's just another form of flannelling, isn't it?'

'I suppose so, sir, yes . . . But things were a bit hectic for most of yesterday, and by the time I was free you'd already gone home.'

'It's your job to keep in touch, Mike. You know that well enough.'

'Yes, sir.'

'Good.' Hastings pulled out a chair. 'I've said my piece. Now it's your turn to talk. I don't care how long it takes, I want to know the lot. Just where do we stand in this Northgate case?'

It took half an hour. The Chief Super listened intently, making notes all the while on a sheet of paper. At the end he leaned back and laced his fingers together underneath his chin. 'This man Grant,' he said. 'You've conclusive evidence that he was the one who murdered Edward Bolton?'

'Yes, sir. Absolutely conclusive. I've had two reports this morning that make that quite clear. The hairs that Dr Ledward found on Bolton's fingers came from Grant's head, there were others retrieved from the clothes found at Holkham, and Ted Merrick's been testing a pair of his dungarees found in Thankerton's garage. They revealed minute fibres from Bolton's shirt and Mrs Scott's blouse, and once we trace his van I've no doubt that Forensics'll turn up some bloodstains.'

'If you find it and they're traceable. It's probably been crushed at a breaker's yard.'

'We're checking them, sir. That's all we can do.'

'And Bolton's brother?'

'We think he may be our man. His alibi for the time of Grant's murder seems far from convincing. We've had to let him go for the moment, but he's under observation. I think it's only a matter of time before we prove he's been lying.'

Hastings looked grim. 'Well, let's hope the time's short, because ours is running out. The Chief Constable's already champing at the bit. If we can't present him with the head of Grant's killer on a plate, and sometime today, it's more than likely that he'll want mine for breakfast tomorrow. And maybe yours too. So you'd better get to work.'

3.

Tench slammed his office door and slung the files on his desk. At that moment he was closer to agreeing with Lubbock than at any time in the five years he'd known him.

It was all very fine for those at the top to set their deadlines and tell everybody else to get down to work, but his old Chief was right. Investigations took time, they couldn't be rushed, and there were days when a case seemed to hang in suspense and the only sane thing to do was to sit tight and wait.

Patience. That had always been Lubbock's watchword. 'Patience, laddie, patience. Let the case simmer. It'll come to the boil in its own good time.'

He was right there, too, and this was one of those days. It didn't matter a toss what the deadlines were. All he could profitably do on this teeming wet Saturday morning in Norwich was to sit at his desk and wait for the scattered members of his team to phone in with their reports.

Apart from Lock, who was manning the phone in the CID room, and Gregg, whose job was to make contact once again with Jeremy Clyde, every single one of them was out in pursuit of the truth about Grant—Sue Gradwell in Burnham Northgate, checking on the Catherine Agnes Grant who was buried in the churchyard; Rayner and Spurgeon seeking the facts about his time with Ted Bolton at Thankerton's garage and the incident that had left him with a plate in his leg; Ellison doing a round of the breakers' yards on the trail of his van; and McKenzie, of course, keeping track of the man who, for all their suspicions, claimed he hadn't set eyes on Grant for the past dozen years.

He, Mike Tench, was waiting for all of them. He was waiting, moreover, for Lester's scene-of-crime reports, and, more vital than all the rest, he was waiting for Merrick to ring from the lab. His was the evidence, if only it could be found, that would nail Terry Bolton to the murder of Grant.

He looked at his watch. It showed twenty past ten.

Reaching for the phone, he rang the canteen and told them to send up a large pot of coffee.

It might well, he felt, be a very long morning.

It was. Very long.

He pulled out all the reports on the case, and read through every file from beginning to end while the phone remained stubbornly, frustratingly silent.

He rang the CID room and spoke to Des Lock, but Lock was waiting too. No, he said, there'd so far been no replies to the appeal in that morning's *EDP*.

Tench swore beneath his breath, took a turn round the room, stared at the wet roofs and spires of the city, then sat down again and glared at the phone.

It didn't even tinkle.

At ten to twelve he rang for more coffee, but it wasn't till a couple of minutes past the hour that at last, at long last, the phone came to life and, snatching the receiver, he heard McKenzie's voice.

'That was quick,' McKenzie said.

'You'd be quick if you'd been waiting for two bloody hours. Where the hell are you?'

'The Blakeney.'

'The Blakeney Hotel?'

'The same. And they're both here, Bolton and his lover girl. She picked him up in his own car and drove him down from Wells. Seems she booked in last night about half-past nine for an indefinite stay.'

'We were right then?'

278

'Looks like it. As soon as we let him go, he must have rung her and told her to get a taxi to Earlham Road. Then he ran her down here, left the car at the Blakeney and either caught the last bus to Norwich or else hitched a lift.'

'A bit out of their league, isn't it? The Blakeney?' said Tench.

'A hell of a way out.' McKenzie was scathing. 'Reckon she must have told him if she couldn't go dancing, he'd better find her something better than a grubby b & b.'

'Where are they now?'

'Tucked away in her room. D'you want me to march in and nick them?'

'No. Not yet. I'm still waiting to hear from Merrick. Just keep tabs on them. Go and sit in the lounge and keep your eyes skinned.'

'There's a problem,' McKenzie said. 'I've got waterproofs on, and I'm bursting for a leak.'

'Then you'll just have to cross your legs and hope for the best,' said Tench. 'We can't afford to lose them.'

4.

McKenzie had no intention of crossing his legs.

There were things, he felt, that a man had to do, and to hell with the world.

He made a dash for the door that flaunted the word GENTLEMEN in bold black letters,

279

pushed it open, struggled out of his waterproofs, and sought blessed relief.

It was the most enjoyable minute he'd spent all morning, and he was tempted to linger and let life pass by.

It was as well that he didn't. A second battle with the waterproofs took him longer than he'd expected, due to sleeves that had somehow turned themselves inside out, and as he emerged into the lobby, still struggling with them, he was just in time to catch a glimpse of Bolton and his lady love, armed with a couple of distinctly heavy suitcases, disappearing through the revolving doors.

Five minutes later he was peering through the mist at a black Morris Eight as it reached the coastal road and turned left towards Cromer.

He knew the road well. The 149, though classed as an 'A' road, was mainly two-lane and contained in its sixty-mile stretch from Lynn more twists and turns than any other 'A' road in the whole of the kingdom. Their frequency and its narrowness made it dangerous to overtake and difficult to achieve any reasonable speed, but with Bolton at the wheel, the Morris seemed intent on courting disaster. It sped down the dip towards Cley and then, brakes squealing, turned left and then right, weaving a perilous passage through the narrow main street, swerving madly round a milk float, slewing past the windmill, and out on the edge of the marsh towards Salthouse. Here it picked up even more speed. Bolton, so it seemed, unlike his inamorata, was intent on reaching his unknown destination in double-quick time. With McKenzie grimly clinging to his tail-lights, he tore through the mist along the twisting, tapering ribbon of road, till, rounding the final bend before Salthouse, another set of tail-lights flashed into view.

The lorry, stacked high with what appeared to McKenzie to be large wooden crates, was travelling itself at no mean speed, and the crates swayed from side to side as it straightened from the bend. There was another screech of brakes as Bolton slowed down to a legitimate thirty and tucked in behind it, swearing no doubt in the knowledge that he'd have little chance to overtake for the next ten miles.

He never enjoyed even that slim chance. The first bend was followed by yet another, as the road, between the marsh and the village green, swung to the left in the opposite direction. The crates swayed again, tilting to the right like the sails of a yacht caught in a sudden squall, and with a crack their rearmost retaining rope snapped. The result was catastrophic. The top four crates, released from their bondage, slid from the load and, spinning uncontrollably, hit the ground with such force that they splintered apart, discharging their contents, untold thousands of flat-headed nails, on to the roadway.

McKenzie had time to brake and turn on to the green, but Bolton was too close to swing either left or right. There were two sharp detonations as his front tyres deflated, and then two more as the rear pair suffered a similar fate, and the Morris, down to its wheel rims, slewed first to one side, then to the other, and clattered to a halt on the edge of the green.

McKenzie sat for a moment, surveying the chaos with something approaching a mild amusement, then he pulled the bike back on its stand and began to pick his way across the gleaming sea of nails. The lorry had stopped some hundred yards ahead, and the driver was already walking back towards the car, and as McKenzie reached it, Bolton clambered out. He was almost apoplectic. 'Did you see that?' he shouted. 'Stupid bastard! He should never be allowed to drive on the bloody road! Not with a load like that!'

McKenzie bent down and peered inside the car. The woman was still sitting there, staring at the windscreen. 'You all right?' he asked.

She turned towards him and gave a little laugh. 'Oh, yes,' she said. 'I'm fine. It's happy hour at the seaside. Just tell him if I've laddered my stockings I'll sue him.'

Bolton was already squaring up to the driver of the lorry. 'You stupid sod!' he yelled. 'You could have bloody well killed us!'

McKenzie let him rant on. He reached down and, dragging out a suitcase, set it on the ground. Then he took two steps forward, tapped Bolton on the shoulder and, as the man turned to face him, lifted his goggles. 'Planning a little holiday, Mr Bolton?' he asked.

5.

Recognition flashed across Bolton's face, and with it the kind of panic that prompts a man to take immediate action. With a couple of swift movements he kicked McKenzie hard, first on the left shin, then on the right, and took to his heels across the green, making for the lane that led up to the heath.

McKenzie gave a roar like an enraged Spanish bull, hobbled back to the Norton and, wincing with pain, kick-started it into life and roared off once again in pursuit of his quarry.

Heads were appearing round the jambs of cottage doors and, as he sped across the green, leaving behind him a trail of blue smoke, he raised a hand towards them. 'Call the police!' he yelled.

*   *   *

The narrow lane where Bolton had disappeared into the mist rose steeply past the village to Salthouse Heath, a mile-long, flinty

283

tract of high ground, overgrown with gorse and bracken and thorn, from which, on a sun-drenched summer day, there was a magnificent panoramic view across the village and coastal road to the salt marsh and the sea—a wild, beautiful place, full of birdsong and light.

But there were days, and this was one, when the heath was a very different place: a lonely, desolate stretch of waste land, where a man could take half a dozen faltering steps and lose himself in the wet, clinging mist; where the clumps of gorse became crouching figures, and where, tripped by the bracken and scratched by the thorns, he could wander for hours without ever stumbling on one of the tracks that criss-crossed the wilderness.

As the Norton spat and snarled its way up the slope, McKenzie peered at the road, desperate to catch a glimpse of Bolton's fleeing figure, but with every yard he covered, the mist seemed to grow thicker. It closed around him like a blinding grey curtain and, conscious that the man had a good head start, he swore at the Norfolk weather with a savage ferocity as he was forced to slow down and crawl up the hill.

Edging painfully forward, yard by reluctant yard, the bike crackled up the slope till, nearing the crest, on the edge of the heath, the mist suddenly parted, there was brilliant sunshine and, little more than a stone's throw ahead, he saw Bolton's toiling figure. As he did so, the man glanced back across his shoulder and, turning aside, darted on to the heath; and it was at that precise moment, as McKenzie opened the throttle, that his pride and joy gave a cough and then spluttered and died.

Few of McKenzie's colleagues remained for long unaware of the breadth of his invective, but even the oldest hand among them might have learned something new in the next few seconds as the sergeant fought vainly to bludgeon the Norton into some spark of life. At last, still swearing at the callousness of fate, he pushed the bike to the side of the road, pulled it back on its stand and, struggling out of his creaking waterproofs, set off up the hill, making for the point where Bolton had disappeared.

There was a track there, leading off across the heath, but no sign of the man he sought. McKenzie took half a dozen cautious steps and crouched down among the ferns.

He listened. No sound. The sun shone down on the tufts of gorse, but nothing so much as stirred. The heath lay as still as the Bronze Age dead beneath the burial mounds that rose here and there like stranded whales above its ragged surface.

He crept forward, stopped and listened again. Then he heard it, close at hand to the right. A faint rustle of leaves and a choking sound, as if someone was fighting to hold back a sneeze.

285

There were times when McKenzie could move silently and swiftly. He eased himself up, and then, as the man yielded at last to his long-suppressed urge, he dived forward like a rugby player scoring a try and dropped on top of him with every ounce of his fifteen stones.

Bolton, his face catapulted into a thorn bush, had no time even to recover his breath. McKenzie had dealt with too many violent criminals to take any risks. In a trice, the man's wrists were handcuffed behind his back, and the sergeant was dragging him up by his hair. 'On your feet!' he growled.

He swung Bolton round and kneed him in the groin. 'Resisting arrest,' he said. 'Now walk, you murdering bastard! Walk!'

6.

Tench stared at the phone.

Where the devil had McKenzie got to? It was more than an hour since he'd called from Blakeney.

'Ring, damn you!' he said. 'For God's sake ring!'

As if in immediate response to his command, the phone bell suddenly shattered the silence. He snatched at the receiver.

'Mac?'

'That's me.'

'Where the hell are you?'

'I'm in what's commonly known as a

286

watering hole.' McKenzie sounded irritatingly cheerful.

'I might have guessed.' Tench wasn't yet prepared to match his mood. 'Which watering hole?'

'The Dun Cow at Salthouse. I'm relaxing with a pint of full-bodied Norfolk ale. Well earned, I might add.'

'Where's Bolton?'

'He's here and he's not going anywhere.'

Tench swallowed hard. 'Don't mess me about, Mac. What d'you mean by that?'

'Exactly what I said. He's shackled to the rail at the edge of the bar. If he tries to go anywhere, he'll take half the pub with him.'

'You've arrested him?'

'Too bloody true.' McKenzie said. 'I've nicked the bugger. He kicked me on the shins. I'm charging him with assault and resisting arrest.'

'He kicked you on the shins and he's still alive and kicking?'

'Well, put it like this. He's a bit the worse for wear. Collided with a thorn bush, and suffered a more intimate kind of inconvenience, but he's fit enough to be tied to a stake and grilled.'

'And what about Mrs Shooter?'

'She's not going anywhere either,' McKenzie said. 'I think she's quite happy to be where she is. She's sitting at a table, sipping a very large brandy-and-soda and chatting to a very large constable from Cromer.'

'Stay with them,' said Tench. 'I'll send a car to pick them up. And forget about the charges. Sore shins don't rate for much in the catalogue of crime. Once we get Bolton here, I'm going to charge him with murder.'

IX

CLOUD OF UNKNOWING

All we know is still infinitely less than all that still remains unknown.

William Harvey: *De Motu Cordis et Sanguinis*

1.

'Please sit down, Mrs Shooter.'

Tench's office was bathed in afternoon sunshine. He looked across his desk as the woman smoothed down her skirt and took the opposite seat. She was blonde, possibly in her early thirties, attractive though in a brash kind of way, and seemed to be more amused than disconcerted by the sequence of events that had brought her face to face with the Chief Inspector.

'You're not in any trouble, Mrs Shooter,' he said. 'Let me introduce myself. My name is Tench. Detective Chief Inspector Tench. I think you've already met Sergeant McKenzie.'

She gave him a winning smile. 'Oh, yes,' she said. 'I have. A most charming man.'

Tench's eyebrows flickered for an instant. 'Yes, indeed,' he said. 'I've no doubt he treated you with the utmost courtesy.'

'Oh, he did, Chief Inspector.' She gave McKenzie a smile that was even more winning.

'I'm glad to hear it, ma'am.' Tench's tone was dry. 'Then perhaps you'll be willing to help us solve a problem.'

'Of course, Chief Inspector. If I possibly can.'

'We're trying to discover what happened this week that led to today's little accident at

Salthouse . . . You were travelling with Mr Bolton. Did he tell you by any chance where you were going?'

'Oh, yes,' she said. 'Paris.'

'Paris?'

'Yes, Chief Inspector, Gay Paree. That was what he said. He'd booked a week's holiday for both of us there.'

Tench leaned back in his chair and frowned. 'Let's go back a bit, Mrs Shooter. According to Mr Bolton, he often spends the night with you at Wessenham. Is that true?'

She tossed her head. 'No.'

'He never stays there with you?'

'Oh, he stays, but not often. Just from time to time. It's up to me, not him. If I want him to stay, he stays. If I don't, he doesn't.'

'I see.' There was another flicker of the eyebrows from Tench. 'Then please cast your mind back to Wednesday, Mrs Shooter. Did he stay the night then?'

'Oh, no.' She was firm. 'He never stays Wednesdays.'

'Is there some reason for that?'

'Yes, it's girls' night on Wednesday. Friday's out too. I go dancing on Friday.'

'But last night you didn't go dancing, Mrs Shooter. Why was that?'

'Well, he rang me up, didn't he? Lunch time on Thursday. Asked me what did I think to a week in Paree?'

'And what did you say?'

She gave a little laugh. 'Oh, come on, Chief Inspector. What girl in her senses would turn down the chance of a week in Paree?'

'But you stayed last night in Blakeney, Mrs Shooter. Why did you do that?'

She sighed. 'It's a long story, Chief Inspector. Do I really have to go into all the details?'

'It would help us a great deal, ma'am, if you did.'

'OK.' She shrugged. 'He said we had to catch the overnight ferry from Dover on Saturday, but he was booked to drive a bus down to Wells on Saturday morning, so it'd give us more time if we set off from there. He had friends in the town who ran a boarding house. He could run me down there Friday night, leave the car with me, and I could pick him up from the Buttlands at midday on Saturday . . . I asked him what about my dancing, and he said it couldn't be helped, I'd just have to miss it.' She looked at them and laughed again. 'That was when I put the screws on. I told him I wasn't going to stay the night in some bug-ridden bed-and-breakfast place. If he wanted me to spend a week with him, even in Paris, he'd better think again and book me in at the Blakeney. And a good job I did. If I'm not going to see gay Paree, then at least I got something out of the deal.'

Tench seized on the word. 'If it was a deal, Mrs Shooter, then what did he expect from

293

you in return?'

She laughed again. 'Surely, Chief Inspector, you don't need to ask me that. What d'you think he expected? A stick of Paris rock?'

'Did he ask you to say that on Wednesday night he stayed with you at your cottage in Wessenham?'

'No. Why should he?'

'You're sure about that?'

'Positive,' she said.

It was McKenzie's turn to take up the questioning. He frowned. 'Mrs Shooter,' he said, 'did Bolton mention what he did on Wednesday night?'

'No.

'Didn't you ask him?'

'I didn't need to, Sergeant. He always goes out drinking with the lads on a Wednesday.'

'And you believe that's what he did?'

'It's what he always does.'

'Does he often invite you to spend a week with him in Paris?'

She gave the same little laugh as before. 'You must be joking,' she said.

'So when he made the offer, it was something of a shock?'

'I'll say it was. Yes.'

'Didn't you wonder then why he'd made it?'

'Not out loud I didn't, no.'

'But you asked yourself why.'

'Maybe. For a moment, but that was all.'

'And did you give yourself an answer?'

'No, Sergeant, I didn't. I didn't bother to find one. He'd offered to take me to Paris for a week. That was good enough for me. I wasn't going to ask him to give me a list of reasons.'

There was silence for a moment. Tench glanced at McKenzie. The sergeant gave a shrug.

'Well, thank you for your help, Mrs Shooter,' Tench said. 'Perhaps you'll be good enough to make a brief statement to Sergeant McKenzie and sign it. I'll arrange for a car to take you back to Wessenham, but please let us know if anyone else offers you a holiday, even if it's only as far as Blakeney.'

She gave another little laugh. 'That'll be the day,' she said. 'But I'm always open to offers'—her eyes strayed to McKenzie—'if the right person asks.'

2.

It was half an hour later that McKenzie returned.

'Well?' said Tench. 'Did you?'

'Did I what?'

'Invite Lady Shooter to take a stroll by the Seine?'

'No, but I was tempted.'

'Then resist it, Mac. She's a material witness. We don't want Bolton getting off on a technicality.'

'He won't.' McKenzie was grim. 'If I have

295

anything to do with it, he'll finish up dangling on the end of a rope . . . If she ever set eyes on Paris, she'd have found herself ditched and left to pay the bill.'

'If she ever did. He was cutting it fine. He must have known that once we found he was missing, we'd put a stop on the ports. And there's another thing, Mac. If he was intending to drive down to Dover, why didn't he take the direct road from Blakeney? Why did he wander along the coast road to Salthouse?'

'Perhaps he'd got a faster car lined up at Cromer. He wouldn't have made much speed in the one he was driving.'

'Or perhaps he never had Dover in his sights. Once out of the area, he could have stopped for a snack somewhere on the road, gone for a Jimmy Riddle, and left her stranded with a cup of tea and a bun.'

'Well, he's the only one who can tell us,' McKenzie said. 'Do I bring the bugger up?'

'Yes, bring him up,' said Tench. 'Interview room. And bring Sue along with you. We need to have everything taken down.'

He saw McKenzie's face. 'And I don't mean what you think I mean, Mac. So get cracking.'

3.

The afternoon sun streamed down through the windows of the interview room and fell straight on Bolton's face.

296

It wasn't a pretty sight. As McKenzie had said, it was a bit the worse for wear. His collision with the thorn bush had etched on it a criss-cross pattern of scratches, and the more intimate inconvenience was still clearly causing him some discomfort. He shifted from side to side on the hard wooden chair, and flinched from time to time.

Not that he seemed to be in any way chastened. His expression was at once both sullen and mutinous, and he scowled across the intervening table at McKenzie.

Tench appeared not to notice. He opened a file, turned a couple of sheets and, without raising his eyes, said, 'I have to remind you, Mr Bolton, that you're still under caution . . . You are Terence John Bolton of Ronaldsway House, Earlham Road, Norwich. Is that correct?'

Bolton ignored him. He pointed an accusing finger at McKenzie. 'I want him charged with assault,' he said. 'He kicked me in the goolies.'

'Answer the question,' McKenzie growled.

Tench repeated it. 'Is that correct?' he said.

'Of course it's bloody well correct. You know that.'

'You told us, Mr Bolton, that you spent last Wednesday night with Elizabeth Shooter at Blackbeck Cottage in Wessenham, but Mrs Shooter now informs us that that isn't true. So I ask you again. Where were you on Wednesday night?'

297

Bolton breathed deeply. 'All right,' he said, 'I were out at a stag night.'

'Were you indeed? And whose stag night was this?'

'Alf Chambers. Works at Pegasus.'

'And where was this little celebration held?'

'Crown and Thistle, off Dereham Road.'

'Then tell me this, Mr Bolton. If, as you now claim, you were nowhere near Wessenham, why did you lie to us and say that you were?'

There was silence for a moment.

'Shall I tell him?' McKenzie said.

'Why not?' Tench leaned back in his chair. 'Perhaps it's time we shared a few secrets with him.'

'Right then.' McKenzie was clearly relishing the prospect. He glared at Bolton. 'You may have been drinking at the Crown and Thistle, but you lied to us because, after you left there, you went somewhere else. You went to Thankerton's garage, and sometime between ten o'clock and midnight that night, you murdered Joe Grant.'

'You're barmy.' Bolton was dismissive.

'I don't think so,' McKenzie said. 'Have you got an electric razor?'

'What the hell's that got to do with anything?'

'Just answer the question.'

'No, I bloody well haven't. Never could get on with the things.'

'I presume, when you stay at Mrs Shooter's,

298

you shave.'

'That's another stupid question. Course I do, yes.'

'Then what do you use?'

'An ordinary safety razor . . . Look, what is all this?'

'And shaving cream?'

'Yes. I'd look well hacking my face to bits without.'

McKenzie reached in his pocket, and produced a plastic bag that held the tube of cream. He pushed it lazily across the table. 'Is that yours?' he asked.

Bolton stared at it. 'It could be.'

'What d'you mean? It could be.'

'It's like what I use.'

'It is yours, Mr Bolton. It was found in Mrs Shooter's bathroom.'

'So what if it was? I stayed there. I told you.'

'It contains a very clear set of your fingerprints, Mr Bolton. So can you explain how those same fingerprints came to be found on the bonnet of the car that Joe Grant was repairing in Thankerton's garage?'

4.

Bolton shrugged. 'No, of course I bloody can't. Last time I were in Thankerton's were back when Ted were working there. There must be some mistake.'

'There's no mistake, Mr Bolton.'

'Why not? There could be. Maybe the prints on that tube there aren't mine.'

'If they're not yours, whose are they?'

'How the hell should I know? Someone else could have stayed at Wessenham and used it.'

Tench leaned forward. 'I think perhaps I should make something clear, Mr Bolton, before you concoct another string of lies. The prints are yours, no one else's. We've matched them against others taken from your car, from an identical tube of shaving cream taken from your suitcase, and from personal possessions found in your house on Earlham Road. We shall, in due course, be insisting you provide a sample yourself, and I've no doubt that those also will match. They prove beyond question that you were in Thankerton's garage on Wednesday, so any attempt on your part to deny the fact is pointless.'

Bolton was still protesting. 'How can they be mine when I've not been near the bloody place?'

'That's for you to explain,' said Tench.

'So you'd better start explaining, and fast,' McKenzie added.

He sat back and waited. Bolton, tight-lipped, stared at the table.

'Nothing to say, Mr Bolton?' Tench was almost cheerful. 'Let me help you. Perhaps I can refresh that failing memory of yours . . . We've found your prints in other places too. On the wing of the car in Thankerton s garage, and also on a monkey-wrench found underneath it. A wrench which, apart from a very clear thumbprint belonging to you, also showed traces of Joe Grant's blood. You may have thought you'd wiped it clean, but in your haste you were a little bit careless, Mr Bolton. It's surprising what Forensics can find on a thing like that . . . Oh, and one thing more. There were scuff marks in the dust at the side of the car. Signs of a struggle. So, if I were you, I'd think very carefully before you decide to say nothing at all. Silence, Mr Bolton, is likely to be viewed as an admission of guilt, so, if you have any explanation, this is the time to say so.'

Bolton took a breath that seemed to be dragged from the bottom of his lungs. 'It weren't murder,' he said sullenly.

Tench narrowed his eyes. 'Are you admitting that you killed Joseph Grant?'

'It weren't murder.'

'No? If you killed the man, Mr Bolton, how could it not be?'

'He come at me, didn't he? Waving that wrench. He were mad, raving mad. If I hadn't hit him with it, I'd have been the one dead.'

'You're claiming it was self-defence?'

'The stupid sod were going to kill me. What the hell would you have done? Course it were self-defence.'

Tench closed the file. 'I think, Mr Bolton, you'd better start at the beginning. Were you telling the truth when you said you were drinking in the Crown and Thistle on Wednesday night?'

Bolton nodded twice.

'Please answer out loud, Mr Bolton. Was it true?'

'Course it was. D'you bloody well want it in writing?'

'Sooner or later, yes,' said Tench. 'What time did you leave?'

'It were round about quarter to eleven.'

'How much had you had to drink?'

'Not much. Couple o' pints, that's all.'

'And where did you go after that?'

'Set off back home, but it were long afore that.'

'What was?'

'The beginning.'

'You mean something happened before last Wednesday?'

'Aye, it did.'

'Then what was it and when?'

'It were soon after Ted come on leave. There were this chap, standing outside the house and staring. Stranger to me. Didn't know him from Adam. He were back next day doing just the same thing. Ted weren't around, so I went out and asked him who the hell he was and what the devil did he think he was doing. "Ted's on leave?" he asked. I told him yes, he was. "Then tell him to stay away or I'll kill him," he said.'

302

5.

Tench frowned. 'Are you telling us that a complete stranger appeared out of nowhere and threatened to kill your brother?'

'He were a stranger to me. I'd never afore set eyes on the chap. At least, that were what I thought.'

'But you had?'

'Oh, aye. More'n once.'

'He told you his name?'

'No, he scarpered afore I could ask him again. I only found out who he was after he'd done it in for Ted.'

Tench stared at him. 'You mean . . . it was Grant?'

'Right on the nail.'

There was another frown from Tench. 'Mr Bolton,' he said, 'I'm finding all this very hard to believe. You saw Joe Grant, a man you must have met before on countless occasions, and yet you failed to recognize him?'

'I hadn't a hope in hell of telling he were Grant.'

'How long was it since you'd seen him?'

'A dozen years. Thereabouts.'

'But surely young men don't change that much, even in a dozen years.'

'He had,' Bolton said.

'He limped?'

'That were one thing.'

303

'There were others?'

'Just one. That were what did me. He'd shaved off his beard.'

'Grant had a beard?'

'He had when I knew him. A full beard, an' all. Started to grow it as soon as he could. It were while he and Ted were working at Thankerton's.'

There was quite a long pause before Tench spoke again. 'Did you warn your brother about this man?' he said.

'I told him all I could.'

'And what did he say?'

'Told me to forget it. He'd be off to the coast in a couple of days, and out of the country soon after that. He wasn't going to have his leave hit for six by some screwball he'd never met.'

'He didn't suggest that the man might be Grant?'

'Never mentioned Joe Grant. Said so afore, didn' I?'

'So when did you find out this fellow was Grant?'

'Not till Wednesday morning. I were driving through town. Got held up in traffic, and this chap in a Lancia pulled up aside me. Never turned his head, but I knew it were him, so when we moved off I followed him, all the way round to the back of Thankerton's. He turned up the track to the garage and parked the car outside. Then he unlocked the door and went

304

in. That were what started me thinking, and I thought about it all bloody day.'

'And,' McKenzie said, 'you were still thinking about it when you left the Crown and Thistle.'

'It were driving me round the bend.'

'So what did you do?'

'Didn't think there were much I could do. Not at that time o' night. But it's a short cut from the Crown to Earlham Road to go by the back of Thankerton's, and I just wandered round there.'

'And saw the light and the car parked outside.'

'Aye, that's right.'

'And you just wandered up the track, found the door open, wandered in and murdered him.'

'It weren't like that.'

'What was it like then?'

'He were underneath the car with his legs sticking out. I said, "Is that Joe Grant?" "Yes," he says, and he shoves himself back and stands up with the wrench in his hand. Once he sees me, his face changes. "What do *you* want?" he says. "It were you as did for Ted," I said, "weren't it?" "What if it were?" he says, all vicious like. "He deserved all he got." "Look," I said. "This just doesn't make sense. You and he were the best of pals." "Not any more," he says, and when I asks him why not, he gives me a look as if he'd like to treat me the same way as Ted. "He killed her," he says. Well, that flummoxed me completely. "Killed who?" I asked him. "Cath," he says. I stared at him. "Cath?" I said. "Who's Cath?" "My wife," he says. "He killed her, and he killed my child too. Both of them. He killed them. Don't you understand?"'

6.

McKenzie's bushy eyebrows lifted a fraction. 'You're telling us Grant confessed to killing your brother?'

'That's what he said.'

'And then went on to accuse him of murder?'

Bolton nodded. 'That's right. Clear as a bell, he were. I'm not bloody deaf.'

'And what did you say to that?'

'I told him he must be mad, stark, staring mad. Ted weren't that sort of chap. He'd never hurt a fly.'

'Go on.'

'Well, he wouldn't have none of it. "You weren't there," he said. "I was and I saw him, so don't tell me I'm mad. I'll not have anybody saying I'm mad." I looked at him, standing there, waving that wrench. "You're as mad as ten bloody hatters," I said. "You ought to be locked up."'

Bolton made a despairing gesture with his hands. 'It were that as sparked him off. His

306

eyes blazed as if he really were mad, and he charged at me, swinging the monkey wrench. Well, all I could do were dodge, and when it came down it couldn't have missed me by more than an inch. He came at me again, and I grabbed his wrist and twisted it. He yelped and dropped the wrench, but he caught me off balance, and the next thing I knew I were down on the floor and his hands were round my neck. I knew that he meant to kill me just like he'd killed Ted, and I had to fight for my life. I could see the wrench lying there on the floor, and somehow I managed to roll over and reach it, but he were up on his feet, trying to stamp on my hand. I scrambled up too and shoved him hard in the chest. He went back against the wall, but he were up and at me again in a flash, trying to grab the wrench, and I had to shove him off a second time. I weren't for using the wrench except for holding him off. I were hoping he'd calm down and just pack it in. But he didn't.'

He paused and shook his head, as if in disbelief. 'He just kept coming at me. He were baring his teeth and snarling like some wild beast out of the jungle, and I had to back off round the side of the car. He stood still for a moment, gathering his breath, then he charged at me again.'

There was another long pause.

'He must have tripped over one of the tools on the floor, because he stumbled forward and fell face down across the bonnet of the car, and that were when I hit him. I didn't mean to kill him, I swear to God I didn't, but he lay there and didn't move, and when I turned him over, his eyes were wide open, dead, but I could see them blazing at me. Even when I reached out and closed the lids, there they were, still blazing.' He shuddered. 'They followed me, those eyes, and when I came to lay him out in the churchyard, they were both still ablaze, staring straight into mine. There were a terrible hate in those eyes. I couldn't stand them accusing me, telling me I'd done what he wanted me to do. That were why I covered them up with his hands. So I wouldn't have to see them.'

He looked up at the two detectives. 'It were self-defence,' he said. 'It were either him or me.'

'And you made bloody sure it wasn't you,' McKenzie said. 'And what did you do after that? You thought there was a chance you could get away with murder, and so, like the stupid oaf that you are, you made a clumsy attempt to cover your tracks. Why the hell, you thought, should anyone suspect you, harmless Terry Bolton, the man who swore black and blue that he'd never believe Joe Grant murdered his brother?'

'It weren't like that,' Bolton protested.

'Don't try to deny it, Mr Bolton,' said Tench. 'We found your fingerprints on Grant's garage door at Newton St Faith, and inside the garage there were more on Grant's car.'

He pushed back his chair and stood up. 'Terence John Bolton,' he said. 'I'm charging you with the murder of Joseph Grant.' He repeated the caution. 'You'll be questioned again tomorrow. Till then you'll remain in custody. Take him down, Sergeant.'

McKenzie gave a grin of anticipation, like the wolf when he first set eyes on Red Riding Hood. 'My pleasure,' he said. 'On your feet, Bolton, and make it double quick. I'm not one for wasting my time on killers.'

7.

The bells of Cley church, ringing out across the Green for Sunday evensong, filtered faintly through the windows of Lubbock's cottage as Tench sipped his coffee.

His old Chief laid down his pipe and poured a second cup of tea. 'You believed him?' he said. 'You think that was what happened?'

'Probably,' said Tench. 'It's true that to begin with he told us a whole pack of lies, but I don't think Terry Bolton's the kind of man who'd set out to do a cold-blooded murder. I think he was genuine when he talked about having to fight for his life.'

'You say he used Grant's own car to take the body to Burnham Northgate?'

'Yes, we proved that. And also that he drove

309

it from there to Newton St Faith, and left it in Grant's garage.'

'And then walked home to Norwich? It's a good four miles.'

'No.' Tench shook his head. 'That was where Grant inadvertently helped him. At some time or other he'd fitted a roofrack to the Lancia, and he kept an old bicycle stowed away at Thankerton's. Bolton roped it on top of the car, used it to ride back and then left it where he'd found it. Then from Thankerton's he walked just the few hundred yards to his own place on Earlham Road.'

'He knew that Grant lived out at Newton St Faith?'

'No, not at first. He told us he'd no idea just where the man lived—thought perhaps it was somewhere in Norwich—but Grant had left his jacket hanging up in the garage, and his driving licence was in a wallet in the pocket. Up to that point, he said, he'd been in a panic, wondering how he could possibly cover things up, but once he found Grant's address, a plan began to work itself out in his mind. Strip him of his clothes, bundle him into the boot of the Lancia, lock up at Thankerton's, dump him out at Burnham and, since he must have a garage at Newton St Faith, hide the car there. It was all very simple, or so he thought. There'd be nothing, come the daylight, to show that anything was wrong either at Thankerton's or at Newton St Faith. Both places would be locked, as they usually were first thing in a morning. It might well be hours before anyone discovered what had happened, and even when they did, who was going to guess that he, Terry Bolton, had had anything to do with it. He knew that Grant's keys to his house and the car must be somewhere around, and of course they were—in his back trouser pocket where he always kept them. The trouble was that his plan turned out to be not so simple after all.'

'He forgot about fingerprints.'

'No, according to him, he didn't. He was well aware of the damning evidence that prints could provide, but two things defeated him. First, he couldn't remember where, in the heat of the struggle, he'd planted his hands; and second, he had to work fast and work in the dark. The window at the back of the garage had no blinds, and he could only hope that no one had already looked in and seen him struggling with Grant. It wasn't likely, but knowing what he still had to do, he couldn't risk being exposed any longer. To try and cover the window with whatever was handy might only arouse suspicion, so he had no alternative but to work in the dark. The key to the garage was still in the door, so he turned it in the lock and switched off the light. But, of course, there were prints that he missed.'

'There were bound to be,' said Lubbock, 'but he was careless too, wasn't he? You found

311

some on Grant's car, and there must have been a light in the garage at St Faith.'

'Oh, there was,' said Tench, 'but justice has strange ways of catching up with killers. When he found the switch and clicked it, the light bulb blew.'

Lubbock reached for his pipe and knocked it out in the battered tin ashtray he kept at his side. 'That's not justice, Mike,' he said, 'it's simply retribution.'

Tench gave a shrug. 'Is there any difference? I sometimes wonder.'

'There's a world of difference, laddie, a whole wide world. Justice is man's work. Retribution's always best left to the gods.' He struck a match and rekindled his pipe. Billows of smoke swirled up and away to the old cottage rafters. He peered at the younger man and suddenly frowned. 'Look, Mike,' he said. 'A week ago I stepped into Burnham Northgate churchyard and found two bodies laid out on a grave. Since then you've solved three murders. One of the killers is dead and the other's in custody. That's no mean achievement. You should be drinking champagne, not just sitting there, staring at a cup of coffee that must be stone cold. So, what's the trouble? Come on, laddie. Tell me.'

Tench emptied his cup and set it down on the table. 'Someone in ancient times once talked about being in a cloud of unknowing. Well, that's where I am. In a cloud of unknowing. And I find I don't like it one little bit.'

8.

For the first time Lubbock showed a flash of irritation. 'Oh, that's all it is, is it? That hoary old chestnut. You're simply trying to tell me you're left with a load of questions that haven't any answers. Every time we reach the point where we can happily close the file on a case, you come down here, toy moodily with a cup of coffee, and complain that things aren't all neatly tied up with a bow of red ribbon. "I don't know this," you say. "I'm still not sure about that." Well, that's just too bad, laddie, because you're probably never going to find any answers. I've told you more than once and I'll tell you again, murder investigations are all about guesswork. We begin them by guessing, and we end up still guessing. We can never uncover the whole of the truth. So just settle for what you've got, and be thankful for that much. Forget about the rest.'

'I can't,' said Tench.

'Of course you can. You've done it before.'

'Maybe, but not this time.'

'Why not? Come on, Mike. What don't you know that's so vital it's making you toss and turn all night? You haven't found Grant's clothes. Is that what it is?'

Tench shook his head. 'No. We know where

313

they are. Bolton hired a boat at Wrexham and dropped them in the middle of Wroxham Broad. There's a team of divers out there now. They'll find them.'

'What else then? His van's still missing?'

'No. We've laid hands on that. Ellison tracked it down to a breaker's yard at Fakenham.'

'You need more evidence to provide cast-iron proof that he murdered Ted Bolton?'

'No. We've got all we need. Merrick provided it. Blood, hair, fingerprints, fibres, the lot.'

'Then I give up,' said Lubbock. 'You know that Joe Grant murdered Ted Bolton and Mrs Scott, and now Bolton's brother's confessed to killing Grant. What more d'you want? Certificates from all three victims to certify death?'

'I know Terry Bolton murdered Joe Grant, and I know why he did it. I also know that Grant murdered Bolton's brother, Ted. The trouble is that in his case I still don't know why.'

'But you do know why. He told Terry why. For some reason or other he got it into that deranged mind of his that Ted had killed both his wife and his child.'

Tench leaned forward. 'Yes, but what was the reason? Why on earth did he think Ted had done something like that?'

'Does it really matter? He murdered him.

314

That's enough.'

'It's not enough for me.'

'Close the file, laddie. You've got both your killers.'

'I can't. Not yet. I keep asking myself the same question. Why? What happened between them to lodge that outrageous idea in Grant's mind? And I need to find the answer. If I don't, I'll still be wondering in thirty years' time.'

Lubbock slowly, methodically refilled his pipe. 'Look, laddie,' he said. 'I've worked on hundreds of murder investigations, and I'm still left with hundreds of unanswered questions. Do I fret about them? No. What's the point of fretting about questions I can't possibly answer, even if I search and search again until doomsday? . . . In this case there are only three people who know what happened—Ted Bolton, Grant and God. Two of them are dead and, unless you've got a direct line to God, he's just as inaccessible. So take my advice. Trying to grasp something that's way out of reach is a waste of time. Forget all about it.'

'I can't accept that. There must be someone else who knows.'

'Why should there be? No one saw Grant murder Ted Bolton, and no one saw his brother hit Grant with a wrench. So explain to me. Why should anyone have seen what happened between Grant and Ted Bolton to drive Grant to murder?'

'It's not a case of seeing.'

'Then what is it a case of?'

'Hearing. If a man believes that someone's murdered his wife, he doesn't keep quiet. He talks about it. Tells people . . . Grant must have talked. So somewhere there must be someone else who knows.'

Lubbock sighed. 'And you propose to find him?'

'Yes, if I can.'

'And you want me to help in this madcap search?'

'You're in a better position to find him than I am.'

'Why?'

'Because,' said Tench, 'you were in Norwich during the blitz, and I'm pretty sure that whatever happened to make Grant accuse Ted Bolton of murder happened in Norwich on the day that followed the first of the "Baedeker" raids—the afternoon of the 28th April, ten years ago.'

9.

'You're sure about that?'

'Yes. I can make a rough guess at the time if you like.'

'Then you know something more than when you were last here.'

'Something, but not enough.'

316

'Well, if you want me to help'—Lubbock blew a smoke ring up at the rafters—'I think you'd better tell me just what you do know.'

Tench seemed to hesitate. 'The question,' he said, 'is where to begin.'

'You know the answer to that one, laddie. Start at the beginning and simply carry on.'

'Well, first of all you were right about the Catherine Agnes Grant who's buried in Northgate churchyard. Apart from McKenzie, Lock and myself, the whole team was out yesterday, trying to add to our knowledge of Joseph Grant, and it was Sue Gradwell's job to contact the Rector, consult the parish records, and follow up any pertinent facts that she found . . . She uncovered quite a lot. Catherine Agnes was Grant's wife, as you suspected she might be. Her maiden name was Howes, Catherine Howes, and she was born at Great Bircham where her father had quite a substantial farm. The connection with Burnham Northgate came through her mother, who'd been born and brought up in the village, and lived there until she married Samuel Howes. Her grave, as a matter of fact, is adjacent to Catherine's.

'She died in September 1939, a week after war broke out, and six months later Samuel Howes followed her. He left the farm to Catherine who was then twenty-one, and with its subsequent sale she became a comparatively wealthy young woman. At that

317

time she was working in a bank at Lynn, but like so many other girls she felt she wanted to do something more useful, and early in 1940 she volunteered for the Wrens and was posted to Portsmouth. It was there that she met Grant.'

He paused for a moment. Lubbock's eyes were closed, and he gave every indication of having drifted off to sleep. Then, quite abruptly, he drew on his pipe and expelled another rolling billow of smoke. 'Well, get on with it, laddie,' he said. 'I'm listening. What on earth was Grant doing down in Portsmouth?'

Tench relaxed once again in his chair. 'That was where we made a mistake,' he said. 'We assumed that, like both the Boltons, he'd served in the army. But he hadn't. In the autumn of 1940, he volunteered for the navy, trained as a naval mechanic, and was posted to work in Portsmouth dockyard. It seems he met Catherine Howes at a canteen dance, and it was a case on both sides of love at first sight. They married at Portsmouth register office in June '41, and by August she was pregnant. That meant, of course, that she was discharged from the Wrens, and as a short-term measure she went to stay with Grant's sister in Tipworth Street. Apparently the two women got on well together, and she was still there at the time of the blitz in '42. By that time she was eight months pregnant.

'We know a number of things for certain,

thanks to Gregg and Spurgeon, who between them managed to reconstruct what happened on the night of the first raid, 27th April, and the following day, the 28th. We know that Grant was home on leave, that he and Catherine were together in the house at Tipworth Street, and that they were lucky to escape when most of the homes around them were reduced to rubble and theirs suffered only a couple of shattered windows and minor damage to the roof. We know too that his sister, his only surviving relative, was working late at the Lido dance hall on Aylsham Road, and was killed on her way back to Tipworth Street by one of the first bombs to fall. And we know, moreover, that at approximately three forty-five on the following afternoon, a team of St John Ambulance workers found Grant and Catherine half-buried beneath the collapsed wall of a building near Exeter Street, that they were taken to the Norfolk and Norwich, and that there Catherine Grant was pronounced to be dead and her husband was detained with a severely complicated fracture of the leg.'

Lubbock waited, eyes closed. 'And that's all you know for sure?'

'Not quite all, no, but even that much helped us to solve a couple of problems. The fact that Grant was in the navy meant that he didn't have to shave off his beard, so he'd still have had it at the time of the bombing, and it meant in addition that up to last week Ted and Terry Bolton had never seen him clean-shaven since he was an adolescent working at Thankerton's. That confirmed what Terry had told us—that when he saw Grant standing outside the house in Earlham Road, he didn't recognize him. And it also explained why Ted didn't either that night in the bar of the Queens Hotel at Holkham. Strip a man of his beard and he's an altogether different person. Ted wouldn't have known him, even if he'd been interested enough to take a look at him, and at that time he clearly wasn't. All his attention was focused on Mrs Scott.'

Lubbock nodded. 'Fair enough. So what else did you discover? D'you know when it was that he shaved off his beard?'

'No, but it may have been only last week, when he got to hear in some way that Ted was home on leave, but we did discover something more that posed yet another problem. Gregg and Spurgeon between them managed to trace not merely one of the ambulance workers, but also a couple of nurses at the Norfolk and Norwich who were on duty at the time when the Grants were brought in. It seems that they'd been trapped underneath a heavy beam that had fallen across Catherine, killing her and the child outright and crushing Grant's leg. He was in considerable pain and half-delirious when he was admitted, but both nurses said that he kept on repeating time and time again, "He never stopped! The bastard never stopped!" It seemed to be the one thing he had on his mind.'

10.

Lubbock opened his eyes. 'And you're wondering if Ted Bolton was the bastard he was talking about?'

'Well, it seems likely, doesn't it?'

His old Chief peered at his pipe in some dissatisfaction, and knocked it out once again in the ashtray. 'It seems just as likely it was someone else altogether.'

'But it could have been Bolton.'

'It could have been, yes.'

'Well, let's suppose it was. And let's link it to something else Gregg discovered.'

'Which was . . . ?'

'That when she was killed, Catherine Grant was already in the early stages of labour.'

Lubbock frowned. 'And?' he said.

'I've a vision of a man who'd just lived through a night when all hell was let loose and a morning when houses lay in ruins all around him, when the streets were choked with rubble and the city was half-paralysed—a morning when news reached him that his sister had been killed. And at the end of all that, he was faced with the knowledge that somehow he had to get his wife urgently to hospital. I've a vision of him struggling through once-familiar streets that he could barely recognize, desperately trying to find a way through the debris, helping her over piles of fallen bricks and through the shells of shattered buildings till, without any warning, one of them collapsed, and he knew that, for all his efforts, he'd failed.'

There was silence for a moment, then faintly, as if from many miles away, they heard the sound of voices raised in an evening hymn.

'But there's one thing,' said Tench, 'that I can't quite discern, no matter how hard I try. Somewhere along that tortuous route something happened that lodged itself in his mind, and the only clues I have are the words that he kept on repeating to the nurses. "He never stopped!" he said. "The bastard never stopped!" . . . And I'm still left wondering. Just what did he mean by that?'

Lubbock reached for his tobacco pouch. 'Sounds very much to me like a case of hit-and-run. One of them was struck by some vehicle or other, and the driver failed to stop.'

'That's what I thought at first, but no, it wasn't that. There were no injuries on either of them consistent with such an accident.'

'Then perhaps he tried to flag someone down and they ignored him.'

'And if that someone was Ted Bolton? Wouldn't that account for Grant's bitterness towards him? If he recognized Bolton, then Bolton must also have recognized him . . . And if Bolton had stopped and picked them both up, then Catherine would never have been trapped by that wall. "He killed her," he said, "and he killed my child too. Both of them. He killed them." ' Tench paused again and looked straight at Lubbock. 'But if that was what happened, why didn't Bolton stop?'

'Any number of reasons. Perhaps he never saw him. Perhaps the driver wasn't Ted Bolton after all. It could have been any one of hundreds of people . . . You shouldn't really need me to tell you this, laddie, but you're making the one mistake no detective worth his salt should ever allow himself to make. You're manipulating the evidence to fit your own solution, and that's the last thing any of us should ever think of doing. The solution should fit the evidence, not the other way round.'

'But my solution may be right. I'm just trying to find the evidence to support it.'

'Face the fact, laddie. It may not exist.'

Tench remained stubborn. 'You may think so. I don't. There must surely be a chance that someone in Norwich witnessed what happened or heard about it later from somebody else.'

'And what d'you propose that I do? Question everyone in the city? All the hundred and thirty thousand?' Lubbock looked down his nose. 'No, laddie, I don't think so. Just take my advice. Forget the whole thing. It's not worth the candle. You talk about being in a cloud of unknowing. Well, that's nothing new. They float around, these clouds, at the end of most murder cases. I've found myself left in dozens in my time, but do they bother me? No, of course they damn well don't. And why? The answer's simple. Given time, clouds disperse. That's a fact. It's nature's law. So settle for what you know and forget about what you don't and if you think I'm going to spend my dotage tottering around Norwich asking a load of questions, forget that as well. I've got better things to do with the rest of my time.'

He heaved himself up from the chair and stretched. 'Come on, lad,' he said. 'You and I are going to take a stroll on the beach. It'll do you a world of good. There's a warm summer breeze wafting up from the south. It'll help to disperse the cloud.'

EPILOGUE

THE MURDER COLUMN

When we want to read of the deeds that are
done for love, whither do we turn?
To the murder column.

George Bernard Shaw: Preface to *Three Plays
for Puritans*

1.

It was early one evening some three weeks later that the phone rang on Tench's desk, and lifting the receiver he heard an all too familiar voice. 'How's that cloud of yours, laddie? Still hanging around?'

'Persistently,' said Tench. 'It hasn't shown any signs yet of wanting to disperse.'

'Then it might be a good idea to come down to the Riverside. There's someone here that I think you should meet.'

'Who is it?'

"That's for you to wait and see. But I'll give you one clue. He's a neighbour of yours. Lives near the bridge at Cringleford.'

'Do I know him?'

'Apparently not, but you've heard of him. I've mentioned him often enough, and it's odds on that you must have seen him around. He's been there five years.'

'What's his name?'

'Let's just say he's an old friend of mine. So get your skates on, laddie. I've told Meg to serve up a pot of strong coffee. If your cloud of unknowing's still as thick as it was, let's try and do something to blow it away.'

*   *   *

The Old Riverside restaurant was run by Meg Dennison, Lubbock's only sister, indeed his only surviving relative. With her husband—a fisherman—she had, for many years, owned a fish-and-chip shop on the seafront at Cromer. Then, between them, they'd bought the Riverside, an old disused watermill by the Wensum in Norwich, and converted it into a restaurant; and when he'd been tragically drowned in a storm, she'd continued to manage the place on her own, making it pay; despite all the rigours of wartime rationing, by exploiting her connections with the fishermen of Cromer, building up a trade with the local farmers, whispering in the ears of Norwich grocers, and achieving a reputation as a formidable cook.

When Lubbock's wife had died from a virulent form of 'flu early in the war, she'd presumed it her duty, both to God and the law, to ensure that her brother was adequately fed, and that was why, from the start, she'd set aside a little room at the back of the Riverside as a private place where he could roll his tongue around poached egg and haddock—his favourite dish—light up his pipe, consume inordinate quantities of tea, and discuss with his colleagues the ins and outs of their latest case.

Raw-boned and tall, she treated him with a kind of affectionate cynicism, giving him from time to time the rough edge of her tongue—a sisterly privilege—but never complaining when sundry other members of the Norwich police attached themselves to him and spent hour after hour in her little back room, thrashing out their problems.

*　　　*　　　*

It took Tench less than a quarter of an hour to reach the street door. As he pushed it open, the bell on its steel ribbon danced up and down, tinkling into silence as he closed it behind him. Steering a zigzag course between the crowded tables—Meg did a brisk trade in evening meals—he waved at her and she jerked her head towards the back. 'They're in there,' she said, 'all three of 'em, puffing away at their filthy old pipes. The place is like a smoke house.'

'Three? Who's he got with him?'

Meg shrugged her bony shoulders. 'God only knows. Never seen 'em before.'

She was right about the smoke. He stood in the doorway, wafting it away, trying to see through the fug. Seated at a table were Lubbock and two other indistinct figures, one of them tall and thin, white-haired and straight-backed, the other much younger, but of similar build. All three were assiduously stoking up their pipes. And before them, on the table, stood a large pot of tea and an even larger one of coffee.

Lubbock raised a warning hand. 'Don't start complaining, laddie,' he said. 'Just pull up a chair and pour yourself a coffee . . . This is Danny Webster, and this is his son, Frank . . . You've heard me talk about Danny. He was my DCI back in the thirties. He's been retired now for a dozen or so years, but we worked together on the Hackleston case, the one that we linked to that affair last year at Taddenham.'

Tench shook both their hands, sat down and poured a coffee. 'Yes,' he said. 'I remember.' He turned to Danny Webster. 'You carried out quite an extensive inquiry.'

The white-haired man smiled. 'To no avail, I'm afraid.'

'Let's forget about that for the moment,' Lubbock said. 'When Danny retired he was living in Norwich, and we met up from time to time during the war, but then we somehow lost touch, and when I happened to meet him again yesterday, we hadn't seen one another for more than five years. We got to talking, reminiscing about the old days, and he asked me what I thought about this business at Northgate. One thing led to another, and he mentioned that his son had served with Ted Bolton during the war. Well, laddie, that was a bit of a turn-up for the book, so I asked a few more questions, and Danny said yes, they were both together here in Norwich in 1942. That was good enough for me, so I asked him to get

330

Frank down here tonight. I think you'd better hear just what he has to say.'

There was silence for a moment. The young man looked at Tench. 'It's true, sir,' he said. 'Ted and I were both here on the day that followed the first big raid. We joined up together back in '38, went to France with the BEF, and just about managed to squeeze out alive. We were both in a pretty rough state by then—the whole unit was—and they packed us all off to re-form at Colchester. At that time there wasn't much to do but sit tight, and we were still there in April 1942. That was when word came through about the blitz on Norwich, and they despatched us right away to give what help we could.'

He paused. 'I don't know exactly what it is you want to hear, sir, but I'll tell you all I know.'

'Just carry on, laddie,' Lubbock said gruffly. 'Take your own time.'

'Well,'—the young man looked at each of them in turn—'we got here round about midday. The town was in one hell of a mess, and they set us to work helping to clear the roads and shift all the rubble. We weren't far from the cathedral, but some streets were so badly smashed up I couldn't point to a map and say just where we were. Ted and I and half a dozen others were working as a team, and we'd been going hard at it for something like an hour and a half when a cry went up that

331

Ted was needed, and Captain Widdowson, our officer, came striding towards us round piles of fallen bricks. "I need a good driver, Bolton," he said, "and you're the best we've got. It's a ticklish job, and you'll need someone else with you." . . . Well, sir, that was that. Ted and I had been through so much together that I wasn't going to let him do this on his own . . . "I'll go with him, sir," I said.

'We were detailed one of those big army trucks with a canopy at the back, and instructed to find the best route we could. That was one of the things that made the job such a ticklish one. The streets were choked with all sorts of debris, we could only go at a snail's pace, and we had to twist and turn and backtrack more than once, but at last we came out on the Dereham Road and managed to step up the speed just a bit. I thought perhaps we'd got through the worst of it, when suddenly I saw this chap waving at us from the side of the road. A bearded chap he was, and he seemed to me to be supporting a woman. I don't think Ted ever saw them. He was hunched over the wheel, and what with all the stuff that was lying around he couldn't take his eyes off the road for a second. And even if he'd seen them, he wouldn't have dared to stop, not with the load we were carrying in the back.'

Tench never moved. 'What was it?' he asked.

'Two bomb-disposal officers nursing an unexploded bomb, sir,' said Frank. 'It was a monster, that bomb. One thousand kilograms. A whole ton of random death and destruction. Our orders were to get it out of the city as fast as we could to some open space where the men could defuse it.'

He stared straight at Tench. 'Believe me, sir,' he said. 'I still get nights when I wake in a cold sweat, thinking back to the journey we made that day.'

2.

Once the Websters had left, the little room fell quiet.

Lubbock lifted the teapot lid, peered inside, and poured himself a tepid cup of tea. 'Accept it,' he said, 'laddie. That's the closest you're going to get to the truth of what happened.'

Tench gave a sigh. 'Well, perhaps you're right, but it's ironic though, isn't it? Grant must have worshipped that wife of his, yet his love for her brought death to an innocent man.'

'That's another thing you need to accept,' Lubbock said. 'Love's a more prolific killer than hate. It's a strange emotion, love. Sublime in its purest form but, once perverted, it kills with all the inevitability of a well-directed shot . . . Yes, it's clear enough that Grant loved his wife, but he loved her to distraction, and that's the key word. Every night he went back to that shrine of his at Newton St Faith, and brooded on his loss. He allowed his love to fester, and as it festered it drove him mad. It turned him into a bitter man, bent on revenge, and when that happened, laddie, there was little enough that anyone could do. He had the motive to kill, the means were always to hand. All he needed was the opportunity to do what his twisted mind told him to do. And when Bolton showed himself, what followed was merely the tainted fruit of a love that years of brooding had savagely corrupted.'

'And the victims were an utterly blameless man and an equally blameless woman.'

'That's life, laddie. Life as it always has been, ever since Cain rose up and slew Abel . . . And don't start asking why. It's a profitless exercise.'

'I was only wondering . . .

'Then don't, and don't expect me to go wondering with you. As far as I'm concerned, this case is now over. It's finished and done with, as it should be for you. Close the files, Mike. Tie them up neatly with bows of red ribbon, and stow them away at the back of a cupboard. Let them gather some dust.'

Tench looked doubtful. 'There's just one thing . . .

'There isn't,' Lubbock said. 'Forget it. There's nothing. Look at it my way. We've wrapped up three murders in the course of a week. What more do you want? Between us, we make a good team, you and I. We work well together. In a way, you know, it's a pity I retired.'

Tench cupped a hand to his ear. 'What was that last word?'

'You heard,' Lubbock said.

'I didn't quite catch it. What does it mean?'

Lubbock looked down his nose. Then he pushed back his chair. 'You need a fresh pot of coffee, laddie,' he said. 'I'll get Meg to serve one up, twice as strong.'